FURY OF A PHOENIX

The Nix Series Book 1

SHANNON MAYER

The characters and events portrayed in this book are fictitious. Any similarity to real persons dead or alive are purely coincidental and not intended by the author.

Copyright © 2017 by Shannon Mayer

All rights reserved. No part of this publication may be reproduced, distributed, or transmitted in any form or by any means, including photocopying, recording, or other electronic or mechanical methods, without the prior written permission of the publisher, except in the case of brief quotations embodied in critical reviews and certain other noncommercial uses permitted by copyright law. For permission requests, write to the publisher, addressed "Attention: Permissions Coordinator," at the address below.

Hijinks Ink Publishing

Box 512

Qualicum Beach, BC,

V9K2L8 Canada

www.hijinksinkpublishing.com

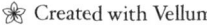 Created with Vellum

ACKNOWLEDGMENTS

This book would not have been possible without the encouragement of a very good friend. I had lost faith in the writing process, in the words and the character because of one person's opinion, and this good friend reminded me *why* I write. She reminded me that it was my story to tell, and that one opinion did not control my destiny. Thank you, Denise, for helping me get my legs back under me, and kicking me in the ass when I needed it.

CHAPTER ONE

The world slid sideways as the truck lost traction on the snowy hill, and there was nothing I could do to stop the momentum, not even if I'd been in the driver's seat. Bear— my sweet boy— reached across and grabbed my hand with his much smaller one, his fear a tangible beast between us, his brown eyes wide. "Mom?"

"Dad's a good driver." I looked him in the eyes and gave him a smile. "It'll be okay."

Something shuddered underneath us as the truck careened faster and faster down the long hill. I clutched his hand tightly.

It would be okay.

Time slowed.

A flare of magic rippled around the truck, dark green and vibrating with a life of its own.

What fresh hell was this?

THE QUESTION for me was not if I'd die of intense anxiety, but exactly how long it would take for the burning heat in my face to *actually* cause the rest of my body to spontaneously combust. Sweat dripped down my sides and clung to the inside of my long-sleeved sweater, and that sweat was probably the only thing keeping me from truly overheating. My hands itched to touch the grip of a gun to help me find my center.

Justin put his hand on my lower back as he guided me through the throng of people. "You're doing great, sweetheart. Just keep moving. These are our friends and neighbors. These are *our* kind of people, you know that."

I nodded, knowing there was more to the words. These were normals. Not a single supernatural in the bunch, which should have soothed me. Well, that wasn't entirely true. There was one, but she hid it well.

Still, the crush of people on me was hard to take. Not because I didn't know them, but because I knew the truth of human nature.

Normals or otherwise, human nature was an ugly beast.

Of all the people in my life—and not that there were many anymore—I trusted three. Justin. Bear. Zee. If nothing else, my past had taught me that trust was too easily given, and even easier to cast aside when the right deal came along.

A woman drew close with enough hairspray holding up her bouffant that the intense scent of Aqua Net curled through the crowd and up my nose long before I could see her. Princess Bouffant called out to us.

"Oh my *gee-osh*, you got her to *cah-m*! How lovely!" She drawled out her words in a pattern that had me fighting to keep the smile on my face. She was an abnormal, though of what flavor I wasn't sure, and didn't really care. The differences in her were subtle. She tried to cover up her scent with the Aqua Net, and the way her eyes darted with heavy amounts of makeup. Every abnormal was a little different in their tells, but they all had a smell that was part animal, part magic.

But that was not my business anymore.

I bit back the snotty retort that hovered on my lips, then caught Justin's wink out the corner of my eye. The grin on the side of his mouth was all it took for me to follow his train of thought.

"Perv," I whispered and gave him an elbow.

"Get your mind out of the gutter, Bea." He pinched my ass, and someone called to him.

"Justin, we need to talk." One of our neighbors waved him over. He gave me a pair of raised eyebrows in a silent request to leave me, and I rolled my eyes. "Go. I can deal with her. Make sure he isn't wanting to use our pastures again."

Here she came, the only abnormal in the bunch.

Goddamn it. I steeled my spine. I could do this. I'd handled tense, uncomfortable situations before. Hell, I'd dealt with shit that was beyond intense since I was a kid. But Zee and my other tutors had never trained me to deal with someone like Mary-Ellen Mayberry and her insatiable need to try and squeeze every, last drop of my past out of me.

Her hair was backcombed so she gained at least an extra three inches in height to her barely five-foot-five frame, which put her on par with me. She waved both hands, cheery as always. "I am *so* glad you came tonight, Bea. This time of year, it's good to be with our *loved* ones."

I kept the smile pasted on my face while I struggled not to bolt. Crowds were a bad place to be, a bad place to find yourself if you were looking out for someone else. Like a child who could disappear in an instant. Like my boy.

The grin held on my lips with great effort and I spoke through it carefully. "I'm so sorry, Mary-Ellen, but have you seen my son?"

She splayed her hands against her chest. "That precious *boy* of yours is upstairs in the rumpus room playing video games with the other kids. Don't *worry*," she took a step toward me and pressed her hand to my forearm like tiny sharp talons, "we don't allow any violent or inappropriate games in our home. Movies, either, so you have nothing to worry about."

"Of course not." I fought to keep the words polite. Just because she irritated me, just because she was an abnormal didn't mean I had to be a bitch to her. "Even so, I don't think we will be staying long. We have a long drive back out to the ranch, and I have mares due to foal soon."

Only a slight exaggeration, the mares weren't due until spring, but she didn't know that.

Mary-Ellen's smile dipped. "Oh, that's a shame. Shoot, we were even going to have *Santa* come in and hand out some little *gifts* to the kids. We hired him specially for tonight."

She waved a hand at the big pane glass window that looked out into the yard, directing my gaze. True to her words, there was a man dressed in red with a big fake beard stuck on his face and a bag over his shoulder. He loitered around the vehicles, waiting for his signal to come in, no doubt. Every step he took had a slight sway to it, like he was drunk. God, a drunk Santa. Fabulous.

I opened my mouth to thank her and decline staying longer when the lights in the house flickered. A nervous roll of laughter went through the visiting friends and neighbors. My right hand shot to my lower back, clutching the small knife handle I kept there, always, no matter where we were. A ghost of green light touched the edges of the window, there and gone before I could be sure of what I was seeing.

"All day that's been happening." Mary-Ellen blew out a rather un-ladylike snort, but my eyes were not on her. The movement of the crowd, the sudden intense feeling of being watched roared up my spine like a spider scuttling along wooden floorboards.

Magic, and those who used it, were not my friends. I

tolerated Mary-Ellen because she tried to be as normal as possible.

The lights flickered again, then came back on fully, this time with no green addition. The other normals barely seemed to notice the second flicker.

I had to be seeing things. It wouldn't be the first time my paranoia got the better of me.

I took a slow breath in and out, but that did nothing to the sudden sense of foreboding that filled my belly, and it took effort to let go of the blade handle, my fingers unsticking from it one by one.

Leftovers of a past that never fully let me go still hovered at the edge of every day and on the cusp of every nightmare. Rationally, I knew nothing was going to happen to us here in the middle of Wyoming at a Christmas party with a bunch of teetotaler Mormons. There was no way my past would ever find us here.

The magical world didn't like the interior of the country, which was why I'd chosen this place. A mantra began to roll through my mind.

We were safe.

I'd broken free, and for over a dozen years, I'd stayed that way.

But still, there had not been a day in the last twelve years I didn't look over my shoulder at least once. That I didn't wonder if I heard an unfamiliar vehicle roll down our long driveway, if someone new moved into Jackson Hole, someone that had come looking for me.

That a flickering of lights and an image of green aura didn't make me tense all the way to my asshole.

Twelve years wasn't enough to erase the past and the demons I'd left behind.

Before I could stop her, Mary-Ellen slid her arm around mine. "I hope you know we would *love* to have you and your boy come visit when Justin is *away* next month. Maybe you could come for dinner *after* church?"

She steered me through the great room with the vaulted ceiling toward the kitchen at the back of the house. I tried to find Justin in the crowd. At 6'6", his height normally gave him away, but he was off somewhere, no doubt talking about his next skiing trip coming up. Or still dealing with the pushy neighbor. That was more likely.

There he was. He turned and caught my eye. Again, both brows raised almost to his hairline. Our silent question for each other. Was I okay?

I pursed my lips and gave him a single blink. I was okay, and glad he was checking.

"Well, thank you. I'll think about it." I said the words with zero intention of ever coming back to Mary-Ellen's on my own. It wasn't that I didn't like her. Or that she wasn't kind and generous.

More of one of those 'it's me not you' conversations that I just didn't want to have. I'd seen Mary-Ellen break down once when she talked about her son going away for two years as a missionary for their church. Not only was it uncomfortable to watch, she'd found the nearest woman and clung to her long after I left the scene.

Then there was the whole 'I know magic exists and you want to act like there is no such thing even though you are abnormal' conversation that hung between us.

Emotions were not something I understood, except when it came to my boys. That was different. They were the first ones who showed me what real love was and had helped me understand that I could have it in my life despite everything I'd done.

"Lovely, that's lovely. Maybe we can have the *missionaries* here, too, if you don't *mind?*"

Oh, shit.

I cleared my throat to cover the muttered curse on my tongue before I spoke. "Of course not, but we are quite busy with the horses, you know. It's a *busy* time of year." I tried to get her hand off my arm, carefully, without hurting her. She was having none of it, her long fingers digging in harder. Staking her claim on me. Damn it all.

"Of course." Her smile never wavered, but her eyes took on an edge.

My own edge pushed to the surface and I locked eyes with her. A staring contest was not something she was going to win with me.

She'd been trying to *save* me and Justin since she met us. Nicely, of course, plying us with food and friendship, but always there was the undertone of us being heathens. And her being better than us. If she'd known who I really was she'd have probably tried to kill me, rather than feed me.

There was a moment, half a breath, where she held my gaze as I let the emptiness in me well up, the blank space that only my boys and their love made go away.

Inside my head the sound of people was replaced with the white noise that preceded the pop of a silencer, the thud of a well-placed bullet, the drip of blood from a wound, the hiss of a monster dying.

As quickly as that, she blinked and looked away, swallowing hard. "We'd just . . . Bear is such a sweet boy, and he reminds me of my boy gone on his mission—"

I got my arm free with a hard yank. Normally, I try to fit in and all that shit. It was a harder gig than one might think. But I was done playing.

Clearing my throat, I searched the crowd for Justin for a good five seconds again as I softened my tone as much as I could. "Look, Mary-Ellen, I know you mean well, but honestly, we aren't interested in your church. No matter how sweet Bear is."

"Of course, of course!" She moved so she was in my line of vision again. But to the left of her in the crowd was a familiar messy head of hair. He came up to my chest, his hair a deep black that held the colors of the rainbow when the sun hit it right. A sweet rush of relief flowed through me at the sight of him.

As if the flickering lights had been an ominous foreboding, like the start of a horror flick, and seeing him was a ray of light dispelling the shadows, and my innate suspicions.

I shook my head at the thoughts running through my mind. Stupid, I was being stupid and paranoid and I didn't need to be.

I held a hand out to Bear, calling to be heard over the steady thrum of noise. "Bear, come here." My son would be a lifeline in a sea of bodies that I wanted to get away from so badly, my skin itched. Being a loner was not something I'd been able to change from my past, one of the few things.

Though to be fair, the rest of what I'd changed had been superficial, allowing me to hide in plain sight, as it were.

A man bumped into me, sloshing punch onto my cowboy boots. The smell of his cologne, Old Spice, hit me almost as hard. He didn't even apologize, just kept on walking through the crowd, the sway in his step making me think he was drunk.

My jaw tightened, but I reined in my anger. It was just punch, after all, and would wash out.

The thing was, none of these people knew how close they walked to death. How close they walked to me.

If they did, they would have either prayed for me, or gone running in the opposite direction.

Bear bobbed and weaved through the last few feet of the crowd between us, oblivious to the tension between me and Mary-Ellen, for which I was grateful. I had shielded him as much as I could from who I really was, from a past that would swallow him whole if I wasn't vigilant.

The monsters would come for him, if they knew he was mine.

He flashed a smile up at me. "What's grooving, Mama?"

I tugged him to me, slinging my right arm over his shoulder, leaving my faster hand free at my side. "Drop the second 'g' if you want to be cool, little Bear."

He laughed and gave a half-hearted effort to pull away from me. I bent down to his ear. "I need your help for just a minute. Do you mind?"

He brightened immediately. Help was the magic word for him. He was everything I could have wanted in a son, and then some. How I'd gotten him, after all I'd done . . . that much I would never know.

"Yeah, sure, I'm your guy." He grinned up at me, dimples showing in the layer of baby fat he still held on his cheeks.

I laughed, and the irritation and need to escape eased a little as he lit up my world, and for a moment the flood of people, the anger, the intense need to run, slid away.

"Oh, that makes me think of Deacon." Mary-Ellen burst into tears behind us. Deacon was her boy who was still on his mission for another year yet, and I took that as our cue.

Time to go. On the other side of the room, Justin was moving too in our direction.

I grabbed Bear's hand and hurried us to the front door.

"I need help bringing in the food for the potluck." I stopped by the door, took my coat off the hanger and slipped it on. Justin reached up and popped a package of cigarette's out of his shirt pocket. "I need a smoke break."

Bear tipped his head sideways at me, a single eyebrow arched high. The look was so reminiscent of his grandfather my heart stuttered.

Bear was nothing like my father. He was *nothing* like that miserable bastard.

I CLUNG to Bear's hand as the truck slammed into the first tree on the passenger side. "Hang on, baby. I got you."

Justin wrestled with the truck, but the steering wheel didn't respond. "Brakes are gone. Deep breath, we're going in!"

A screech of trees clawing at the sides of the truck did nothing to slow our headlong rush off the side of the road, down the hill to the icy water of the lake below. A swirl of green slid through the truck, touching on each of us.

This was no accident.

We were strong swimmers, all three of us, we'd make it out. We'd make it out, we would, as long as we could dodge the magic swirling around us.

"Deep breath, baby!" I kept my eyes on Bear, kept him looking at me, my head trying to tell me what was happening while my heart refused it. Fear had never been like this before. Eating its way through me from the inside out like a violent maggot.

Something exploded right under the truck halfway down the hill, and we were thrust into the air, the green light deepening until it was nearly black, filling the cab with smoke. Smoke that smelled like rot and death. The truck rolled, and my hand was yanked out of Bear's as he slammed against his side of the truck.

Over and over we flipped, the truck smashing harder with each rotation, the metal bending, the truck that should have protected us in a crash turning into a twisted death trap. Metal squealed as it tore, shooting through the cab like rusted spears.

The hill leveled out as it reached the edge of the lake and the truck slowed its rapid, violent descent, and turned into a slalom that sent us into the lake.

The crash was over, as suddenly as it started. The truck was silent except for the burble of water under it, beginning to reach into the cab.

My body and mind wanted me to be still, to take stock of the damage to my legs and torso. My heart wouldn't allow it.

I scrambled as true, thick gray smoke began to fill the cab through a hole in the floor. I fought to get my seatbelt off, to reach for Bear ... a rumble that sounded like thunder rippled through the air.

Thunder where there was no storm.

The magic had found me.

"What's that look for?" I brushed a finger down the middle of Bear's nose, a replica of my own.

He laughed and shook his head. "I have a surprise for you. But I'll wait."

"A surprise?" I made a mock grab for him. "Well, I bet I can torture the information out of you."

Justin laughed and followed us out as we ran across the yard. He strolled to where our old Ford was parked, looking perfectly at home amongst all the other trucks and four-wheelers. Bear ran around the truck once and I chased him, sliding on the hard-packed snow. Justin cheered us on back and forth. All the irritation in me was gone in a single breath because this was where I belonged. Here with my boy and my husband, in the open fresh winter air, free from everything. I was not the killer of my past, but a mother now. A mother with a son who was her whole world.

I caught Bear on the second go around the truck and swept him into the air despite his size. Working with horses and continuing with Zee's training had kept me fit and strong. Planting a kiss on his cheek, I didn't mind that he squirmed. It wouldn't be long before he would be too big for his mama's kisses. My heart gave a twinge at the thought of losing that.

My boy was growing up far too fast for my liking. One day, I might have to tell him who I really was, and about the family I'd left behind and why. I did not relish those thoughts.

"Mama, are you crying?" He reached up and touched my cheek, concern etched into his young face. Only Bear and Justin . . . they were the only ones worthy of my tears. Justin was there in a flash, his hand warm against the back of my neck. I looked at him, let him see the sorrow for a split second.

I cleared my throat. "Snowflake in my eyes."

Bear laughed and rolled his eyes. "Sure."

We grabbed—or I should say I grabbed—the single pot from the back of the truck. A batch of homemade pierogis I'd learned to make from an old recipe book were still warm. I was not a natural cook, but I made sure it looked like I was with every meal I made. Hell, it was no different than putting together a fine-tuned poison that couldn't be detected until it was too late. Follow the recipe, don't deviate and it would turn out fine.

Justin put his cigarette out in the snow, and blew a final puff of smoke. His arm snaked around me waist and he tugged me against him. "Okay?"

"Yeah, just trying not to smack Mary-Ellen."

He kissed the side of my head. "You haven't yet, I think you can hold out until dinner is over."

I rolled my eyes at him and shook my head.

Bear settled in to walk beside me, matching my slow pace as we headed toward the house. "You left the food out here in the truck for an escape, didn't you?"

Justin grunted. "Smart boy of mine."

I glanced at him. "Yes. Well, I thought it best for all parties involved for me to have an out." Before I started lashing out at people, before I started in on the paranoia. Control was something I had in spades after all this time, but that didn't mean I wanted to push it. There was always that possibility I would snap back to where I'd been before. Shoot first, ask questions later.

He nodded his eyes wide. "That's cool. You can always tell me we need to talk. People wouldn't question that, would they? Like maybe I'm in trouble for something?"

I slowed and then stopped and looked at him. Seeing all that I could have been if not for my training. Innocent. Loving. Giving. "That's . . . the best gift you could have given me."

His grin was all I needed to get moving again. Unlike me, he loved the limelight. He had to get that from Justin and his desire to be seen by the world. The one thing that had almost turned me away from his father when we first met.

He ran ahead of us and Justin tightened his hold on me. "If it's too much with the crowd, we can go."

I let myself lean into him, let him carry some of my anxiety for just a moment. Let him be my rock. "I'll be okay."

"I love you, Bea." He pressed his mouth to mine gently, catching me off guard. Not that he wasn't affectionate, but because public displays of affection were not common for either of us. In his own way, despite loving the limelight, he was a private kind of guy. I kissed him back, the kiss anchoring me, taking me back to the first time he'd kissed me and I'd actually felt something in return. The first time I began to understand that not all men were assholes.

He stepped back and winked. "That hold you until later?"

I couldn't help the laugh. "Warming me up, are you?"

He waggled his eyebrows and swept a hand out to indicate I should go ahead of him.

Stepping into the house, the noise and crush of people didn't seem as overwhelming as the first time in, though I knew the numbers hadn't changed. The clear cold air had wiped away the sense of foreboding. I handed off the pierogis to the ladies in the kitchen with Bear at my side. When his friends called to him he looked to me.

"Mama, can I go?"

Maybe, but I heard the real question: Did I need him? My heart swelled as I ran a hand over his soft thick hair. "Go have fun. I'm fine. Your dad can keep me company."

He was gone in a flash and Justin stood there with me watching. "We got lucky with him."

I turned in his arms, not caring that we were in public. "Our son is damn amazing."

"Hey, don't cuss here. You'll get us kicked out before the food is served and it looks like quite the spread." He tweaked my nose gently. I looked to his face, my eyes tracing the scars that ran down the side of his face from a skiing accident years ago.

This life was not what I'd ever thought I'd have. Normal. Safe. Loving.

I laughed softly—the sound of my own laughter still strange to my ears—and put my head against his chest. He tightened his arms around me. "I talked to Noah earlier. I have to go to California again next week. Hollywood, if you can believe it."

A sigh slid out of me. "He may be your best friend, but I think lately he's been trying to see if he can spend more time with you than me and Bear. You cheating on me with him?"

He laughed and shook his head. "His legs aren't as nice as yours."

A sigh slid from him, and with it went the mirth. "It's another promo possibility. The sponsors won't sign me if I don't show the right amount of willingness. You know that. And we could use the money. The roof is going to need to be replaced in the spring."

I did know that. Justin was a world-renowned stunt skier and had more than his fair share of magazine spreads. But . . .

he was getting older, and the competition was getting younger. What money he made now had to see us through a very long time.

That or I'd have to explain why I had several million dollars of unmarked bills buried in the barn. Money I took not to spend, but to keep out of my father's hands. Money I took to punish him more than anything else. Money that I had suspected would be tracked back to us if we used it.

"Don't worry." Justin kept his arms around my shoulders. "It won't be a long trip, and if it goes as planned, I won't have to do more sponsorships. We'll be set for life."

"Are you serious?" The urge to pepper him with questions rushed through me. Why hadn't he said anything earlier? He grinned at me, the dimples that Bear had inherited showing up through the two-day stubble.

"Trust me, baby. This is the score I've been waiting for."

Score. I snorted softly. As if he were some sort of bad-ass.

The money he'd made through the years was always enough, but barely. Seventy-five thousand was standard for him, and I made sure the foal crop each year paid for itself and then some. Not a lot, but at least I wasn't taking away from what he made.

"I wanted to surprise you when I came home with the check. Maybe I could cash it and we could roll around on all the bills naked on the bed." He winked at me and I shook my head, laughing again. Laughter . . . so absent before, and my life was filled with it now.

"You are something else, you know that?" I arched an eyebrow at him.

He grinned down at me. "That's why you married me, isn't it? 'Cause I'm a special guy."

The green myst swirled around the truck and pushed the hulking weight from the edge of the water, out until it was over the depths. The ice cracked under the weight of the truck as it slid, rolling across the shoreline until a weak spot gave. The truck went sideways and down until the entire driver's side was under water, leaving the passenger side sticking out at an angle. Justin and Bear were on the driver's side, and the water swirled up around them, filling their side slowly. I blinked through blood running down the side of my head, the smoke and taste of death magic burning my lungs. I reached across for Bear, but I couldn't move my legs.

Justin wasn't making any noise; he wasn't fighting to get out. To get us all out.

"Justin." I croaked his name out, even though I knew . . . the angle of his neck was one I'd seen too many times, and it was far from natural.

I twisted in my seat, and pushed Justin from my mind because there was nothing I could do for him, and Bear needed me. My son whimpered and reached for me with his right hand, but my seatbelt had tightened, jerking me back against the seat. My left wrist was broken, I was sure of it, but worse, I was pinned by the side door. It had bent inward from one of the revolutions of the truck and had both my legs jammed tightly under the metal.

"Baby, I'm here." I pushed with my unbroken hand against the metal around me as I reached for him with my left.

"Mama . . ." His whisper faded with each syllable.

"I'm here, Bear." I stretched for him. Stretched for his hand that he was no longer lifting to me as it flopped into the water filling up around him, circling around his chest, creeping up to his chin where it stopped.

"Bear, Bear, talk to me!" I fought my seatbelt and the metal trapping me, holding me away from my Bear. Panic surged, and I fought to get my hand to my lower back, to my knife. My fingers found the handle and I ripped it out, cut the seatbelt in a single slash, but I was still trapped by my legs.

Removing the seatbelt gave me the inches I needed to grab his arm, so I could circle my hands around his. I pulled him and his body flopped toward me. Flopped. Flopped. Limp. Dying. Words and emotions scattered through me like explosions gone wrong.

My heart. My boy. The skin of my legs tore, as I fought to get to him, so I could do CPR. It wasn't enough, my movement didn't free me enough to pull him out.

"Mama . . . it hurts," he whispered. So softly, slipping away from me. I was going to lose him.

I screamed for him, screamed his name. "Bear, you hang on, baby, hang on!"

The click of a weapon cut through my screams, taking me to my past in an instant, a tendril of green swirling in around my face.

The tip of the gun slid through the front passenger window in front of me. I clamped my mouth shut and swallowed the screams as Justin's head jumped, a bullet slamming through it. His blood sprayed the water, invisible against the black ink of the lake.

A second click of the weapon, the brush of magic against my skin and I closed my eyes. At least I would be with my boys. With my Bear.

I let a breath out and waited for the sound of the hammer to fall.

There was nothing, just a quiet sloshing of feet and legs through the water, loose chunks of ice bumping against the outside of the truck and then my head exploded with bright white light and shattering pain and my head slid under the dark water.

CHAPTER TWO

Dreams, just dreams. The accident wasn't real. We had made it home from the Christmas party with no problems, no hint of magic or death. How often had nightmares of losing Justin or Bear visited me over the years? Often enough that I shouldn't have been surprised that I'd had another.

I told myself that simple and yet so very complex lie as I swam upward out of the mire that was a drugged sleep, the heavy taste of chemicals coating my tongue that screamed I'd been put out and not knocked out. Sleep, but more like the sleep of the dead. No, not dead. Just tired. I let myself live in the lies a little longer.

We must have stayed too late at the party. Had I drank too much? No, that wasn't possible at a Mormon party. I knew I was lying to myself, but I let the lies stay at the front of my mind because that was safer. That was a better place for them as I struggled to put the pieces together. I needed time to let the truth sink underneath the fog of almost awake, while I still clung to the edges of sleep and the reprieve it held for my fear.

There had been no accident. Justin was alive. Bear was

alive. Maybe I'd been thrown off one of the three-year-old colts as I introduced him to the saddle. That would explain the pain in my back and legs. The thrumming pound of my head. The ache in my wrist.

But it did not explain away the ache in my heart, nor the taste of magic at the back of my throat.

I groaned and tried to shift my position—when had our bed been this hard under my back? A sharp pain made me suck in a breath, the pain of a knife cutting through my ribs, sticking me hard.

A deep voice I almost recognized, with the accent hailing from the East Coast, rolled through the shadows of my slow awakening.

"The wife is alive, boss. You want me to finish it?"

Finish it. Those two words reverberated through my brain like a gong and the accident welled up in my mind, washing away the last of the lies I so desperately clung to.

The truck rolling and going into the river, Justin's neck, the gunshot, the green swirling auras of magic . . . Bear. Reaching for me, crying for me. Screeching metal, cracking ice, the cold of the water seeping around me, the blood dripping into the slow lazy current, the violent explosion under us as we slid down the hill . . .

I opened my eyes, found myself looking at an unfamiliar ceiling, pocked with scars like someone had thrown pencils up to stick into the cheap panels, over and over. Cracks ran through the dirty gray panels, and I stared at them while my consciousness caught up to the fact I was no longer asleep.

I made myself turn my head to the right where the voice had been speaking, only to see the edge of the speaker's body as he left the room. Dark pants underneath a doctor's lab coat, but the unmistakable outline of a gun under the back of that white coat. Tall, easily over six foot, but lean, not the beefy muscled man I'd already imagined. I watched the door, waiting for him to come back, and when he didn't, I couldn't deny where I was any longer.

Or why I was there.

Hospital. Accident. Death. Magic.

I couldn't close my eyes, because when I did I saw my boy. I saw his hand reaching for me, then slowly, slowly dropping into the water as his life slid away from him.

"Bear." His name was on my lips, and I knew the answer to the question I was asking because my heart didn't beat the way it had yesterday. Today it was hollow, empty as it had been before my boys.

Grief roared over me like a lion swallowing me whole and I couldn't see past it. I didn't want to see past it. I let it take me, and I don't know for how long. I only knew the light in the room from the only window shifted over time, slowly darkening. A nurse came in and tried to give me something. A sedative.

"Get the fuck away from me!" I screamed the words, hurling them like the weapons I wanted in my hands. The nurse rushed out of the room with high spots on her cheeks, the needle clutched in her left hand. I leaned forward, watching her, suspicion slicing through me. Did she throw the needle out? Had she been told to give me that sedative? Was it even a sedative or something more dangerous? I put my hands to my head, rocking slowly. The killer I'd been reared up inside of me. The one that had been taught to survive no matter what. To be a weapon. I'd put her away and thought she was gone forever.

Hard.

Violent.

Dangerous.

I'd cast off those chains when I'd met Justin, when I'd found my first taste of love and safety. When I'd first felt Bear growing inside me and I had more reason than ever to fight for a life I'd never thought was possible. Whatever love I'd learned with Justin was nothing compared to what Bear's life had brought to me.

But he was gone. Dead. They both were.

I threw up, the nausea hitting me so suddenly that I didn't have a chance to even look for a bucket. I turned my head to the side, splattering the sheets and the floor with clear liquid.

"I'll get a bucket." Someone said, I assumed a nurse. I didn't even look up, couldn't move from where I was.

Despite the pain in my ribs and legs from the angle I lay, I stayed in that position.

Pain was good, it cleared my mind like nothing else. It always had. It would allow me to set the mind-numbing grief aside long enough to make sure I was seeing what had happened clearly. That I wasn't remembering wrong the things that had happened as the truck went out of control. That I wasn't putting things into my memory because I wanted to blame someone for what happened. That my paranoia hadn't got the better of me.

I played the accident over and over in my head, looking at it with a calculating, experienced eye, avoiding the scenes of Bear and Justin and focusing on the feel of the truck as it slid, the way it had flipped, the man outside the truck. The color that had suffused the truck, the way the green swirls had held us in the air.

The brakes had been tampered with, of that much I was sure, but that had only been the beginning of things.

Three of the tires had blown out, which was impossible, unless there was a spike belt, which would have blown all four tires. They had to have been shot. Which meant there had been at least two shooters, and one of them had been able to work death magic.

The explosion that had gone off under us had been powerful, yet directed. The only way to manage that was with someone who had great control over their abilities. Had the magic been under the truck, attached, or launched at us in the last seconds? I pulled the sensation of the explosion going off through me again. No, the magic had been in the bush under us, not on the truck itself, I was sure of it.

That girl I'd been, all that training I'd thought I'd left behind, shoved everything else aside and showed me what I didn't want to believe.

Justin's and Bear's deaths had not been accidental. Not for one heartbreaking second.

The past, who I'd been . . . I didn't want to be that girl, and I'd run to escape what I'd been made into. There was no way my father had found me. Yet . . . the truth was in front of me.

I needed to get out of here. Because the girl from my past was laughing maniacally, enjoying the pain I writhed in. She knew the truth and so did I. Someone *had* found me, and the deaths of the two souls I loved more than my own life was the result.

Pain and grief rapidly shifted into dangerous territory inside me. Rage fired at the edges of the grief and burned away the emotion.

Another nurse came in, this one with a bucket and mop. He cleaned up the mess at my feet, a sad smile on his face. He was young, maybe twenty-five, with a hairline that was already receding, and I knew just by the edges of his face he was an abnormal. The hair grew wonky along his jaw line, like a beard gone wild. But the hair was coarse, and multiple colors. I looked him over for the lines of a weapon under his scrubs but saw nothing. He didn't notice my intense perusal of his body, or if he did, he ignored me. More like he was used to being checked out. Abnormals were rarely trusted.

"You have a visitor," he said. "Says he's your uncle. You good with him coming in once I've got this cleaned up?"

The tremor in my legs and arms was nothing I could control. If it was my uncle, all was good. But that was what the hitmen I used to work with would say to get close to their marks. They could be your uncle, your godfather, your cousin. Anything to get within striking distance. And if it was a magic user, I was royally screwed. I had none of my tools to block the magic, none of my weapons to stave off a power that I'd never had, nor ever would have.

Adrenaline surged, and the pain faded from me like the edge of the nurse's hairline from his face.

"Give me a minute," I whispered, doing my best to go back to the quiet wife I'd pretended to be in public. The orderly's face softened further and he wiped up the last of the vomit with the mop, offered me a cool rag, and then went out into the hall.

I wiped my face down, but kept the cloth over my mouth, partially hiding my face as I went over my options. I didn't have much choice but to face whoever was coming in, and the state my body was in didn't give me much in terms of a hand-to-hand fight. Surprise would be all I would have on my side.

A part of my brain tried to tell me this was crazy, that things like this didn't happen. But I knew better.

I knew the dark underbelly of the world of normals and abnormals better than anyone.

There was the soft murmur of voices, the quick give and take of words. I had fifteen seconds at best to get ready.

Gritting my teeth, I pushed myself up straighter and hissed through the pain. I couldn't stop the tremor in my hands as I put my left hand over the IV that was attached to my right arm. I pulled it out, not even feeling the sting of the needle sliding from under my skin, not caring that the blood dripped down my arm. With my left arm in a cast, it was hard to move fast. I tossed the cloth the nurse had given me over the bleeding wound from the IV, then tucked the needle into the palm of my right hand.

Improvisation. If the man with the gun came back, I wouldn't have more than a split second to use the needle on him and grab the gun. If he was an abnormal, I would have even less time. Going for the eyes would be best, or the neck if he didn't bend down far enough.

My heart . . . God, my heart wanted to shatter. It wanted to give up. I wanted to grieve for my boy and husband and lie in bed and cry until there were no tears left in my body. A part of me wanted to lie down and die right there, to let whoever was coming in finish the job they started. I used to think tears and grief were weakness, but already I found a new truth.

Grief was not a weakness. It was fuel for my anger. Grief was a luxury I did not have and that left me nothing but anger to run on.

If I was right—and I was sure I was—the accident wasn't an accident, and someone was at fault for my two boys' deaths.

Which meant someone was going to pay for their lives with their own, piece by piece, if I had to.

The door to my room creaked open and I lay back on the raised bed, closing my eyes until they were open a mere slit. A man slipped into the room, the door shutting with a shush behind him. Silent as a shadow, his footsteps didn't squeak once on the clean floor. The dark pants were the same as those the strange man had been wearing, and I kept my small amount of vision on his legs as he walked toward me, carefully. As if he didn't want to wake me.

The legs stopped at my bedside, close to where I clutched the hidden needle.

I let a slow breath out, readying myself for the pain it

would cost me to sit up fast and jam the needle into one of his eyes.

"You ain't sleeping, doll face."

My eyes sprung open. "Zee."

It *was* my uncle and not some unnamed hitman. Or at least, everyone knew him as my uncle, and even Justin had believed that for the first few years of our marriage. A necessity to keeping my husband safe. Or so I'd thought. When I'd finally told him about who I truly was—or at least who I was related to—and that Zee was uncle in name only, he'd not only taken it in stride, he said it didn't matter. That it wouldn't have mattered if I'd been Lucifer's daughter, he would love me still. At the time, I'd laughed, and cringed because I'd not been able to tell him the rest. That I was about as close to being Lucifer's daughter, or at least as close as one could get on this side of the grave, in more ways than one.

I looked over Zee, trying to see if he'd been hurt while I'd been away. To see if he'd had to fend off some sort of attack on the ranch. While his neck was scarred from an attempt on his life years ago, and his face was as craggy and rough with a half-grown beard, I couldn't see any new injuries. Long before I'd met him, he'd been a special ops man overseas, and that was where he'd learned much of his training and skills that he'd passed onto me. One of those skills was the ability to push all your emotions away, to not show a drop of compassion, empathy, or caring, even if you were shattered inside. To keep going, even when you wanted to lie down and die.

To be fair, though, Zee was also the only abnormal I'd met that I trusted. He was a Hider. One who could make things vanish, disappear even though they were right in front of you.

The only reasons I'd ever trusted him to begin with were that I'd known him since I was six years old, and my mother had loved him dearly.

He held out a rough knuckled hand and I took it, holding it as my last lifeline, as a sob slipped out of me, horrifying me. His eyes were shiny with tears, but not one dropped from him.

"Shit, this doesn't seem real," he said. Not *I'm sorry*, he would never say that. Because he knew, like I did, this was not his fault.

I sat up and leaned into his one shoulder no matter that the movement cut through my injuries. "Tell me they're alive, Zee. Tell me this is a bad dream and that Bear is going to walk through that door. Tell me if he is gone, that you can bring him back. *Please*." My voice cracked on the last word, my last attempt at continuing to be the woman with the normal life. The woman who knew nothing of the darkness the world held.

"I never lied to you yet. You think I should start now?" He carefully tightened his hold over my shoulders. "You survived this accident, let's try and keep it that way."

I lifted my eyes to his, looking for the confirmation of what I already knew, but didn't fully want to believe. That the accident was anything but. He gave me the faintest of nods, his eyes incredibly sad, but also hard. Hard and understanding, and . . . angry.

Closing my own eyes, I worked to push the tears away, to cap the grief that would consume me if I let it. I could be a sobbing mess, and I deserved that time. I deserved to grieve for Bear, for Justin . . . but if I let that take me over, as I knew it would, that would leave me unable to do what I had to do. Something I'd trained most of my life for, something I'd run so far and fast from that I thought it would never catch up to me.

How very wrong I'd been.

I bit my lower lip and sucked in a sharp breath. "Get me out of here, Zee. I want to go home."

"Already done. Have your discharge papers here . . . three broken ribs, cracked pelvic bone, severe bruising across both femurs, broken left wrist, concussion, and then the usual cuts and nicks." He flipped a file folder at me, open wide. I glanced over it, noting no signature under the discharge section. So, I had not been discharged, but it didn't matter. I was leaving, and no doctor was going to tell me otherwise.

I had work to do, work that would keep me from thinking about my boys, thinking about Bear reaching for me, crying for me, as he died. Thinking about how much pain he must have been in as he'd died—

My throat tightened and I swallowed hard over the sudden growing lump. Zee crouched in front of me. "You aren't me, doll face. You're allowed to let it out."

I glared at him, letting the anger carry me. "And if I can't stop letting it out? Then I'm useless, and I won't be that, Zee. I refuse that option."

He gave me a smile that I knew would send chills through any other person. "You think they'll get away with this? You think I believe you—of all people—would let them? You grieve, and while you grieve, we'll prepare for what's coming." He slid a hand over my head, cupping the back of my neck. "I know you as if you were my own blood, and I know your heart is too big to not let this pain out. It's why you had to get out of the business. It's why you could find a way to live a normal life for so long. It's why you loved that boy more than your own life when everything you've been through pointed to you being unable to love."

I should have known he would understand me better than I knew myself. He got up and went to the cracked cupboard across the room. "I brought you clothes yesterday when I came to check on you."

He pulled out a pair of light gray sweatpants and an oversized hoodie. He helped me dress, as comfortable with me as if he had been my father, his hands gentle on my wounded body.

I wished he had been my father. Maybe I wouldn't be here now if that had been the case.

No, I would have been an abnormal like him then, and hiding from the world. Running for my life, or working for the tyrants of the world to make a living, tyrants like my father.

A hiss slipped out of me as I lifted my right leg. I could barely get it a few inches off the floor. Zee bent without a question and maneuvered my foot into the leg hole. "Haven't had to help you dress for a good twenty-five years. When you took a tumble off the obstacle course, and broke both your arms. Remember that?"

I kept my silence, but appreciated that he was trying to distract me. I stood as he slid a pair of my oldest runners on my feet, then waited as he laced them up. "Haven't done this for about the same length of time either." He patted my calf when he was done, then stood, head and shoulders above me.

I slid an arm around his back and leaned into his body, letting him help me stand as I let myself acclimate to the pain. "Let's go."

Zee walked at a pace I could keep up with, but even so, by the time we reached the front doors of the hospital, my breath came in hard gulps with the exertion and sweat rolled down my face. Broken ribs . . . they would take time to heal. So would the pelvic bone issue and the wrist. But none of that mattered. Zee understood that I had to take time to heal, and in that time, I would make my plans.

He got me into his truck and strapped me in. I let him do it for me, because the feeling of sitting in a vehicle so like Justin's old Ford froze my body . . . I couldn't stop the flashback from happening.

Flashbacks were not new to me and I gritted my teeth as this one washed over my senses.

I could see the inside of the old Ford, could feel it rumble under me. The sensation of being in the truck as it careened down the hill, and then when the first tire had blown, to be followed so closely by the second and third. I made myself focus on that part, the stark details of the accident that had been set up, and ignored the rest of what had happened. I would not think about Justin and Bear.

I put a hand over my eyes as Zee started the truck up, my spine tingling with a rush of adrenaline that had nowhere to go.

"You going to be sick?" Zee didn't put the truck in first gear.

"No. Just get me home." I wanted my bed. I wanted a place I was familiar with, away from the hospital. I should have known things wouldn't be that easy.

I should have known that Zee . . . that he was trying to help in his own way.

We were ten minutes into the drive when he cleared his throat. "The doc sent home some good sedative painkillers to help you sleep. Percocet by the looks of it."

I didn't look at him, just kept my hand over my eyes, trying to keep my mind blank, nothing. "Anything else?"

He cleared his throat again. "I got the initial police report. There was no tampering on the brake lines. Nothing. And there were no tire blowouts. I know you want someone to blame, and I know your past is the easiest place to do that."

What was left of my emotions froze over in slow sections so that my body felt like it was being pushed through ice, piece by piece. My silence only seemed to encourage him, when all I wanted was for him to stop talking. Because he was wrong. I hadn't told him about the gunshot. Or the man at the truck, or what I suspected was the same man at the hospital.

"Bea—"

"No." I threw the word at him. "That is not my name."

"That has been your name all these years. You going back to Nix now?" The weight of his eyes flickered from me to the road and back again.

I nodded. "Yes. I never stopped being Nix. No point in hiding it now."

He let out a slow breath. "Look, I get it. I do. When your mom died, I wanted to blame them all, every last fucker I'd ever dealt with. I wanted *them* to be the reason she was gone. They weren't. She was sick and no healer would touch her because of your father, and so she died. Just like this was an accident. The reality is your family and your past has forgotten about you. The way you wanted, the way we planned."

My stomach rolled, his words acid drops in my belly. "In the hospital, you said . . . they wouldn't get away with it. You said—"

"I said what I said to get you moving." His tone was hard. "I said what I said to get you up and out of that bed, Nix. I know this pain. I know it well. It will consume you if you let it, it will drive you crazy if you let yourself sink into a belief that this was no accident."

I put my hands over my eyes and leaned forward so that my forehead was on my knees. My back and hips protested the movement but I barely noticed. "It *wasn't* an accident. I know it wasn't. What about the report on Justin?" Why was he even arguing? He knew my family, and he knew their reach and the lengths they went to protect their money and power.

I was a loose cannon they'd never tracked down, a weapon they'd lost somewhere in the wild that had taken a large sum of blood money right out from under their noses. I'd avoided all the hunters they'd sent after me, both normals and abnormals, and there was no reason to think that Zee wasn't right.

If he was right, then I could grieve. Except he wasn't, which meant I couldn't let it out, not yet, and maybe not for a long time.

Zee's fingers drummed a terrible staccato on the steering wheel with one hand and a matching beat on the stick shift with the other. "Justin died with a broken neck."

"That's it? No gunshot wound to the head?" I sat up, my eyes narrowing.

"Nothing in the reports," he said, his words as careful as if he were treading glass shards. "The official autopsy report won't be out for a few weeks at least."

"They can be faked. You know that."

He shook his head. "What happened was a terrible, shitty accident that never should have happened, but it did. You've picked up after you lost everything once before, you can do it again." He slowed for what was one of the only intersections in town, took a left, and we were heading out toward the place I'd called home for ten years. Ten years of peace.

Ten years of no blood or death, or magic or monster slaying that wasn't putting food on the table. Flashes of my past tried to reach for me, to remind me of what I'd walked away from, of what I'd tried to protect my small family from.

And they'd been killed anyway.

I worked to practice the breathing that was supposed to help with flashbacks, only it wasn't a flashback I was trying to calm, but an intense and fast-growing rage.

Rage that built at an alarming speed within my body, going to spill over my lips. "You don't know that it was an accident, Zee. You weren't there, I was. There were gunshots, there was an explosion under the goddamned truck and we were lifted with some sort—"

"Yeah, and you hit your head hard enough to be out cold

when the paramedics and first responders showed up, your face in the water. You almost drowned!" He threw the words at me as his face bloomed a dark red and the veins in his throat pulsed.

"There was death magic, Zee. Green and dark and vibrating. I saw it at the party, just a glimmer and I thought I was seeing things. I . . . I should have checked." Oh my God, if I'd only checked, maybe my boys would be alive now. My stomach heaved.

Everything Zee was saying was a lie. I knew it in the depths of my gut.

I'd been awake in the truck, I'd been reaching for Bear. I'd seen the green swirling aura around us, and I'd heard the gun click as a bullet slid into the chamber.

I'd been hit in the head, but not because of the accident.

"Fuck you!" I slammed my good hand onto the dash of the truck. "There were *gunshots* and *death myst*, Zee. I think I know a goddamn gunshot when I hear one."

Finally, I had his attention. He slowed the truck and looked at me.

"Death myst and gunshots. Are you absolutely sure?"

I clenched my hands in my lap. "Three tires, Zee. Which means at least two shooters, likely one of them was an abnormal. The brakes went out, and we both know that is no simple thing. Not for them to fully fail like they did without interference. I was *there*. Justin was pumping the brakes and getting nothing. You think I don't know what destructive magic looks like anymore? That I've forgotten? After the crash, Justin was shot in the head, I *watched* it happen. Why are you fighting me on this?"

Zee's eyes flicked over me. "Because . . . our past, *your* past would make you believe this a murder no matter if it was an accident or not, because you know how ugly the world can be. There is no way your family found us, Nix. There is no way they got past my wards around you and the house. Those wards extended to Bear, you know that."

I let out a breath. "But not Justin."

"I had to pick two people." He looked to me and then away, shame coloring his face. I shook my head.

"Zee, I wouldn't have had it any other way."

His ability to hide things was stronger than most others in his genre of magic and I'd trusted my life to it. But I'd known the risks. I'd known Justin would be left in the open. I'd thought he'd be safe, though, because I'd met him long after I'd left my family.

I struggled to swallow, seeing Justin's head explode once more inside my own mind. "If it was my family that did this, I would be dead, too."

He nodded. "Then there is no reason for this to be anything but an accident. An accident you want to believe is something more so you have someone to hate for it. Magic happens, Nix. It does. Maybe Justin pissed off the wrong person on the circuit." His words were incredibly soft. More than he'd ever been with me. He was using caution.

My jaw was so tight, my teeth ached. What if he was right? I blew out a slow breath, thinking.

Zee stayed silent, letting me work through things on my own. I couldn't take my mind away from the gunshots, from the death myst, or the man who'd shot Justin through the window.

I didn't look at him. I didn't want to see pity in his eyes. Pity for me. For the girl who'd been beaten and abused as a child, whose father had turned her into a killer, and who'd finally found peace in the arms of an everyday man, and hope and a love she never thought possible in the heart of a boy who'd been her world. A groan slid from me, shaking my teeth, shaking my entire body.

"Goddamn it, Zee. I don't even know if I want to be

wrong." The thing was, I knew what I'd seen. It was burned into my mind like a brand.

"I know, doll face," he whispered. "I know."

The balance of the truck shifted as we started on a short slope downward, one that would quickly rise and then we would be on the hill. I sat straighter and stared out the side window. The snowy white scenery flickered by as we crested the hill, the hill that had been dark and too slick for a truck that held my most precious cargo.

I closed my eyes. I was not resilient enough to see the skid marks if they were still there, to see the impression at the edge of the water and know that my boy had bled out, breathed his last breath, and I'd been helpless to save him.

No . . . I had to be strong, now more than ever. I had to find out why Bear and Justin had died. They deserved that much from me.

Carefully, I let out the darkness I'd kept caged for so long. I let Phoenix Romano out, and allowed myself to truly see through her eyes. Who I'd been before. She was strong enough to do this, because she didn't love anyone.

The sensation was strange, but in seconds, I felt the truth slide under my skin. Phoenix was a predator and it would take that kind of mentality to track down the truth of this.

There were clues here on the hill, clues to what had truly happened. "Pull over, Zee."

"You sure?"

"Do it." Nausea rolled upward in my guts and I pushed it down with a simple image. A raging fire rolling through a forest, roaring at the edges, wiping out everything in its path. Emotionless, and driven by nothing but nature and the desire to consume.

My heart rate slowed, and the gut-wrenching grief and nausea bled away drop by drop.

Zee pulled over and put the emergency brake on. He got

out and came around to my side. I grabbed his hand and let him help me out as I took stock once more of my injuries. My pelvic bone was the worst, aching with every step. I focused on that, on the peripheral as I let my eyes sweep the area.

We walked to the side of the road and looked over the embankment. The trees that were shattered by the weight of the truck, the drag marks where the Ford had been towed out of the water and back up the bank. A tremor slid through my armor, but I made myself look at the scene with an analytical eye. If this had been a job of mine, there would be no clues left, but there were very few people as good as me, even when it came to the abnormals. That was where I had always come in.

Abnormals were cocky, thinking they could never be caught because of their abilities with magic. I was good enough to know everyone could be caught—magic or not.

Even me.

I needed to find something that backed up my memories to prove to Zee I was right. Maybe even to prove to myself I was right, that it was not some paranoia-induced memory that clung to me. If not, I would be forced into believing the accident was a lie, when I knew in every fiber of my being it wasn't.

Jaw tight, I searched the area, looking for tracks. Anything would have worked for me: another vehicle's tire treads, footprints that didn't fit, the tripod marks from a long-distance rifle of some variety. It had been several days since the accident and traffic through the area had not been light so I wasn't hopeful.

No doubt the local police force had screwed over the crime scene with their ineptness.

"You said there was an explosion? Then there should be some evidence, either on the truck or in the bush, of some residual magic." Zee let my hand go and started to scrape at the packed snow in a few spots on the side of the hill. "They could have buried the leftovers, but then there should be scorch marks still, even if they tried to hide it." He didn't dispute me again, for which I was grateful. The last thing I wanted was to fight with him. I'd tell him if he were right, if we found nothing. I would swallow my pride.

I nodded, thinking. "We were halfway down the hill when it happened." I made myself walk slowly, taking each step with care back up the hill.

Zee let me move on my own for a bit, then returned to my side. We were near the top when we turned and looked down the slope.

"I'm not seeing it, Nix. There is nothing here." He drew a breath and I shook my head.

Hands clenched, I scanned the slope over and over. He was right, there were no obvious scorch marks, no huge pot holes, no residue. But I would have never left something so obvious either. I would have covered my tracks.

The breath in my lungs hitched as my eyes landed on something subtly out of place on the slick slope.

"Then what is that?" I pointed at a slightly humped section right in the middle of the hill. Snow had been packed hard, almost like a speedbump, then half-heartedly covered with a few bare branches to help it blend in.

"Snow pack, that's what it is," Zee said, but he was sliding down ahead of me, hurrying. I followed slowly. The truth now was at hand, and this was either his belief or mine that would be proven.

Mine. I was right about this, as horrible as it was to be right, I knew I was.

He dug into the snow pack with the heel of his boot until blackened scorch marks appeared through the pristine white. He went to one knee and slid his fingers through the soil that flickered with tiny green crystals, then lifted his hand to his nose.

"Fuck." He whispered, "I wanted you to be wrong. Death myst, you were right."

I stopped next to him and put a hand on his shoulder.

"You believe me now?"

"Yeah." He stood and put a hand under my elbow. "All the more reason to get out of sight."

"They could be waiting at the farm," I pointed out.

"Not with my wards in place. If they try to get through, they will be fried."

They. Until we knew who had done this, it would be the nameless 'They' we would focus on.

"They'll get a shock and a half if they do." He growled the words. "Who do they think they're messing with? They can't possibly know who you are, or I am, for that matter. If they did, they never would have left you alive in the truck."

Those were my thoughts exactly. Pieces of this didn't match up. If people from my past, or Zee's, had shown up and caused this, why had they left me alive? Why hadn't I been the one who'd been shot in the head? Why was I the one that the death myst had ghosted over?

It didn't make sense.

And I didn't like when things didn't add up, especially in a world where death and magic could hide in plain sight.

Minutes later, we were back in the truck, and Zee had us moving fast, no longer drawing out the drive.

A flash of yellow 'do not cross' tape fluttered at the bottom of the hill, and I twisted my head to look at Zee so I didn't have to see the reminder.

His face was tight, his lips drawn, and his eyes narrowed. Anger radiated off him in waves, like I'd only seen once before. When we'd received news my mother had died.

He'd loved her. I knew that. But she'd been my father's

second wife, and she and Zee could never have a relationship. My father didn't like his things taken from him.

Bear had been Zee's nephew in all but blood, the only family either of them would ever know outside of me and Justin. A part of me wanted to reach across and take Zee's hand.

That was who I'd learned to become over the last twelve years: a person who could give comfort and love. A woman who was soft and kind, and full of social anxiety. That was who Justin knew. He'd never known I was a killer under all that, I'd let him believe I was my older sister. Seeing as she was dead, it was a convenient ruse.

Almost as if he were reading my mind, Zee cleared his throat and asked a question I wished he hadn't. "You aren't crying. Why not, doll face?"

Why wasn't I crying when I was facing the worst thing anyone could? I fought to find the words that would make sense. Maybe more for myself than for Zee.

I looked away from him. "I was always worried they would be taken from me. That . . . I would be found by my father and punished for everything I'd done, for the money I took from him. I thought he'd send the Stick Man after me, and that my boys would bear the brunt of my past." I shrugged and let the woman I truly was take hold of the reins once more. "Justin and Bear are gone. I have nothing to worry about anymore."

Even I heard the flat tone in my voice, the monotone that belonged a lifetime away.

"Don't go back to being her, Nix. You didn't just run from them, you ran from what they turned you into."

I looked at him, letting my eyes harden. "Then they shouldn't have woken the monster slayer that lay silent for so many years."

CHAPTER THREE

I realized Zee had drugged me after I woke. One of the Percocet likely slipped in my food, given the aftertaste in my mouth. The pain in my pelvis and arm were barely registering, a three on the pain scale. Easy to work through for now.

The only good thing I could see was we were home, in the ranch house filled with memories.

When we'd gotten home from the hospital the day before, we'd checked the perimeter of the house. Zee had taken the two farm dogs with him. The Belgian Malinois were trained not only to help with the herding of the horses, but in protection as well. A leaner version of a German shepherd, they were highly intelligent and loyal to the death.

They also had a serious aversion to magic. It had taken a long time for them to be comfortable around Zee.

Abe, the younger of the two dogs, watched me from the foot of my bed. His whole head was black, as were his legs up to where they joined with his fawn-colored body. Even the tips of the lighter color were black, giving him a two-toned look. He was big for a Mal—as the breed was known—sitting right at eighty pounds of solid muscle. His dark eyes were locked on me. He whined softly and his bushy tail thumped once.

"Abe, *kriech*." I snapped my fingers and he army-crawled up the bed until his body was stretched out along mine and his long muzzle rested on my shoulder. Both dogs were trained using German commands for guard dogs. *Kriech* meant to crawl.

Another whine slid from him.

He'd been Bear's dog, sleeping with my boy every night from the time we'd brought him home as a puppy. Abe was too smart for his own good.

I bit the inside of my cheek, the sharp pain holding the grief at bay.

The sheets were tangled around my limbs, and damp with sweat like I'd been thrashing. I sat up slowly, groaning as my body protested. Abe sat up and sniffed my hair, his big nose ruffling the mess of boxed dye blonde. I pushed him away gently with my good hand, then ran a hand over my ribs, touching carefully where the light swelling indicated the breaks. Sun streamed in through the big sliding glass doors that led out onto the back deck. Even in the dead of winter, the brilliant blue sky could be seen from any window in the house. One of the reasons I'd chosen Wyoming to run to and hide when I'd left my father's employ.

That and, as far as I knew at the time, my family had no ties to the place I was hiding. It didn't hurt that most abnormals liked the two coastlines. I didn't know the reason, and I didn't care. It worked in my favor and that was good enough for me.

Sure, there was a healthy dose of religion between the Mormons and the Catholics, but overall, it was tolerable. They were good people when they weren't too busy trying to save my soul. Something I was quite sure wasn't possible anyway.

My heart tried to take me back to grieving, showing me a memory of Bear slinging open the sliding glass door with a cringing bang, yelling at me to get up and play in the snow with him.

"Come on, Mama. Get up. We've got stuff to do!"

I swallowed, or tried to, past the lump in my throat. "Bear," I whispered his name, the view out of the sliding glass blurring for a moment as I struggled to hold back the tears. Abe whined again, as he leapt from the bed and ran to the bedroom door. He sniffed at the floor and then sat down and looked over his shoulder at me. His eyes accusing. Bear wasn't there.

"I have to let you go for a bit, baby. I . . . I'll be with you soon enough, but I have to let you go for a little while. To do what I must. Will you let me, my boy?" The words were not much, a prayer to my child in a way. An angel taken far too soon, yet I felt as though he were beside me still. I had to do what I had to do, and that meant no tears, at least for a little while.

Of course, there was no answer. I wasn't that far gone as to expect one, or be disappointed when none came.

Still, something eased in my chest, a relief of the pressure on me. That I was expected to grieve until I melted away. Of all the people in my life, Bear had understood me the best. One day I would have told him about who I'd been. I would have told him about the hidden world, when he'd been old enough. The truth of it, all of it. More than I'd ever told Justin. Because being of my blood, he needed to know his history. I'm not sure Justin would have still loved me if he'd known I'd been Phoenix Romano. He'd talked about me once.

"Did you have much to do with your sister, the Phoenix?" Justin sat next to me on the bed, his chest bare.

I shook my head. "No. We ran in different circles. She was the killer, I was the girl being groomed to be married off."

"So, you didn't like her?"

I shrugged, going for casual. "I didn't have anything to do with her, why?"

"I did a little digging after I met you." He shrugged. *"I heard some bad shit about her. That she's a psycho barely leashed by your father. That she killed a bunch of kids for kicks. Just to prove she was a bad ass."* He shook his head. *"I have a hard time believing you are related to her."*

I closed my eyes and laid down on the bed, pulled the covers up and faked a yawn. "Don't believe everything you hear, Justin. She probably wasn't all that bad."

He snorted and flicked out the light. "Killer's never change, Bea."

I put a hand over my face. I'd done enough online psychology courses over the years to be able to self-analyze my ability to compartmentalize.

Or maybe I was the cold calculating bitch I'd been accused of being more than once. That was a distinct possibility too. *Psychopath* had been a taunt thrown at me on a regular basis.

The monsters didn't like me killing them.

The normals feared me.

My family hated me.

I slid from the bed and to the door that led down the hall to the kitchen. Each step I took sent a shot of pain along my hip. Each breath was a slow burning heat through the broken bits in my chest.

The smell of bacon drew me forward. I wasn't hungry, but I had to eat if I was going to gain my strength back. There were rules to healing. Food. Rest. Slow training. More food and rest. I had time, there was no rush on this job. No one had hired me to find the killers. I wasn't on a deadline.

Even so, I itched to move, to get after whoever had done this and string them up by their innards. But I knew I had to be patient, as much as I wanted to run off after them and smile as I cut their hearts out, I had to be strong enough and that would require things like sleep, training, and food.

The kitchen was designed around a classic farmhouse style with pale blue cabinets and a barn board on one side of the oversized island. The ceiling was marked with dark timber beams and more grayish barn board. I hadn't picked out those colors, that had been all Justin.

I put a hand on the dark gray granite of the island. "Zee. You give me Percocet again without my permission and I'm going to sic Abe on you."

Abe gave a soft woof from my side in agreement, his eyes locking on Zee.

Zee didn't look up from the stove, and did nothing but grunt. With one hand, he waved a spatula at the far side of the island. "Crash is in the paper today again. Chief of police said it was faulty brakes, of course."

I slid around the edge of the island and grabbed at the paper. Already open to the page where Bear and Justin smiled up at me, their heads pushed together as Bear hugged his dad around the neck.

I looked away from their faces, to the words highlighted in bright yellow. Zee's doing, no doubt.

"Accident. Frozen brakes. Dead on impact. Lone survivor lucky to be alive." I crumpled the paper as I spoke. "The police are in on it. They have to be."

"Of course they are. Or at least one or two of them are. But are they abs or norms on the take?" Zee did look at me then. His eyes were tired around the edges, and something about his movements made me watch him a little closer.

Stiffer? No, there was a tremor in his hand holding the spatula. Maybe he was just overtired, but I didn't think so.

"Stayed up while I slept?" I tossed the paper aside as he slid a plate of food to me.

"We have to take shifts at night, at least until we know for sure who did this." He sat on a barstool across from me and we ate in silence except for the clink of cutlery on the china. The food tasted like nothing to me and I almost had to poke it down to make myself eat it all.

Food and rest. I needed to heal to be strong enough to hunt.

Zee finished ahead of me. I handed the last of my bacon to Abe who took it carefully from my fingers. Abigail lifted her head from the living room, her ears perked forward. She'd always been more of Justin's dog. Her eyes slid to the front window, waiting for him.

"There is something you haven't considered." Zee took my plate and his and put them into the dishwasher.

"And that is?" I arched an eyebrow and leaned back on my chair in an attempt to ease the pain in my hip.

He shut the dishwasher and turned it on. "That their deaths had nothing to do with you or me. That this happened because of something not at all tied to the Romano family."

Those words hovered between us. My family thought of themselves as mafia because of their connections with them. They thought of themselves as untouchable because of my father's deals he made with someone far more dangerous than the human mafia.

I frowned. "How is that even possible? Why would we be targeted otherwise?"

Zee put his fists on the granite countertop. "Tell me again what the man from the hospital said."

I drew a breath. "He asked if he should finish off the wife."

"Exactly." Zee leaned toward me. "Clearly if it was you he was after, even if he decided to hold off for some reason, they'd have used your name. One of them anyway. Bea, Nix. Something. But you are just *the wife*."

I sat there thinking about what he'd said, letting the words sink in. "Then . . . they were after Justin all along?"

Zee's face was grim. "That's what I'm guessing. And if you didn't have the Percocet in you, you'd have beat me to that conclusion."

I mulled over his words. You didn't refer to targeted hits as *the wife*. You used their names. Or you called them the mark. Or the hit. Or any number of other things, but nothing so generic as *the wife*.

"Could it be a rival skier who wanted him bumped? That next sponsorship, he told me it was a gold mine. Could it have been enough to put him in danger?" Zee kept cleaning the kitchen as he spoke, letting me follow my own threads.

I shook my head. "No, he was friends with everyone he met. You know that. He and Noah . . . they were like the good guys. The ones everyone wanted their picture with, the ones everyone wanted to party with."

Zee nodded, but I knew he wasn't convinced any more than I was. Reality was, hits didn't happen for no reason, they were never random, and there were so few mistakes that I couldn't chalk this up to that.

I rubbed my good hand over my face.

"I don't want a funeral for them."

His shoulders hunched. "About that. I didn't, but . . . Mary-Ellen took it over."

My jaw twitched hard and I swallowed the words that fought to spill out. "When?"

"Tomorrow. The chief of police . . ."

"What?"

"Shit, don't shoot me, Nix," he muttered. "The chief had

Bear and Justin cremated. To be fair, Mary-Ellen fought him on it, on your behalf."

Cremated.

I couldn't even say goodbye. Mary-Ellen was an interfering busybody, but I had no real anger for her.

It was the chief of police I wanted to skewer. Cremation meant there was no way to prove the gunshot to Justin's head, no way to detect any of the death myst on the clothing. Whoever had done this was covering their tracks. I'd give them that.

"Autopsies aren't done that fast," I said. "Not two days after an accident."

"I know," Zee said. "They're pushing this through hard."

I closed my eyes. A funeral, I was going to have to go through that regardless now. Of course, Mary-Ellen would think she was being helpful. There was a choice; I could either go into town and flip out on her and shut the whole thing down, or I could go through with it and have it done. I didn't want to plan a funeral. I didn't want people's pity or sympathy.

I wanted to start hunting whoever had done this to my boys.

Without another word, I slid from the barstool and hobbled back to my bedroom with Abe on my heels. I dropped a hand to his head and let him take some of my weight. "Good boy. You stick with me now, okay."

He pressed a little harder against my leg, giving me his silent and unwavering support. Back in the room, I fumbled out of my pajama bottoms and into my jeans, tugged on a couple pairs of thick wool socks, then an undershirt and thick sweater that barely fit over my cast.

I caught a glimpse of my face in the large mirror next to the bed and over the dresser. My normally tanned skin was pasty, pale, and my dark roots were showing through the blonde.

The contacts I wore made my eyes green. I reached up and popped them both out. Dark eyes looked back at me now, dark with flecks of amber in one of them. I turned away from the mirror and Abe matched his pace to mine as I headed to the back of the house. Zee didn't try to stop me; he knew me well enough to let me be.

Justin would have tried to baby me, to tuck me back into bed and tell me he'd take care of me. Look at where that had gotten us. I'd hidden away from the world, trusting him and Zee. And now something he was into had gotten both Justin and Bear killed.

Bundled up in boots and a heavy coat that again barely fit over my cast, I headed out to the barn and the quiet refuge of my horses. They nickered to me, their soft muzzles reaching for my hands, looking for my touch. There were four mares in foal, and one young stallion in the barn, and I took my time with each of them before I let them out into the bigger pasture for the day.

Moving hay, cleaning stalls, filling water buckets, grooming the pregnant mares and checking on their progress took hours, and tired me out physically even if my mind was far from exhausted. So much for letting myself rest. I should have known I couldn't just stay inside and sleep.

I kept pushing through until I could do nothing but sit on a bale of hay, sweat running down my face.

Abe lay on the floor in front of me, his ears and eyes alert as he constantly scanned the area. I drew a breath, pushed to my feet, and headed to the tack room at the back of the barn. The smell of leather enveloped me as I stepped in, the warmth of the heated room cutting through the chill on my limbs. I stripped off my heavy coat and tossed it to the side, then walked to the far wall where the saddle racks hung.

I stood there, staring at the wall, seeing the perfectly etched lines where the door into a hidden room had been placed on one of Justin's first skiing trips after we'd moved here. Because I didn't want him to know he'd married a freak who couldn't give up her weapons entirely.

I went to my knees and stuck my hand under the lowest saddle rack, feeling for the spring mechanism with my fingers. I found the small, cold steel lever and tugged it once, unlatching the door.

The rack of saddles opened outward. I pushed to my feet and stepped around the door and down into a narrow room. There was a dangling light cord somewhere, and it took me a moment of grasping in the dark to find it. I pulled the string and the hundred-watt light came on in a blinding flash. Abe sniffed at some of the gear piled up near the floor.

There was a rustling, the sound of a yawn inside the room. I drew a slow breath. "Ladies, you awake?"

A mutter, but nothing else.

The walls were covered from floor to ceiling with guns of all shapes and sizes, from a variety of handguns to long rifles to AK-47s and even an Israeli Galil. There was a rocket launcher at the top of my reach, not that I'd had to use it, but it was a nice backup weapon. Knives, grenades, flash bangs, tear gas, and then my rack of poisons. I ran my hands over the tools of my trade. I had my favorites, of course, and they were in the center of the wall in their own sheaths. My two best guns were Beretta style in shape and look, but they were custom-made handguns with a few quirks.

And there was one small feature that set them apart from the rest.

"Oh, look who shows up after how many months?" Dinah all but bounced in her holster as she threw the words at me.

None of the other weapons talked, only Dinah and Eleanor had been cursed with a strange kind of sentience.

They didn't think it was a curse—yes, I'd asked them—but I wasn't so sure. Sometimes I wondered if they were real people, whose souls had been trapped inside the inanimate weapons as punishment.

Mostly though, I chose not to think about them as anything but weapons.

Matte black and threaded for silencers, they had their names etched into each smooth metal grip. Eleanor on one and Dinah on the other. I picked up Eleanor and ran my thumb over the etching. "Long time, bitch," I said softly.

"Screw you," she muttered.

Eleanor had earned her name because of something my mother had told me as a child. She said when you died, you saw a bright, shining light coming for you and that was death. Eleanor was my preferred killing gun, and since the name meant bright, shining one, I'd always felt it fit. I frowned and continued to feel the edges of the name. I'd thought I'd left her behind for good.

"What made you come back to us now? Haven't seen you for months." Dinah's voice was lilting almost, what you'd think of from a fairy in a kid's movie. She was also the chatty one.

"Someone killed my boy," I said as I opened the chamber on Eleanor, checked it, took a clip and slammed it home. Unlimited rounds—a perk of the girls—with a laser sight, was deadly at a lot of ranges. I flicked the laser on and slowly turned, letting the red dot dance on the wall and across the other weapons, flicking here and there before turning it off.

"Your son?" Eleanor asked quietly.

I nodded. They didn't have eyes but they seemed to be able to "see", for lack of a better word. Or maybe they sensed the world around them. I wasn't truly sure.

Dinah was just as much of a bitch as Eleanor, though

technically, Eleanor had more kills. I put the clip into Dinah just as hard. She gave a shiver in my hand.

"I want to kill something. Tell me we are going hunting," she whined.

Dinah was named after an old biblical character and her name meant judgment. More often than not, I used Dinah to inflict wounds, and slow people down, much to her displeasure. Not to say that she didn't ever kill people, just that I preferred Eleanor for that. She was less . . . needy about the blood being spilled.

"Yes, Dinah. We are going hunting."

"Yippy, it's about damn time!" She all but squealed the words.

I took the black leather holster from the side wall, stripped down to my thinnest shirt and put it on, weaving my cast through the loops. I tightened the straps, adjusting them to my shape so they hugged my body tightly, then slid both guns into their spot. They fit in my custom shoulder holster, over my lower back, which meant they were perfectly hidden if I wore the right coat.

Extra magazines and ammo for the guns went onto the shoulder holster's straps made specifically for that. The two guns wouldn't be enough, but if I was going back to being that woman I'd left behind, I would start with the guns that had protected me the best, despite their attitudes.

Eleanor shimmied in her holster, settling in. "Who did it?"

"I don't know. But we're going to find out." I looked over the rest of my gear I had put together in the last twelve years.

Even out of the business, I'd never stopped thinking I might need to protect my family at some point. Knives adorned a whole section, tactical gear, survival gear, climbing gear . . . camouflage, dark clothing, bulletproof vest and riot gear. Even riot gear for Abe and Abigail, which consisted of thick leather dog coats edged with Kevlar. All of it just in case.

I shivered in the sudden realization that all that prep had not done me any good, because ultimately, I had let my guard down. All it would have taken was a simple check of the brakes before we left the Christmas party.

"Whoever did this was at the party." I whispered the words to myself.

An image of the Santa, all dressed up in red outside the house, slammed into my brain. It was him. He had been the one to do this. I was sure of it in a way I could not explain.

My body heaved, and the last of my breakfast fought its way up my throat. I clenched my teeth and held it at bay.

Someone at the Christmas party. The flickering lights, the whisper of green myst through the house. While the lights had been out, Santa had been outside, and that's when the brakes had been tampered with. I knew it without a shadow of a doubt with the gut instinct that came from being trained in the business.

I took my cell phone from my pocket and dialed Mary-Ellen.

She picked up on the second ring. "Hello?"

"Who was the Santa at the party?"

"Who is this?" Her tone was anything but nice. Which was odd for her. I gripped the phone harder.

"It's Bea. *Who was the Santa at the party?*" Perhaps my tone finally reached through to her. Then again, maybe not.

"Oh, Bea, I'm so sorry your sweet boy—"

"Who was the goddamn Santa?"

There was a huge intake of breath. "I'm sorry, I can't have you talking to me like that."

I bit my lower lip to keep from screaming at her, and I clenched the edge of the doorframe to keep from storming off, driving to her house and putting Dinah to her temple.

Dinah sniffed, her voice muffled from my back. "I'd shoot her in the face if it was me, then she'd start talking."

I swatted my hand to my lower back to shut her up.

"Who. Was. The. Santa?" Every word was quiet, but full of heat. It was the best I could do at staying polite.

"I hired him. He was here visiting family. Said he had played Santa before."

"Did he have a name?"

"John Smith. But it doesn't matter, he never came in, never even gave the kids their toys. He just took my money and left."

Of course, he hadn't followed through. I rolled my eyes. That was a false name if I ever heard one, which meant there would be very little to go on. He would have spun a web of lies to hide his tracks. I would still have Zee look into him and have him check at Mary-Ellen's place for any leftover magic. Just in case.

I hung up on Mary-Ellen without a goodbye. So much for finding anything useful there.

"You should be nice, or I'll misfire on you," Dinah lilted from her holster.

"You would never give up the chance of killing someone," I snapped. My guns were amazing, but they were also a serious pain in the ass when they wanted to be.

Dinah sniffed again but went quiet.

I made myself go to the back wall and the full-length mirror. To the side of it was another latch with a code pad. I plugged in the numerical equivalent of Bear's name. 2327. There was a click and the latch opened. I swung the mirror open to reveal six shelves each a solid foot deep. The top shelf held all my fake IDs, passports, names, and information I'd stolen from my father along with the money.

Money which filled the remaining five shelves. Five million dollars that I'd planned to never use. I didn't need it. I didn't want my father's help for anything, even though I knew he owed me at least that much money for my services rendered and rivals slain.

My back twitched, pulling at old scars.

Hundred-dollar bills packed tightly in bundles of a thousand each. I grabbed two stacks and tucked them into a duffel bag. I would come back later for more weapons.

With difficulty, I pulled the string to the light with my casted hand, plunging the narrow room into darkness before I stepped into the tack room. I pushed the saddle rack shut, the only sound, the latch clicking closed once more.

Back at the house, Zee sat on the back porch waiting for me.

His eyes were narrowed as I approached, flickering over the bag slung over my shoulder. "Feel better now that you've pushed yourself?"

I shrugged. "I had to get a few things."

"That's why you aren't freaking out about the funeral? You think someone might show?" His eyes widened.

"I'm surprised you didn't think of it." I lowered myself into the chair next to him, wincing at the throbbing pain in so many parts of my body.

"I'm getting old, Nix."

Dinah snickered from her holster. "He is old."

"Don't be rude," Eleanor chided. "I always liked Zee."

He lifted both eyebrows. "The ladies are in fine form, I see."

I shrugged.

Another time, he would have laughed off the comments. But not today. And I didn't correct him, not after seeing the tremor in his hands. I glanced at him. "Something you want to tell me?"

"Not right now. We have other things to worry about." He looked out over the pastures covered in white, the fences dotting the farm, dividing it. "You should try to sleep. You're going to need your strength for the funeral tomorrow."

I shook my head. "You first. I'll be good until tonight."

He started to argue, opened his mouth, thought better of it and then stood. "Fine. I'll be in the living room on the couch."

Abigail, the older of the two Malinois, went with him. Abe watched her go, but didn't move from my side.

"That's it, then? You're my best boy now?" I ran a hand over his head and he put his muzzle on my lap with the softest exhalation of breath, a doggy sigh.

Nothing else could bring the emotion up through me like the understanding that Abe was missing Bear, too, that somehow, he knew his boy was gone forever.

I pulled one of the magazines from my right pocket and carefully checked it over. I stayed where I was on the porch and pulled Eleanor and Dinah apart on the table next to me. They grunted and sometimes laughed while I cleaned them and put them back together. Mostly they laughed at me for struggling to work around a hand done up in a cast. But the task kept my mind on something other than the grief that wanted to consume me at every turn.

I would not succumb to it. I refused to let my boys' deaths slow me from finding those who'd done this to all of us. Nothing was going to stop me from making those at fault pay.

Hell hath no fury like a mother whose bear cub was killed in front of her eyes.

"I'm coming for you," I whispered to the growing darkness. "Do you know who I am? Do you know what you've awakened?"

Dinah and Eleanor went silent on the table, for once not answering me.

There was no answer, but for the long howl of a wolf in

the mountains. Abe sat up and a growl trickled from his throat as he bared his teeth, his hackles rising along his back. I didn't tell him to shush. He was no longer a family dog any more than I was a wife and a mother.

I wanted to snarl with him, show my teeth and dive into the fray. The time would come. Now I had to be patient. I had to heal.

Then, and only then, would I hunt down my prey and pull them apart while they begged for mercy.

Mercy I would never give them as long as I drew breath, that they would never find in my hands.

"We'll kill them all," Eleanor whispered in the dark. I nodded.

"Every last one."

CHAPTER FOUR

The funeral was held at the Mormon church. Of course, that was all Mary-Ellen. I kept reminding myself she was being helpful, that she was trying to be kind. Of course, she was a sobbing mess as she tried to gather me into a hug within seconds of stepping into the chapel. It was almost enough to make me pull Dinah from under my loose-fitting shirt and hip-length wool coat.

"She wore pants?"

I heard someone whisper those words a little too loudly. I turned slowly, not recognizing the woman and not caring. Judgmental bastards.

Dinah and Eleanor grumbled under my coat. They knew when to keep it down. I did not.

"I'll wear whatever the fuck I want to the funeral of my son and husband, and you'd do well to keep your goddamn mouth shut." I locked eyes with the woman, but not for long because she couldn't hold my gaze. She muttered something that may have been an apology and scuttled away.

Zee was at my elbow. "That was subtle."

Dinah shivered in her holster, a laugh held back.

I nodded. "She was lucky I didn't draw on her."

He grunted. "Lucky it was your left wrist that broke."

I almost laughed because it was a long-standing joke that even though I was right-handed, I drew my weapons faster with my left. I wondered if that would be true now that the left had been broken. I also knew our banter was nothing more than a distraction for what was coming.

We were seated at the front, which meant we had to walk down the long aisle between the pews. I took the chance to look at every person already there.

Not that there were many. Some of Bear's school friends and their parents, Mary-Ellen's family, a few other members of the local congregation and community, Justin's best friend, Noah.

He raised grief-stricken, red-rimmed blue eyes to me. They had been like brothers. That's what Justin had said. How many times had we had him over for dinner? Now when I looked at him, I wondered what he knew about Justin's path, and what he'd tell me if I asked. I gave him a nod and he stood as though I'd beckoned him. Shit. I did not want a hug from him for multiple reasons, the most obvious being I didn't want him asking why I was packing a pair of guns into a funeral.

When he drew close, his hands raising to embrace me, I shook my head and took a step back. "Don't hug me."

"Of course." He dropped his hands, then ran one through his shaggy blond hair. "Look, I know it's hollow, but I can't tell you how sorry I am. I . . . I can't believe they're both gone. I wish . . ."

I nodded, hoping if I didn't speak he'd get the hint. Apparently not.

He glanced at his hands. "I know that you are going

through a lot, right now, and I want to be there for you. Justin would want me to help you with anything you need."

I nodded again, watching him closely, noting how his eyes dipped to the left. The left meant a lie was coming. This was about to get interesting.

"I know he has a ton of his skiing stuff in his office. I can help you clean it out, pack it away, get rid of it. And if it's too much, you don't even have to be there, I can sort it all out, get it packed for you. If you want." His deep blue eyes were sincere, but there was something . . . off. Besides the lie, that was. More like there was an urgency to his offer.

Zee cleared his throat. "We'll let you know when we start that."

Noah turned and gave him a smile. "Sure. You've got my number. I'm in town for at least a week or two now."

In town. He didn't live here. What was he doing here then, staying so long after the funeral? He and Justin always met at their ski destinations. The reality was, Noah didn't live anywhere. He floated from place to place according to Justin. Ladies' man, talented skier, party animal. That was Noah. Again, according to Justin.

I'd never seen anything to dispute it. Even now, this close to Noah, there was a whiff of beer under the cologne he wore, and maybe the red-rimmed eyes weren't from sorrow so much as overdoing the drinking the night before.

Not that I was judging. If he needed to drink to get through his best friend's funeral, so be it. I wasn't much of a drinker; the last thing I wanted was to have my senses blurred.

"I'm surprised you're so . . . together," Noah said softly. He put a hand to the edge of his sport coat. "I have a flask if you want."

I kept my eyes on his, cool. "My mother told me once that if you loved someone enough that it hurt you when they died, you shouldn't try to erase the grief. The grief was what told you how deeply you loved them. So, I'll pass."

Zee grabbed my good arm and steered me away from the now slack-jawed Noah. "Your mom really say that?"

"Yes. Right before I left that life behind." She'd said it right before she'd died.

Finally, we were in our seats after dodging a few more sympathetic smiles and attempts at hugs. No one seemed surprised when I recoiled from them. Hell, I'd been doing it since we'd moved here, so my behavior was nothing new.

I closed my eyes and tried to listen to the sounds around me outside of the speaker at the pew talking about life and death and losing loved ones. The cough of someone in the back, the whisper of a child, the crinkle of a tissue.

But it was the scuff of a shoe on the edge of a doorway that turned me around in my seat.

There at the back of the chapel stood a man I didn't know, one who didn't belong in Jackson Hole. Suit and tie, all dark colors as per most funerals, he could have been anyone. Could have just been here to support the loss of a local man and his son.

Except, I was sure it was the man from the hospital.

I gripped Zee's arm, and he slowly turned so we were both looking at the man. Those around us turned too, of course, and the man slipped into the room and sat in the back pew, bowing his head, then lifting it so just his eyes were on mine.

Zee faced the front once more. "Stop staring at him."

But I couldn't. My eyes narrowed and the man . . . he smiled at me, and tipped his head. I was up and moving, and so was he. Away from me, out the back doors of the chapel. I hurried down the pews as fast as I could, to the gasps of the people there. Let them have their fucking show. Let them have their gossip. That man, whoever he was, knew something about the death of my boys.

"Hurry," Dinah urged me, twitching in her holster.

In the foyer of the chapel, the man in black was gone and I didn't know which direction he'd slipped. There was parking on two sides of the chapel. The door closest to me would make sense, but there was no swirl of cold air and snow from the door opening. I hurried down the hall to the other exit. Zee caught up to me and passed me. He didn't ask if I was sure.

I was and he knew it.

He ran, I hobbled, and the rest of the congregation followed at a hurried, whispering, pace. Noah caught me by the arm as I stepped out of the church. "What is going on?"

"Old boyfriend." The lie was easy and out of my mouth without hesitation. "I told him not to come, but . . ."

"Oh." His hand slid from my arm and I walked out to the parking lot where Zee stood watching a black sedan drive away.

"Plates?" I asked softly.

"No, they were blacked out."

Of course.

The bishop ushered us all back in, and the funeral was wrapped up in what I suspected was record time.

Bear would have laughed; he would have thought it was great fun that Zee and I had broken up something that was supposed to be solemn and quiet. That made me smile, the first smile since he'd been gone. Small, fleeting, but it was there. He was still with me, and that would be enough for today.

After that, we followed the hearse to the cemetery. We were the only ones who went to the actual burial, though Mary-Ellen fought to come with us. I denied her to her face, thanked her for all she did and left her there at the church with the plates and plates of food, punch, and gossip mongering.

Seeing Bear and Justin go into the ground . . . this was the part I didn't want anyone else around for, the part where I knew I wouldn't be able to hold back the tears. To say my final goodbye, to lay them both to rest and start on a new chapter in my life.

Zee was on one knee, his hand over the top of the smaller urn. He murmured words I couldn't hear, didn't want to hear, because as he spoke, his shoulders shook and one hand went to cover his face. He kept his head bowed for a long time. A tiny flare of light whispered around his fingers, golden and soft. I didn't know what kind of spell he put on Bear's urn, but I could take a guess.

"No one will be able to take his spirit," Zee said, a frown creasing his face, and then he shook his head as if some insect had landed on his skin.

I nodded, but was unable to answer past the constriction in my throat.

I looked to the sky for strength, to find the words I needed to say my final goodbye. There were no words waiting for me there, which left me looking around the cemetery for something, anything, to get me through this. Instead of inspiration, suspicion met me head on.

A dark sedan, the same one from the chapel, was there, parked far enough away that if I'd been anyone else, I would doubt what I was seeing. Far enough away that if we tried to give chase, we'd lose them.

I lifted my bad hand and flipped them off. If they were watching, they'd see it.

I put a hand on Zee's shoulder and he stepped back, then I went to my knees. I leaned my head against the light-colored wooden urn. "I love you, my boy. This isn't goodbye. I promise you that. Wait for me on the other side because I won't be long, and we won't ever be apart again."

Strange that a killer like me could believe in an afterlife.

Maybe that's why I had been so good at it, though. I didn't see death as being final.

Tears slid down my cheeks but they didn't choke me up, they freed me. There was a strange peace in having the charge to go after his killers. I whispered my love to Justin, pressing my hand to his urn. I would miss him, miss his laughter and his smile. His boundless love and energy, the way he made me smile. The way he'd shown me I was more than the name that had been attached to me for so long.

I turned away and touched Bear's urn again . . . Bear . . . he was part of my heart and soul in a way I'd never understood before he'd been born. Even when I'd been pregnant I hadn't understood the depth of love between a mother and child. My fingers trembled as I clutched at what was left of my son.

"We'll make this right, Nix. We will," Zee said.

"I know." I took a step back and then another and another until I was at the truck and could breathe once more. I looked over to where the sedan had been parked. Of course, it was gone. "They're watching me."

"Making sure of what?"

"I don't know." I shook my head. "That I don't suspect?"

"Well, you blew that at the church." He snorted.

I rubbed a hand over my face as he pulled away from the cemetery. "Then what are they looking for?"

"We've been out of the game long enough that we're getting slow." He gave a rough laugh. "If they're keeping an eye on us, it's because they want to make sure we aren't . . ."

"At home. Could they break the wards?" I whispered and his foot was already on the gas pedal, the tires biting into the snow and drifting us through the first corner.

"If they have another Hider, yes. They could do it."

The drive home was almost an hour in normal conditions, and Zee had us home in half that.

He hit the brakes hard as we reached the end of the driveway and we slid sideways once more. I was out of the truck as soon as it stopped and forced myself into an awkward run up the steps of the house.

Zee spun in a quick circle, his eyes narrowed. "The wards are gone. It has to be a Hider. Watch yourself."

"Abigail, Abe!" I called the dogs and gave a sharp whistle.

There was the faintest of cries from the living room. I bolted through and then skidded to a stop. Abigail lay flat out, her eyes glazed, the bullet having gone straight through her skull, dead center. Abe fought to crawl to me. Blood poured from a wound in his chest, and his breath came in wheezes that splattered his lips with red foam. "Get him to the vet," I yelled at Zee. "Go, go!"

"He's just a dog," Zee yelled back. I spun on him.

"He was Bear's dog. Get him to the damn vet!"

Zee shook his head. "When the house is cleared."

I wanted to scream in frustration, even though I knew, logically, he was right. Which meant the faster I helped him clear it, the faster we'd be moving. "Abe, *bleib*." Stay.

I pointed at the floor and he stopped moving, though the gurgling breath didn't slow. I pulled Dinah and Eleanor out, and the ladies settled into my hands as though they were an extension of my body.

In under two minutes, we'd cleared the house. Only two of the rooms had any obvious damage, and Zee agreed there was nothing more urgent than getting Abe to the vet. We wrapped him in a blanket and Zee slid him into the passenger side of the truck. "Just get him there." I shut the door.

Zee's jaw tightened. "Shoot anything that moves. You won't see the Hider until he's on top of you."

I gave him a nod and he pulled out of the driveway, once more moving at a fast pace. I hoped Abe would make it, but it was out of my hands now. I stepped into the house and made my way to Abigail before I checked out the rooms that had been searched. I went to my knees beside her, touched a hand along her back and then slowly pried her mouth open. The dogs were trained to attack, grab any intruders and shake them until they were on the ground. From there, they were to work as a team, disarming or strangling the intruder. Inside Abigail's mouth, caught on her back teeth, was a strip of material.

I pulled it out and held it up to the light. There was a slight shimmer to it, and as I rubbed my fingers across it, I pinned it down. Black Gore-Tex, something you could find in a variety of clothing. Justin had some Gore-Tex leg gaiters, as did a lot of people in the area for keeping their legs dry in the deep snow.

I slid my fingers over Abigail's body again, pressing against her neck. She hadn't lost all of her heat. I guessed it had been barely an hour since she'd been shot and we'd been gone for close to three.

Whoever had done this had waited until they knew for sure we were gone. With Abigail's body temperature, they hadn't come in right away either. I frowned. Could it have been someone who had been at the funeral to make sure we were there? It would have been easy enough to check on us, and know that we were going to be at least another couple of hours. Even with that they'd have had time to drive all the way out to the farm, search and leave without running into us.

The man in the suit was my first inclination. If it was him, he'd moved fast looking for whatever it was he had been looking for. Maybe the money in the barn? I doubted it, though I would double-check the stash later.

I stroked Abigail's fur. "I'm sorry, my girl." I stood and pulled a blanket from the couch to cover her body. My ribs ached even with the painkillers, and moving her outside to bury her was not a priority. That could wait until Zee came back.

I went to the kitchen and washed my hands clean of the dogs' blood, my mind already working ahead, mapping out my next steps.

Our bedroom and Justin's office had been the two rooms that had been tossed.

I'd check out the bedroom first, because I was sure there would be nothing to find in it. Then I would check Justin's office. That was the most logical place for him to have hidden something that an intruder would look for.

Unlike me, he didn't have a barn or a shop that I would call just his, so the office would be where he'd have hidden something.

I paused at the sink as I dried my hands, the distinct crunch of tires on snow turning me around. From where I stood, I could see out the window into the front yard, but whoever had arrived had parked to the right of the window, far enough that I couldn't see the make of the vehicle or who stepped out of it without placing myself into full view.

I pulled Dinah from my back with my right hand and crept along the edge of the kitchen to where I could see the front door.

"Killing?" she asked.

"Maybe." I doubted whoever had tossed the house had come back this soon. At least, that was what I was hoping.

Then again, whoever was coming up the steps was deliberately being quiet. Most people stomped their feet to remove the snow, which in turn announced their presence. And those who knew us, knew we had dogs that didn't like strangers. It was important to not try to be sneaky with attack dogs on the premises.

Whoever this was didn't know us, and wasn't here on a social visit.

I brought Dinah up and waited with the red dot sighted on the front door at what would be gut level for the average person. I wouldn't kill them right away. I needed answers. But that didn't mean I wasn't going to shoot this quiet, unknown person.

Dinah sighed. "I am so looking forward to this."

CHAPTER FIVE

I stood there, leaning against the kitchen wall with Dinah in my right hand, the left hand still in a cast tucked up underneath the right to help balance the hold.

The front door eased open, slowly, without a creak. I sighted on the red dot, waiting for the perfect shot. I wanted whoever this was fully inside, and the door shut before I put a bullet in them. Easier than trying to drag them inside to interrogate if they fell backward onto the deck.

A shaggy blond head poked in. "Bea, you here?"

"Shit," I muttered and lowered Dinah and slid her back into my holster while she grumbled, all before his eyes swept over me in the kitchen. I glared at him, keeping my position against the wall. "What the hell are you doing here, Noah? And since when do you just walk the fuck into my house?"

He let himself the rest of the way in and shut the door behind him, as if I hadn't just cussed him out. "I wanted to check on you. The chapel scene, not letting anyone come to the graveside . . . Justin would have wanted—"

"I don't care what he would have wanted." I also didn't

care how hard my words were. "He isn't here now, and I can take care of things by myself. I did before him, and I will again. Capiche?"

Noah's eyes widened, but I saw a flicker of something I didn't like. That edge of untruth I'd seen in the chapel. He knew what Justin had been up to, which meant he knew what had gotten him and Bear killed. I could feel it in my gut.

He took a step closer, one hand outstretched and his face a picture of sadness and grief. "Who are you? Where is the sweet wife of my best friend who always greeted me with a kiss on the cheek and fresh muffins from the oven?"

I glared at him. "She died with her husband and son. Who are you, Noah?"

His face paled.

I arched an eyebrow. "What was Justin doing? What was he into that killed him and Bear?"

His eyes darted down and he shook his head. "What are you talking about?"

"What was the big score the two of you were into? Not skiing promos. I'm not that blind now."

He cleared his throat. "Listen, I know you're grieving—"

"Did he tell you who I am?"

That seemed to catch him off guard. His jaw dropped and he stood there as though I'd hit him with a stun gun.

"What?"

"DID HE TELL YOU WHO I AM?" The words reverberated between us, echoing in the vast, empty house.

Noah let out a slow breath, opened his mouth, and I cut him off.

"No more lies. You owe me that. My husband is dead because of lies. My boy is dead because of lies. Tell me the truth or get the hell out of my house and never, ever, come back if you value your life." I breathed the words, almost growling the last of them. I wasn't sure he would be honest with me even now, but I would give him this one last chance.

His lips pursed and he shook his head, finally letting out a big breath. "I know who your father is, yes."

I nodded, wondering just what he meant by that. Did he know I was not my sister? Did he know I was Phoenix? "And?"

He shrugged. "Justin told me one night after a competition. We'd been drinking and he told me because I asked about your family. Said you were treated pretty badly." His jaw ticked.

I'd told Justin about one incident with my older brother Gabe. About how he and his friends had beaten me so badly one night that I didn't remember what else had happened. I didn't know if there had been a rape at the time. I'd suspected, but wasn't sure. That's the thing when you're only twelve. You don't know. Looking back, I knew the truth. I'd been sore, aching between my legs in a bad way that could only mean one thing—that the beating had led to at least one of the men raping me. For all I knew, it had been my brother.

I wouldn't put it past him.

I shook my head. "You going to tell me what you and Justin were doing?" I threw the question at him again, bringing him back to the conversation at hand.

"Bea, I get that you might think this is some conspiracy, and it's probably easier than believing that what happened was an accident with your family history—"

"It's time for you to go." I folded my arms and tipped my chin at the door behind him. "If you don't want to be honest with me, you can just fuck off."

I didn't think his eyes could widen further but they did. "Bea, I know you're grieving but this isn't you. Don't let this change you."

My right hand twitched, and I let him see me put it to my back. "Go, Noah."

"Where is Zee?"

"Out."

The standoff was obvious to me, if not to him. He frowned further. "Where are the dogs?"

"Abe is with Zee." Not a lie.

He frowned. "And Abigail?"

"In the barn."

His eyes narrowed further. Almost like he knew I was lying. But why would he care?

"Bea, is there something going on you want to tell me about?"

I arched an eyebrow at him. "Something you want to tell *me* about? Like why you couldn't wait to get into Justin's office now that he's dead? Is there some fake sponsorship deal hiding the truth of something else? Maybe about that big score? Or something else?"

His jaw dropped. "What? No, of course not!"

I pointed at him for the third time. "Go. I don't want you here right now, and if I find anything for sponsorships, I will send them your way. Justin would have wanted me to do that for you." I couldn't help but throw his own words back at him.

He flushed. "Grief is ugly on you, Bea. Don't let it be the part of your life that defines you." He backed away and shut the door behind him. I waited for the sound of the car to leave before I let myself breathe.

"You are no therapist, and your bullshit psychoanalysis won't work on this girl. Not when I know you're lying about something," I muttered to myself as I walked down the hall to my bedroom.

"He was lying," Eleanor said. "You could almost smell it on him."

"I know," I said.

"Think he's an abnormal?" Dinah asked.

"No. Zee would have known." I sighed as I looked around the room at the mess.

The mattress was flipped and shredded, every piece of clothing had been tossed out and the drawers and the closet had been busted open, shards of the thin wood spread across the room.

There were holes in various parts of the walls, as though the intruder had randomly chosen spots to try out his fist. I went through the few books laid on the bed that had pages torn out. Justin's family bible was missing, but nothing else that I could see. I closed my eyes, thinking about what was in the bible. Some of his family history in the front, but nothing other than a notation here and there. None of the few pieces of jewelry I had were missing, none of the coins that Justin collected in his travels had been taken. Nothing of value was gone.

Not that I thought it was a random robbery, but those details confirmed it. I sat on the edge of the box spring and let myself take the room in, let it soak in that whatever had caused my two boys' deaths wasn't over yet. Whoever had killed them wasn't done with this place.

If they'd been willing to hire a Hider to break the wards, there was money involved, and more magic than I would have liked.

"What the hell was going on, Justin? How deep was the shit you were in?" I ran a hand over the edge of the box spring.

The more I thought about the situation, the more certain I was that this was directly tied to something Justin had been doing. There was no denying it now. Zee had been right all along, if they—whoever had done this—were after me, they'd have killed me in the truck. Or the hospital. Both times, I'd been helpless, and yet I'd been spared.

Spared because I had no connection to whatever it was they were looking for. Bear and I were fodder. It had been Justin and something he'd hidden that they were after. They needed him out of the way first? Or had that been punishment?

The only questions now were why and what were they after? A family bible was hardly a find.

Unless it held something important. Numbers, a name . . . I shook my head. Too late for that line of thinking now. It was gone, and I doubted I'd be able to find it anytime soon. But was that the only thing they had come for? Somehow, I doubted it.

I pushed up with my good hand and headed slowly to the office at the front of the house. There were wet spots on the floor where the boots of the intruders had tracked in snow and ice, the warmth of the house melting it into puddles.

I made myself put my feet in the imprints that had been left, as subtle as they were. Wide, they were spaced wide apart, like a big man. Bigger than the one who had been watching me. That one had been tall, yes, but slender. This man . . . he was built like a brick shithouse on steroids with the straddle of his legs. Like the man in the Santa suit? Possibly.

Unable to stop myself, I considered Noah. He was a bigger man, but he didn't straddle his stance like this one did, which was the only thing that kept me from tracking him down right then and putting Eleanor to his temple.

The office door was kicked in, breaking the lock on it. Not that the lock was anything tough, just enough to keep Bear out of the only room with WiFi. We'd been doing our best to keep us all off grid. I avoided the Internet like the plague, afraid that even a single picture of me or Bear would be enough to tip off those who could still be looking for me.

I shook my head as I stepped inside the room. Whoever tossed it didn't have experience looking for things. A newb at best. I slipped my coat off and laid it on the floor.

The office doubled as a library, and the built-ins along the two sides had been full of books that Justin and I had collected in our years together. Older books, some signed, some rare. They'd all been thrown off the shelves, some of them with pages torn out. It would be difficult to tell which books were missing until I started putting them back and even then . . . "Sons of bitches, you are making this hard, which means you are going to die terribly."

The two ladies in their holsters laughed, bouncing in unison.

I started with the empty shelves. I slid my fingers over the edges, looking for a lip, an indent, anything that would show me a secret hiding place Justin had kept from me.

I grabbed a stool from the kitchen in order to reach the top shelves. The top shelf would seem the obvious place to put something secret, which to me meant it was the last place I'd put anything, but I checked anyway.

My fingers slid over the smallest of cuts in the corner of one shelf at the back. I pushed up on my tiptoes and peered in as I hooked my finger and pushed and shoved at the space. Nothing happened. I shook my head. The whole idea that Justin had been doing something shady was . . . out there, to say the least. I was adept at picking out a liar, and I struggled to fully believe he'd been doing something that had made this all happen.

But the evidence was piling up against him. And I was not blind when it came to the people I loved.

"Justin, help me out here. Where did you hide your shit?"

I spoke out loud because I couldn't make sense of what was going on inside my head.

I could almost hear him laugh. Like this was a game. Only he wouldn't have laughed if he'd understood that it had cost our son his life, too.

"What about behind a picture?" Dinah offered.

"No pictures in here." I did a slow turn of the room.

"Floor boards?" Eleanor asked.

Again, I shook my head. "No, we had them replaced just last year and I helped lay them."

I kept at the shelves even though they gave me nothing.

Half an hour later, the only land line phone in the house rang.

I stared at it a moment, thinking of how it could be rigged to explode, or to have some sort of spell woven into the earpiece. I leaned over it and saw the number calling.

Zee. I scooped up the receiver and held it away from my ear.

"Tell me something good," I said.

"Abe will live. I'm on my way back." He spoke quickly, the sound of the truck in the backdrop, the rev of the engine through the phone line. "The police are on their way to the house right now, I just picked them up on the scanner."

"What? Why?" I didn't think for one instant that he'd tipped them off.

"Don't know, but someone said they thought they heard gunshots out our way."

I stared around the room. That was a long time since the gunshots. This was a god damn set up. "Are you going to make it back before them?"

"By minutes, if I'm lucky."

I hung up the phone and started slamming the books back into the shelves, as fast as I could. The police were in on this; we knew that. And if they wanted a way to keep someone quiet or out of their way, or a scapegoat . . . the spouse of the person killed was a great one to pin something on. I couldn't bring any sort of justice to my boys if I was locked up.

That was assuming they were human and that I wasn't about to face a couple of abnormals for the first time in years.

I scrambled to get the books shoved in, barely finishing the haphazard job when the first set of tires crunched into the driveway.

I hobbled to the living room as Zee burst in through the front door.

"Zee, take Abigail out back to the barn!"

He ran to the living room, and I followed him. There was blood all over the floor from her and Abe. There would be no hiding the stains, not in the time I had left.

Another set of tires crunched over the snow.

The only chance I had was to keep them outside.

I hurried to the front door and stepped out, shutting the door behind me as the two police officers reached the bottom steps of the porch. I wrapped my arms around my waist, cupping my cast with my good hand and gave a full-bodied shiver. "Officers, can I help you?"

They glanced at each other, then back to me. I didn't move other than to shiver again.

The older of the two, with salt-and-pepper gray hair showing at the edge of his hat line, spoke. "There were reports of gunshots out this way. We wanted to make sure you were not injured."

I squinted my eyes to look at his tag and shook my head. "No gunshots since I've been home, Officer Schmidt." I tried to see if there was anything obviously off about him. A hint of magic. I turned so my left side was closer to them. Eleanor had a bit of a nose on her.

She shimmied in her holster. "No magic."

"What was that?" The officer quirked an eyebrow.

"I didn't say anything." Best to play dumb here.

"And the report that one of your dogs was shot?" The younger of the two cleared his throat. "Dr. Rickets let us know."

Damn it.

"We came home and found him shot, yes, that's true. He was probably out chasing deer and got caught by a hunter." I didn't look away from his eyes. "That's life when you live this far out of town."

"You don't know who might have done it?" Officer Schmidt flipped open a small notepad and pulled a pen from the pocket on the front of his coat.

I frowned, trying my best to look confused, and sad, and not at all pissed that they'd showed up on my doorstep. "No, how could I? Half the town likes to hunt this time of year."

He nodded and scribbled something down. "Mind if we come in?"

"Actually, I do. I'm going through my husband's things, right now."

The younger officer's eyebrows shot up. "This soon after his death?"

Fucking insensitive little asshole.

Now I was truly pissed. "Listen, you grieve the way you want to grieve, and I will grieve the way I want. When your spouse and child are ripped from your lives in a split second, I'll be sure to show up on your doorstep and tell you just how to deal with emotional shit. Sound good?"

I think I was screaming at them, the words a torrent that couldn't be stopped. Rage, grief, anger, frustration, it was a dark mixture I could not contain. The door opened behind me. I knew it was Zee by the intake of his breath. He put his hands on my arms, the warmth seeping through me and anchoring me long enough that I could rein myself in.

"Officers, my niece has been through a great deal. Perhaps another time would be better?" His words were polite but the tone was all business. He wasn't really asking them, he was telling them to fuck off as nicely as he could. I let him steer me back into the house as they backed away to their car with promises to return.

"Phone first, to be sure. I would hate for you to see her break down again," Zee said. I wanted to look back, but kept moving into the house.

Officer Schmidt said something but I didn't catch it as Zee slammed the door shut and locked it behind us. I shook from top to bottom, the anger giving me the energy to keep going when my body was beyond exhausted and demanded time to sleep. When the adrenaline faded, I was going to crash hard.

"Zee, Dr. Rickets spilled on us."

He shook his head. "He said nothing. I was there with him the whole time and he went right into surgery with Abe. There was no time, but that means someone else who knew the dogs had been shot told the police."

"Unless it was the police who were here and did the shooting." I was already striding back through the house to Justin's office. "Check the tire tracks against the others. I'm almost done in the office."

Zee followed me for a few steps. "There is no rush now, Nix. You need to sleep."

"I need to damn well figure something out or I won't sleep!" I snapped. "I *can't* sleep knowing that something Justin was doing caused his death, and Bear's!"

Zee let out a sigh, and turned away. I didn't feel bad for yelling at him. There was too much on the line right now. And he of all people would understand what I was going through.

Back in the office, I searched through the papers and

filing cabinet, and when Zee came back in, he stepped up to help without question. There was nothing out of place other than the mess. The sponsorships were all there, the paperwork was all perfectly in order once I put it back together. Magazines with Justin on the cover. I closed my eyes. Had he been a world-renowned stunt skier, or had that been a lie too? Had I buried my head so deeply that he'd pulled that over on me?

"Think it's weird that they didn't take the computer?" Zee pointed out the laptop, untouched on the desk.

"Yeah, that is weird." Confusion flickered through me as I ran a hand over the laptop. I'd avoided technology, mostly so I wouldn't be found. Because all it would take was one random picture and I had no doubt my father would be on me like a wolf on a fresh kill.

I opened the computer and flicked it on. Unless they weren't techie at all.

"Abnormals then?"

"That's my thought," Zee said. He leaned over my shoulder. "What do you think you might find?"

"I've never looked Justin up," I said. "I trusted him. The magazine covers made it real. The money made it real. I need to see how good of a liar he was."

I looked up at Zee and he put a hand on my shoulder. "Doesn't mean he didn't love you."

"You think I was married to a con man, too?" What was meant to be a joke, fell flat between us.

I stared at the screen, pulled up the Internet with the click of the mouse and typed *Justin Stark skier* into the search bar.

Nothing.

I swallowed hard. Funny how the last and most blatant piece of evidence was proving to be the hardest to swallow. All the rest had been theories and conjectures. I tried a few variations of Justin's name, misspelling it. I finally looked up the magazine he was often featured in. *Ski Boldly.*

The website came up with a message across it and I could do nothing but laugh as I read it out loud. "Website no longer active. Ski Boldly has been purchased by Winter Sports and will no longer be run as a physical magazine, but as an E-zine. We hope you continue to enjoy our articles at your leisure from the comfort of your laptop."

I shook my head and shut the laptop slowly. "Didn't you run his information when he and I first got together?"

Zee pulled up a chair and sat beside me. "I did. It all checked out."

"That kind of cover-up . . . how much money would have to be thrown at it?" I raised an eyebrow as I drummed my fingers on the desk.

"More than any normal police investigation. Deep pockets, Nix. Very deep pockets. And likely more than a dose of magic in order to get by me."

I ran a hand over my face. "So, we're talking about what, then, some sort of private investor? What could he have possibly been doing to warrant a full lie about his life? To me?"

My stomach fell as the truth slowly spun out. "Something about me. He was working with . . . something to do with my family?"

Zee shook his head. "Again, that can't be right. If that had been the case, they'd have killed you, or at the very least taken you back to your father. But that doesn't mean it might not have been someone *like* your family. Someone with power and money and no scruples. Mancini. Fannin. Yousef. Just to name a few."

Unspoken between us was the one word, the one kind of family it could be. The Collection. They worked very similar to and sometimes in conjunction with the human mob. My father worked on the edges of the Collection for years, fancying himself one of them because he had power and money and had made a literal deal with the devil. But they smartly never let him into their inner circles because he was a normal. Not to mention, he was too much of a loose cannon, even I knew that. The head of the Collection was Mancini and he wouldn't let my father in for reasons known only to him. In my younger years when I'd still thought my father was the king of the world, that had pissed me off as though it were a slight against all of us. Now, it was just plain amusing.

"No hard evidence yet, though. Let's keep looking. There have to be clues," Zee said. He was right, I felt it in my gut. The pieces were slowly revealing themselves to us, but I didn't doubt there were more revelations coming.

I drummed my fingers on the desk again. "Then we keep looking."

My gaze slid to the drawers of the desk, all of them ripped out and shattered on the floor.

A niggling feeling began at the base of my skull and I closed my eyes to pull up the memory that whispered through me.

"You almost done?" I put my head through the office doorway. Justin was bent over some paperwork. He grinned up at me, and slid the papers into the top right drawer.

"Almost."

"Well, don't dawdle. I can't sleep when I know you're still up working." I gave him a wink. He winked back and stuffed his hand into the drawer again. His family bible was on the desk next to him, open wide.

"Give me thirty seconds. Think you can strip in that time?" His grin was wide as he waggled his brows at me. Laughing, I turned away. His hand was still in the right-side drawer.

Almost like he'd been working on something specific.

I dropped to my knees and looked in the cavity where the

drawer should have been. I slid my hand in, flattening my palm and feeling along the sides first, then the bottom of the shelf. Nothing out of the ordinary.

"Got something?" Zee crouched beside me, flicking on a flashlight from his pocket. I pushed my hands upward onto the top of the narrow space and there was the softest of clicks. I looked at him.

"Yeah, I do."

CHAPTER SIX

The click on the top of the drawer's space seemed to echo between Zee and me. A hidden compartment was nothing strange in my previous line of business. Hell, I had two in the barn myself.

Justin had been no stunt skier, so just what was he besides a con man?

My heart pounded in a way I didn't like, that I couldn't slow down. The top of the empty drawer space dropped down into my hand, a folding compartment. I peered in and Zee angled the flashlight better for me to see. In the thin space of the hidden area, a small sheaf of wrinkled papers lay. Carefully, I pulled them out, stood, and spread them across the desk.

I stared at the papers, counting them. A dozen sheets, and I couldn't make out a single word of it. Letters, yes. Numbers, yes. Even a few symbols I recognized. But the others? "What is this, Chinese?"

"This part is Hebrew." Zee tapped a small section. "That's Russian."

I kept staring at the paper, seeing the bits and pieces of

languages and symbols I recognized. I touched each one as I spoke. "This is Japanese, Egyptian, Korean . . . I have no idea what these are." I swept my hand across several sections of paper, frowning at them.

And then the paper glittered blue, and all the symbols shifted, danced across the page and rearranged themselves.

Zee let out a low whistle. "Now that's a damn code. Magic and human, blended to make it unbreakable."

"Yeah, that's what I'm thinking." I touched a symbol and it flared under my finger and then shot off to another piece of the page.

Zee picked up one of the papers and handed it to me. "Code it may be, but this is a list of some sort, that much is obvious. Even with the symbols moving, they are staying within their constructs."

He was right, there seemed to be a pattern that could be a list, even with the moving bits and pieces. Two lines of coded writing, side by side. No matter how the symbols moved, that much stayed. I closed my eyes, thinking through the ache in my body. My pelvis break throbbed, humming with pain, and I forced myself to think through it, to use the pain to clear my mind.

"The bible was the only thing taken . . . the family bible was his key to this." I tapped my fingers on it. "I'm sure of it."

I took the paper and held it up. I flipped it over. The reverse was same. "A list of what, though?"

He put a hand on my shoulder. "I think this can wait for tomorrow, Nix. It's after dinner. I'm going to make us something to eat, and then you are taking a Percocet whether you like it or not so you will sleep."

My jaw ticked, but I knew when to argue and when to let him lead. The rational part of my brain told me he was right. I was running on empty. "Okay. I'll see if I can find a backup master key for this then."

Dinah laughed. "Oh please, you don't think any of us buy that?"

I tossed her and Eleanor on the desk on top of the papers. They were created by magic deeper than any I'd ever dealt with, and so I knew there were things about them I didn't understand. Talents they had yet to show me. "You two see anything you want to share with me?"

Zee left the three of us in the office.

I flicked on a few more lights and sat at the desk, the papers spread out in front of me, the two guns resting on them.

"You already know it's in code," Dinah said. "What else do you want?"

"Do you recognize any of the magical symbols?" I tapped a finger on the paper, the images dancing away from my skin like fireflies.

Eleanor shivered. "This one is the sign for death."

"And this one for pain," Dinah chimed in.

"Torture."

"Agony."

"Blood."

"Demon."

"Mayhem."

They fired back and forth at rapid speed and then both paused. I knew it would be Eleanor who spoke next even though she'd spoken the last word.

"Devil deal."

I clenched my jaw shut tightly as I struggled to contain the sudden anger at that last. "My father?"

"It doesn't say Romano," Dinah said. "Just Devil deal."

I nodded. "Thank you."

I slid them off the papers and looked over the sheets without touching anything. The movement of the symbols slowed and settled.

They were all written in Justin's hand except for the sheet with the double-sided list. That one was a combination of his writing and someone else's. Justin's scrawl was sharp, angled, and dark. The other was finer, cleaner, like the person had taken their time with the symbols.

I started with making a list of the languages and symbols I recognized. So many, though, why so many? I counted fifteen that I knew, and at least that many that I didn't. None of that included the magical ones.

Bits and pieces all used to make up a code, a code and a set of papers that if I was right, Justin and Bear had died for.

What the hell was on this paper?

Jaw ticking, I went to the shelves I'd so hastily shoved back together. Most of the books were Justin's. He'd had a thing for ancient cultures. For other countries. That's what he'd told me.

I searched through until I found a book on ancient Egypt and pulled it out. Flipping through the pages, I found notations here and there in the margins. Tiny little things.

Parts of the code.

"What the hell were you up to, Justin? And who did you try to con that went south?" I put the book on the desk and kept looking for others while I waited on Zee to call me. I wondered if Justin would have stayed with me if he knew how deeply I'd been in that world. I'd told him I was one of the Romano daughters, and let him believe I was the one who "died." It went well with my desire to disappear from my family, a good cover. I never told him about the money I'd taken. Never told him that I'd been the enforcer for my father, or that my father had quite literally made a deal with the devil. I never told Justin that I'd chosen my enforcer role because it meant I was safe. It meant I could kill anyone who stepped wrong.

A cold shiver ran down my spine, and a wash of fatigue spilled up in its place.

I had to keep moving, keep looking, but there was a time and a place for the search. Whoever was looking for this code would be back. I picked up the papers and tucked them into my shirt.

Dinah and Eleanor were next, back into their holsters. I left the office and wove my way to the back door of the house.

"Putting the papers in the vault?" Zee asked as he tossed a couple steaks on the grill pan.

"Safer there, I think." I slid on my heavy coat and was out the back door in a matter of seconds. Down to the barn, I went. First I checked on the mares, tossed them some food, and ran a hand over their bellies. Only then did I go to the saddle rack in the tack room. I put the coded papers not in with the money, but in a second smaller compartment in the floor. A decoy compartment to keep the money safe. A few stacks of bills, some jewelry, and a couple interesting trinkets were stashed there. I put the papers under them, and shut the trap door. The seams were barely visible, but someone looking would find it.

That being said, if they got this far, I was probably already dead.

I made my way back to the main house, my mind reeling with everything I'd learned and all the possibilities that lay in front of me.

We ate dinner, Zee offered me the Percocet, and I took it begrudgingly. I fell asleep on the couch, not willing to go back to my bedroom, trashed as it was. I woke up the next morning, sore and angry. I fed the horses, checked on the mares, and cleaned the stalls with Zee's help.

That became the ebb and flow of our days. We took care of the ranch. Zee fed me, and I sat in my tack room as I tried to break the code Justin had put together. We fended off the police twice more. Dinah and Eleanor kept me company in the small hours of the night when I couldn't sleep.

Abe came home.

Two weeks after the accident and about a week after an empty Christmas, the phone rang. I answered it without looking. "Hello?"

"Mrs. Stark, this is Chief Lars of the Jackson Hole PD. I have the official report on the accident and wanted to let you know what we found, if you'd like to know, that is."

I wasn't holding my breath that any of what he told me would be true. "What did you find, Chief Lars?"

He cleared his throat. "Well, it's as we thought when we first came on the scene. The brake lines were frozen, which caused a catastrophic failure of the braking system. The brakes were old, and it was truly an accident."

"Bullshit," Dinah muttered from her spot on the desk. I was always impressed at how good her hearing was.

"Can I come to see the truck?" The question was one I'd been waiting to ask. Zee had found nothing at Mary-Ellen's house, and the lead of John Smith had gone nowhere. But the old Ford still might hold a clue. "My son . . . he said he had a gift for me, and I just now realized it would still be in the truck."

"We searched through the truck and found nothing, Mrs. Stark." His voice was anything but conciliatory. Anything but understanding of a mother's grief.

"Still, it would make me feel better to look for myself." I knew he was lying about the cause of the accident. What I didn't know was if he knew he was lying, or if he was in on this scheme. I hung up before he could argue with me.

"Zee, I'm headed into town. Do you want to come?" I grabbed his truck keys from the kitchen island. He had one of the guns from the tack room storage spread out in parts, cleaning it.

"No, I'll stay." He looked up over the scope. "I take it you aren't going in for groceries?"

I shook my head. "No. Going to look at the Ford."

He stopped moving. "What do you think you're going to find?"

I shook my head. "I don't know. But maybe something. Maybe nothing. A clue, something to point us in a direction instead of just spinning our wheels in deep mud."

Zee went back to his cleaning. "Sure. Get me something to eat while you're there. Pizza would be a nice change."

As I walked to the door, Abe let out a soft woof and limped to me. He was still healing too, one side of his body slowly growing in the fur where it had been shaved for the surgery. "You keep an eye on Zee." I scrubbed his ears, and ran my hand over his head. His big dark eyes followed me as I stepped onto the porch.

I drove into town, slowing as I drove up the hill that had changed my world forever. Heart pain clawed at me and I refused its entrance, refused to break down. Not yet, I wasn't done with justice for my boys yet.

My mouth quirked as I mouthed the word *justice* to myself. When had I ever actually given that and not only death? Perhaps this was the first time. Perhaps, I was turning over a new leaf. I snorted softly.

"What's so funny? I want to laugh too," Dinah said.

"Stop pestering her," Eleanor said. "If she wants to share with us, she will."

I tapped a finger on the steering wheel. "First time the three of us are seeking justice and not just death. I found it amusing."

"Well, I don't," Dinah barked. "I want to get more kills."

"Still trying to catch up to Eleanor?"

Dinah grumbled and went quiet after I spoke.

The police station was quiet as I pulled in. It didn't look like they had anyone else visiting. I stepped out of the truck and headed up the short flight of steps. The woman at the front desk looked up as I came in, her hair pulled back in a ponytail so tight, it looked like she'd given herself a small facelift.

"Can I help you?" Her face was expressionless. Maybe there was a true facelift under there too. Or maybe she'd been touched up with myst.

"Here to see Chief Lars." I smiled at her, but it was a hard smile, I could feel the edges of it, and how it didn't reach my eyes.

She glanced down at her book in front of her. "He doesn't have any appointments."

"Excellent, then he will have time to see me," I leaned in and read her name tag, "Doris."

Flustered, she blinked rapidly and backed away. "I'll get him."

I stood quietly, waiting. There at the back of the big open room was Officer Schmidt and his younger partner whose name I'd never taken note of. I lifted a hand to them, waving.

Let them make of that what they would.

Doris was back a few minutes later with a heavy-set Chief Lars huffing behind her. "Mrs. Stark, you didn't need to come all the way into town."

"I did. I told you I wanted to see inside the truck to see about what my son left behind for me. If you didn't find anything, then it's still there."

He shook his head, heavy jowls swinging. "We can't have you climbing on evidence. And anything else is probably in the lake."

I raised my eyebrows. "Evidence? So, it wasn't an accident?"

He spluttered. "It was an accident. But even accidents have evidence."

I took a step toward him. "The truck legally belongs to me now as my husband's will left everything to me."

"It's still in the evidence locker."

I shrugged. "I don't have a problem with that. You can keep the truck for now, I only want to look in it. Of course, I can get a lawyer involved, but I'd rather not. It would look bad, don't you think, to tell a widow that she couldn't try to find a gift her *dead son* left behind for her?"

His jaw worked back and forth as his face reddened, and finally he huffed out a puff of air. "Fine. Follow me."

He stomped through the main section of the police station and out the back door into what looked like a junkyard. A scattering of vehicles, all which had obviously been in accidents of some sort were there in front of me, sprawled out like dead animals. The old Ford was at the far end of the yard.

"Ten minutes," Chief Lars said as though I were visiting with an inmate in a jail. I hadn't decided, yet, if he was on the take or not. I suspected not, or he wouldn't have let me get even this far.

I didn't spare him another glance. As I strode forward through the aisle between the vehicles, I approached the passenger side of the Ford and peered through the window. The crumpled side door wouldn't allow me in so I went around to the driver's side. The driver's door opened on the first yank and I slid into the truck.

I fought to keep my breathing even as I methodically slid my hands over and under the seats, as I opened the dash, as I forced myself to climb into the backseat, as I fought with the urge to bolt from the truck and the memories it held.

"What is in here? What do you think you will find?" Dinah's voice was muffled.

"A clue," I said. "Anything."

Focus, just focus. That was my mantra and I kept it running through my mind on a loop.

The first thing I realized was that the police hadn't done any sort of search of the truck. If they had, they would have found the middle seat in the back could open. Just as I was doing now. The middle seat had been a storage place for Bear's toys when he'd been younger that Justin had put in himself, delighting Bear to no end. I flicked the small latch that held it closed and lifted the lid.

In the bottom of the storage space was a tiny box wrapped in shining red paper and tied with a sparkly green bow, slightly water damaged but otherwise intact. I slid it out and tucked it into my coat pocket. This was not the time to open it, and not even the real reason I'd come. At best, I had only a few minutes left to search the truck. I let myself out of the driver's door and looked to the front entrance of the yard. Chief Lars had gone back inside.

"Fool," I muttered as I dropped to my knees, and slid under the truck. The only thing the chief had right was that the brakes had failed. There was no way they'd frozen. That was one of those urban myths people said happened to them when their brakes were just shitty.

I found the brake lines, slipped my gloves off and worked my fingers over the thick rubber. There.

I found what I was looking for. Not a cut in the brake lines, but puncture marks, subtle under my fingertips. Made with a clamping tool that forced many, many holes into the rubber, allowing the brake fluid to leak out over time.

This particular trick . . . I knew who it belonged to.

Tank Follietta. Punctured brake lines were something he was known for far and wide in the circles I used to run in. Even an abnormal would die in a bad car crash. I ran my hand over the rubber again to make sure, finally taking a knife from my shoulder holster and slicing off a piece. I held it to the light. "Fuck it all, Tank." There was no doubt in what was right in front of me. I tucked the rubber line into my pocket to show Zee. To be sure I was on the right path.

Tank was one of my father's business associates, in a way. One of the thugs tied to Mr. Mancini, the head of the Mancini family in New York. Tank had used this trick more than once to eliminate a rival for his own boss.

I was going to kill Tank slowly for this. Because worse than the fact that it was Tank was that I'd considered him something of a friend in the past. Someone I could almost trust. Or at least I knew wouldn't toss me under a bus without a warning first. Of course, there was that fact that he wouldn't have known it was me, hidden as I was with Zee's ability. "Shit." I didn't want to give anyone the benefit of the doubt. Not even Tank.

I slid out from under the truck and stood to find Officer Schmidt's young partner watching me with narrowed eyes.

"What were you doing under the truck?"

I fished the gift from Bear out of my pocket. "Looking for this."

"Your kid hid his gift for you in the chassis?" The disbelief was obvious, clear.

I shrugged. "He was a smart boy, handy . . . not unlike his father."

I didn't care if he believed me or not. That wasn't the point. The point was that I'd found something solid. I knew who I was going after now.

I pushed my way past the younger officer, then paused a few steps away from him. "You got a name?"

"Officer Ryan."

I gave him a nod, and continued on my way. "Officer Ryan, thank you for checking on me."

He escorted me out of the police station without another word.

My drive home was uneventful; I didn't look at the lake. Didn't even notice the hill. I couldn't, not with the way my mind was racing and where it was taking me.

Punctured brake lines. Tank Follietta. Mancini.

What the ever-living hell had Justin been wrapped in? The answer was not one I had thought for an instant in the last two weeks. I'd hoped in the dark of the night that Justin had been in some sort of gambling ring, that maybe he'd been cheating on me and the woman had him done in . . . but this? To *truly* have ties to the Collection? Despite what Zee had suggested, I'd not thought it possible.

I hated being wrong.

I pulled onto the driveway of my home and sat in the truck, thinking. Apparently, I sat too long because Zee came out to find me. He opened the driver's side door and peered in.

"What? Was there something on the truck?"

I pulled the line from my pocket and held it out to him. "Punctured brake lines. They used a clamp," I said.

He sucked in a sharp breath as he ran his hands over it. "Shit. Follietta?"

"Yeah, my thoughts exactly. Tell me I'm wrong. Justin couldn't have had some sort of tangling with the Collection, could he? I mean . . . wouldn't we have figured it out? He had no magic of his own."

The words sounded ridiculous in the same sentence, and yet they made sense in a horrible, mind-numbing sort of way. The Collection didn't take it lightly if you crossed them. I knew that from working for my father—his ties to them were enough to make him one of them from the outside—but if the Collection was involved with the accident, then that meant there had to be money and power on the line, and no small amount of magic.

The score Justin had been talking about made more sense now. With great risk came great reward. But . . . that also meant Noah was in on this scheme of Justin's.

I made myself step out of the truck and go inside. "There's a way to be sure of what's happening. You know Romano Industries keeps records for Mr. Mancini. His people don't like the tech shit."

"No, don't go there. They will have you killed if you get caught. I can't ward you that well, Nix." Zee followed my line of thinking but I was already way ahead of him.

"Zee, my father's business has enough ties with the Collection and we both know he had spies on the inside. We know because I helped him set them up and get them in." My father was so blindingly arrogant that he kept tabs on the heads of the families he dealt with, not only so he could emulate them, but so he could use his ties with them. He thought maybe he could blackmail them.

That was the thing about my father, nothing was too dangerous or taboo, not if it meant he was making money or gaining power.

That included having his twelve-year-old daughter trained as one of his enforcers. He'd created a weapon that could think for itself in me.

I pinched the bridge of my nose. "The databases would be the place to start. We both know I can get in and out without being caught. I'll go old school, no wards. It won't be hard, and it will give us evidence. If I must kill Tank, I will. But we both know he's getting old. And fat. You think he'd have been able to get under the lowered chassis of the Ford?"

"Point taken." Zee's jaw was tight as we walked into the house side by side. "It's still a shitty idea."

"You got a better one?" I fired at him as I strode away,

down the hall to my bedroom. We'd set the room right, and flipped the mattress so the slash marks were underneath and unseen as if they had never been. I shut the door behind me then sat on the bed. I put my hand on the outside of my coat pocket, feeling the edges of the package within.

Slowly, I pulled the wrapped gift out and stared at it.

I flipped the card over.

You're my best girl, Mom.

Love, Bear.

I put my fist to my mouth and bit down on my knuckles as I fought the pain the words lit inside my heart. Shaking, I stood and went to the dresser, opened the top drawer and put the present in. "Not yet, Bear. I'll open it, but not right now."

I backed away. There was a lot to do to prep for a trip to my father's main place of business. A knock on the door turned me around.

"Come in."

Zee poked his head in. "We need to have a hard talk."

I frowned. "All right."

He opened the door fully and leaned on the frame. Abe pushed past him and placed himself between me and Zee.

"Well?"

"You stole a lot of money from your father headed for Mr. Mancini when you left your . . . position. You sure that isn't the reason all this is happening?"

"You said yourself if this was about me, I'd be dead right now."

His mouth tightened. "The Collection isn't like your father, Nix. He might think he's like them, he might try and be like them, but he isn't. They never would have hired me, an ex-special ops guy with no family to use against me. They train their own, and they don't step outside of their bloodlines. You stealing all that money . . . if they'd found you, they'd want to make you suffer. They'd want to hurt you, Nix."

I stared at him. "You mean they would do this, they would kill everyone I love first."

He gave me a tight nod. "Exactly. And we both know your father would have thrown you under the bus when you walked away. That money was his, and it was going to the Mancini family. *You* were supposed to deliver it. It was your father's payday to get into the Collection, officially."

He didn't have to remind me. I recalled the weight of the cash in the two large bags. I'd been planning my escape, waiting for the right moment to get away from my psychotic father and his cronies, to get away from all those who'd hurt me. I let Zee's words sink in. "Then this could still be partially my fault then. I could still be the reason we were found."

"Yeah, it could, but I doubt that you are all of it."

I hunched my shoulders, guilt and shame swelling through me. I fought through it, pushed my way to the top of the drowning emotions. I forced my mind and not my heart to think this through. "And the coded papers? The fact that it was Justin's spaces, not mine that were tossed? They didn't even go to the barn."

He tipped his head to one side. "You know, I've looked into Justin's life through the years, used my connections where I could to make sure he was safe. Whoever is helping him is better than anyone else I've ever seen. He's squeaky clean. Those coded papers *could* be nothing. Maybe it was a random robbery because people knew we'd be away. That happens with funerals and weddings when they are announced in a paper. Their homes become an easy target for thieves." His eyes were inscrutable. I tried to decipher what he was really thinking and couldn't get anything back.

I rubbed a hand over my face.

"They took nothing but the family bible, a bible I saw on his desk when he was working on that code," I said. "Not much value in a bible printed in the 1960s. Unless there is something of value added to it somehow."

He let out a sigh and I took a step toward him. "Wait, are you just trying to talk me out of this?"

With a nod, he turned away, his shoulders drooping. "You are the only family I have left, Nix. And you are like a daughter to me. I . . . I don't want to lose you, too."

I blinked several times, trying to reconcile this grizzled old man with wounds of war etched into his skin, with the soft words he was saying. He was a killer as much as I was, more so in some ways. He'd been at it longer.

"Thank you. But don't try and talk me out of it again." I kept my tone as soft as I could, but even I could hear the iron in them.

Zee grunted. "If you're really going to do this, then we'd best get your flabby ass in shape."

"Flabby ass! I still run ten miles most days, in addition to the barn work." I glared at him.

He shook his head. "If you're going after the Collection, you need to be in top shape, Nix. And that means you're going to need patience. The mob isn't going anywhere. It's time to hone your edge, and make you a weapon the Collection will fear once more."

CHAPTER SEVEN

True to his word, Zee set to retraining me, treating me as though I were one of his newbie recruits rather than the veteran killer I was. He at least gave me the full six weeks so my arm and pelvis crack healed for the most part, anyway. At the end of the long days, my bones ached like I'd been pummeled. Then again, I had been in some cases.

As soon as my cast was off, he started me back hard, running me the ten miles I'd been doing previously in the deep snow, setting me to weights and full-body workouts that pushed every limit I had. We worked on shooting, setting explosives under pressure, picking locks of every kind, rappelling, and knife throwing. All I had done before, and while some of it was rusty, every piece of it came back into clear focus. The skills were there, and unlike before when I used them for someone else, this time, they were for me. For my boys.

Dinah kept up a running commentary most days. Eleanor helped fill in any gaps she missed.

"You should be working at your reflexes more, you're not as fast as the myst users." That from Dinah.

"She has a point," Eleanor added. "Repetition is going to be key to your speed seeing as you are a normal."

Day in and day out, I worked until I was drained of everything and fell into bed every night.

I could feel it in every breath and flex of my muscles as they grew leaner. Three months after Justin and Bear left me, I was faster than I had been as a younger version of myself.

Valentines passed in a blur that I panned to ignore if not for the bouquet of flowers that had shown up on my doorstep. Shaking, I brought the two dozen red roses with a note stuck to them.

Love to you always my beautiful wife. J.

I leaned against the flowers, knowing that they were from Justin. This was something he would have done, pre-ordered flowers months in advance in case he was not home. In case he was on a trip. Or in this instance, dead. Tears dripped down my cheeks and into the velvet petals. No matter that he may have caused this loss in my life, he'd loved me like I'd never been loved before.

And I missed him, I missed his strength and laughter. I missed his touch.

"Son of a bitch, I hate crying you know that." I whispered into the flowers before setting them on the table and walking away, Abe tight to my side.

Abe healed nicely and ran with me every day as the snow melted and the temperatures rose. Zee added a backpack with twenty pounds of gear to my runs, added torture techniques, applying them to me and forcing me to the edge of my mental limits as he held me under the icy water of the creek. We fitted Abe for his own vest, adjusting it so he could carry extra ammo for me, as well as be safer with the bulletproof dog vest.

Every day, all the familiar training techniques took me back to my childhood. My father had thought to make a perfect solider out of one of his children and I'd volunteered. I'd wanted to escape the torment of my older brothers. I'd wanted to be stronger. I'd wanted a way to protect myself.

Born to his second wife, I'd started out life as a chubby, ugly duckling. My father already had a beautiful daughter, so when we sat at the dinner table that night and he'd asked which of his children would want to be his enforcer, trained by Zee himself, a legend in the family already, I'd stood.

My father had been surprised at first, but eventually consented.

"No one will suspect you of coming to collect, Phoenix. You will be amazing once Zee has trained you." He'd touched my chin, lifting my eyes to his. I'd been twelve. Twelve years old and all I wanted was my father to love me. To protect me. But he wasn't doing either and I knew it was up to me.

"I won't disappoint you, Father." I'd stared up at him, adoring. He was handsome with his dark hair and eyes, identical to my own.

I shook my head as I army-crawled through the thick mud under the electric wires Zee had set up. Abe was beside me, flat to the muck, his tongue hanging out as we worked through the obstacle course.

Two miles of mud, water, walls, near drowning, ropes, nets, up and down. And at the end, I had to go hand to hand with Zee with nothing more than my fists and feet.

This was my last test, the last piece that would show both him and me if I was ready to go back into the world I'd run from. That I thought I'd never have to go back to.

From under the wires, I slid and ran at the fifteen-foot wall. Zee waited on the other side. I sprinted hard, forcing myself up until I could grab the top and hauled myself over, Abe still right beside me, his claws scrabbling as he clung to the top with a grunt. In the past months, he'd connected with me in a way I'd never had with a dog before.

Almost like he knew what I was doing. Like he knew I was going after those people who'd killed Bear and he wanted in on the action, a shot at the assholes who had torn our boy from us.

Zee waited for me at the end of the course, two army batons, one in each hand. I spit to the side. I hated the batons. They left bruises like nothing else, and Zee wielded them as an expert, aiming for my sore spots.

I slowed as I approached him, enough to slow my heart a little, and then I stepped into the circle with him. I gestured for Abe to go to the left. Zee frowned.

"Dog isn't allowed."

I shrugged. "You have your weapons, I have mine."

Abe let out a low growl and crouched as he slunk around Zee, doing his best to get behind the big man.

"So be it," Zee said and promptly disappeared.

"Son of a—" A baton slammed into my gut, cutting me off.

Bent over, I struggled to breathe as I searched the mud in front of me. I dropped to my ass and swept my left leg out in a circle, connecting with Zee's ankles, sending him down.

I didn't think it would hurt him so much as give me an edge. He stood, partially visible with the mud splattering him.

Not perfect, but it would have to do.

"Not enough, Nix," Zee growled.

I blinked and my vision disappeared. "Seriously?"

"They have a Hider. Someone good enough to break my wards and leave no evidence. That means you will face him at some point."

I stayed where I was on the ground. If I could hit Zee hard enough, he'd lose his concentration and his hold on me would slip. Warding inanimate things was much easier than blocking the vision on a person.

"Abe, *fass*." Attack.

There was a rush of Abe's paws in the mud and then Zee howled. There was a cry as he thumped Abe with the baton, but from the sounds, Abe did not let go.

My vision flickered. With only a portion of my sight given back, I leapt forward at the mud-covered Zee. He saw me coming and swept his batons at my head.

I ducked the swing of the first baton, swept my right arm upward and caught Zee's second swing on my forearm. The crack of skin and bone on the weapon rippled through the air, and I went to my knees, a howl on my lips. He wasn't holding back.

I let the blow push me down to help ease the impact. Pain ratcheted through me, but I couldn't stop the fight now. His next blow was coming. From the mud, I kicked out and slammed my heel into his left leg while Abe continued to yank on the right, splitting him apart.

Zee swept the batons both at Abe, aiming for his head. I flipped back onto my hands and kicked Zee under the chin with my heel, mud flying in every direction.

The crack of boot on jaw echoed in the air.

I continued over my flip into a crouch. Zee wobbled where he was, shook his head and slid to the ground.

Moving as fast as I could, I climbed up his body, snagged a baton and pressed it against his throat. I straddled his upper body and Abe pinned his right leg. Blood trickled down my arm, and my vision still wobbled. But I had him. Something I'd never managed before.

"You letting me win, old man?"

He'd never been so slow, even his magic seemed . . . sluggish. He shook his head and I got off him as he coughed and put a hand to his throat. "No. Damn it."

I held out a hand to him and helped him to his feet. I rubbed my arm that had taken the baton blow. It was going to be swollen and aching for days. And I was sure Zee hadn't given me his full force. But was that on purpose? He wasn't helping me if he didn't push me.

He held up his hand. "One more test before you go to New York."

I stared at him. He flipped one hand over and a piece of paper appeared in his palm. "A job. Simple, straightforward, but you need to see if you can still do it. If you can still pull the trigger."

I snorted, snot flying past my lips. "I can still pull the trigger."

"I'm going to insist you do this job. Or I will blind you and make it so you can't go to New York."

My jaw dropped. "You wouldn't."

"I would."

I snatched the paper and stared at the words printed in his hand. "What the hell kind of job is this? Have tea with Mary-Ellen? Is this a joke?"

He shook his head. "She's not what she seems."

"You mean she's secretly Catholic?" I couldn't help myself and the flippant attitude. Zee glared at me.

"No. She's not human."

"Oooh," Dinah did a stage whisper from her spot on the table in the back yard, "How will we ever survive an abnormal?"

I ignored her and kept my eyes on Zee. "Oh, well, I already knew that, so did you." I waved at him and he grabbed my arm, dragging me close, his eyes locked on mine, seeing into me as only he could.

"Be careful about listening to your guns, Nix. They make you cocky, and they are partly what made you hard before. You trusted them too much. You trusted them over the people in your life who cared for you." His eyes bore into mine. "They are weapons, designed to kill and nothing else. You are not. You are not a weapon."

I swallowed hard, feeling the chastisement down to my toes. "Zee, I just . . . I just can't be miserable all the time. I can't. It's killing me. Black humor is at least an attempt at surviving."

"I know. But watch yourself. I see their influence on you. Same as before. It took you a long time to break free of it." Zee glanced at the house where Dinah and Eleanor sat on the table, waiting for me. He was right in a way. The two guns were . . . addictive in their own way. They represented safety and protection in ways I'd never had before them.

"There is a reason your sister killed herself with your guns," Zee said softly. "Remember that, too. We just don't know what that reason was."

I nodded. "I will."

The thing was, I was not Bianca. My sister had magic of her own. Three of my four siblings did because they were born from our father's first wife, Maggie. Gabe was the only one who seemed to have missed out on that perk. My mother was a normal, and so was I.

Bianca had killed herself with Eleanor, and left a note that the guns were to be mine after her death.

Eleanor would not talk about my sister.

I made my way to the back of the house and the table where the two guns were and scooped them up. Within a half hour, I was showered, dressed and headed off to see Mary-Ellen.

"She's an abnormal? That's what you said?" Eleanor asked the question, surprising me.

"Apparently."

"And we're going to kill her?" The hopeful note in Dinah's voice was a little too strong.

"I don't know." That much was true. I didn't hate her. But generally speaking, abnormals were dangerous and only showed up when they were there to kill or hurt you. That being said, Mary-Ellen had been in the valley long before me. Maybe she was hiding too. But if that was the case . . . who was she hiding from?

CHAPTER EIGHT

Pulling up to Mary-Ellen's home in town was surreal. The last time I'd been there was the ill-fated Christmas party. I shifted in my seat, thinking. How the hell was I going to go about this? The Hiding Zee had laid on me and Bear for so many years was gone which meant anyone who knew what the Phoenix looked like would recognize me.

"Any ideas?" Dinah asked.

I fingered the bottom hem of the loose shirt I wore. "Well, there's one way to make sure she knows who I am." The shirt cut down low in the back, showing off my impossible to miss tattoo. Bright wings spread across my back in gold, red, orange, and black, and the pinion feathers ran across the back of my arms. A testament to the only thing my mother gave me that I could truly say was my own.

My name.

"Ahh, the wings. Right." Dinah wiggled in her holster. "So . . . you flash your back, she attacks you, and we can shoot her?"

I pushed open the door and stepped into the spring air. "No. I pull the trigger, remember?"

"Stop pestering her," Eleanor snapped. The two of them bickered low enough against my back that I could only catch a word here and there. I did my best to ignore them as I walked up to the front door of the everyday house, of an everyday family, and lifted my hand to knock.

The door opened before I could even put my knuckles to the hollow wood door.

Mary-Ellen and her bouffant stood in the doorway. "I thought I heard a truck. What are you doing here, Bea?"

"I came to talk to you." I tried to see past the cover of human skin. Zee didn't know what kind of abnormal she was. Which meant I was still going in more than a little blind to this situation.

She blinked a few times. "Oh. Well, come in, please. The missionaries just left. I have some soup and sandwiches if you're hungry?"

"Poison," Dinah whispered. I doubted that was the case, but I appreciated the reminder.

"What was that?" Mary-Ellen glanced at me.

"Didn't say a thing." I smiled at her, holding her eyes. "Here, let me get the door." Her eyes were on me as I turned and shut the door, giving her full view of my back, and the rather distinctive tattoo.

A strangled squawk escaped her and I spun around, Eleanor in my left hand. "I think we need to talk."

There was a violent burst of red myst and I squeezed the trigger, aiming for Mary-Ellen's leg. Eleanor went off, and I was slammed to the floor. Bright colors erupted in my vision and I rolled, throwing Mary-Ellen off as she screeched and squawked. Like some sort of giant . . . bird?

Oh shit.

Her beak slammed into the floor, tearing up the wooden

slats, missing me by inches. I rolled forward. "I want to talk to you, Mary-Ellen! Don't make me kill you!"

Another screech and a pair of talons the size of my head raked the front of my belly, opening the first few layers of skin.

Mary-Ellen was obviously a shifter, her body mostly bird, but her tail lashed long and sinuous like a snake. I lifted my eyes to her head.

A weird mishmash of bird and snake. Beaked with fangs, snake eyes, a crest of feathers on top. I had no name for her. I wasn't sure there was any name for her. Unlike the library of mythical creatures the general populace believed was out there, what really existed was anything but categorized. Not in the least.

Magic did weird shit.

Like making guns talk.

And slamming two animals' DNA together and making it into a monster.

I held my hands up, palms facing her. Eleanor hung from my one finger. "Mary-Ellen, stop flipping your shit."

She screeched at me and backed up a few steps, limping. There was a perfect hole in her left leg.

Eleanor didn't miss, and neither did I.

"You . . ." She squawked and stuttered as she spoke, "you are the Phoenix. You'll kill me. I have children. I have a life. I'm not his anymore."

I frowned. "I'm not here to kill you. I swear it on . . ." I was going to say I would swear it on my boy, but that wasn't possible any longer. "I swear it, Mary-Ellen."

Her big avian eyes blinked several times, the eyelid transparent and freaky as shit. I didn't move. "Whom did you belong to?"

She trembled, her feathers fluttering. "I won't go back to him."

"To whom?"

She shook her head and took another limping step back, then her eyes narrowed at a speed that I could barely follow.

"You're out of shape," she said. "If you knew who I was, you'd kill me."

I spun Eleanor so she was back in my hand. "Then you'd better talk fast so you don't end up in bits in pieces."

Her body expanded with a big breath.

Her legs tensed and her wing tips fluttered.

Fucking hellfire, we were doing this right now. I needed to deescalate this. "Mary-Ellen, you helped me bury my boy and as much as I would really love to blow your brains out every time you asked me to be your friend, I am doing my best not to kill you. Talk to me by the count of ten or I will let you make an up-close acquaintance with Eleanor."

On my back, Dinah groaned softly, "Spoiled brat."

Mary-Ellen slumped, defeated and ready to talk. Zee was wrong, I hadn't lost my edge.

Except right then, I did a damn stupid thing.

I lowered Eleanor.

Mary-Ellen blurred as she came at me, her feathers fluttering, blinding in the speed of her movement. Her fanged beak came straight for my head.

I dove to the right, through the doorway and into the spare room. I hit the floor as I skidded and kicked the door shut. A split second later, she busted through and then the truly strange shit started.

Her body multiplied so I was looking at not one, but four Mary-Ellen lizard birds. They darted around me and I fired as her four beaks shot at me in unison.

The bullet went through the one image of her.

"Damn big bird!" I snatched Dinah out of her holster, as I was hammered in the upper back. Mary-Ellen's beak snapped something in my shoulder and Dinah flew across the room from my suddenly nerveless fingers.

I dropped to the floor and did a wide sweep with one leg, going for her ankles. I swept through two images and then hit her on the third image. She went down with a screeching squawk and I grabbed hold of one of her legs above the talon. She yanked hard, putting pressure on the injured shoulder, forcing my hand to drop her.

Enough of this shit. I swept Eleanor up and shot Mary-Ellen. I aimed for her wings, and her belly.

From where she lay, I hit her evenly, all three bullets driving through her and into the floor. She cried out and her body shifted once more, sliding from a big-ass bird thing, down to a human with wild hair once more.

"Please don't kill me." She gripped her stomach with one hand. Both her arms bled from the shoulder shots.

I didn't lower my gun. "Talk to me, Mary-Ellen."

"Your father owned me," she whispered. "If I had known it was you, I'd have turned you in for the money years ago. It would have bought my freedom completely."

My father. Damn my soul to hell. It always came back to him.

"He would have killed you and we both know it," I snapped. "Don't be stupid. If my father owned you, and you ran from him, he would kill you if you went back no matter the prize you offered."

Her eyes filled and spilled over with tears. "I know. I'm sorry."

Dinah screamed a warning as Mary-Ellen lifted her but I saw it coming. I aimed down Eleanor's sight and squeezed the trigger.

Mary-Ellen's head snapped back as a bullet wound appeared in the middle of her forehead, right between her eyes.

The silence after the last gunshot was deafening. "Thanks, Dinah." I bent and pried her out of Mary-Ellen's fingers.

"No problem. Maybe you can let me kill someone next?"

I nodded. "For saving my life, you got it."

I left Mary-Ellen there and did a search of the house. I didn't know what I was supposed to be looking for, if anything at all. It would not be the first time Zee had sent me to an abnormal that he felt needed killing.

But I didn't believe that was the case here. Something about Mary-Ellen had tipped him off. I only had to find out what.

I wove my way through the house. Mary-Ellen's husband, Hank, worked the day shift at the local hospital as a cleaner. I had a few hours yet.

I was in the back bedroom when I heard the knock on the front door, and the click of the latch opening. I froze where I was.

"Miss Mary-Ellen, it's the missionaries. We thought we'd bring back your container. We ate the cookies already."

Well, this was a twist I hadn't been counting on. "Leave it on the floor. I'm indisposed," I called out in my best high pitched Mary-Ellen voice.

The door clicked shut and I went back to searching the room. Again, I should have known better.

There were no missionaries at the door, but I had to admit later that it was a perfect ruse to make me let my guard down.

Because who would think of two Mormon missionary boys as supernatural creatures protecting their bird queen?

Not me.

The creak of the floor behind me was the split-second warning I got. I spun and dropped to one knee, snapping both Dinah and Eleanor up in unison though my shoulder and back screamed in protest. Life was something I would fight for, even if it hurt me.

"Oh, yeah, baby," Dinah whispered. "Let's blow them to bits."

The two boys were no longer in their suits and ties. They'd shifted to the same kind of bird-lizard thing Mary-Ellen had been. Only they were significantly smaller than her oversized legs. More like baby lizard-birds.

"What are you?"

"Kagusta," the one on the right said. The name meant nothing to me. I kept Dinah on him, Eleanor on the other. "You killed Mary-Ellen?"

I didn't answer at first. I stood slowly, working my way around the oversized bed to the pane glass window. "She wouldn't answer my questions. You going to be that stupid?"

They looked at each other and then shook their feather-crested heads in unison. Their plumage was far brighter than Mary-Ellen's. The colors of their feathers were neon shades of blue, green and orange.

Fucking gaudy if you asked me, but I never did understand why magic created things the way it did. I wondered if it were an entity. If it was it just having a good belly laugh as it slapped shit together and gave it life and legs to walk around on.

"No, we'll answer you," the one on the right said. His bird eyes blinked in that same unnerving way Mary-Ellen's had.

"Any special abilities besides duplicating your image?" I asked.

They shook their heads again.

"Why was she in hiding?" I was all the way around the bed now, and my back was to the big pane glass window. An escape route. I didn't trust them any further than I could throw them when it came to telling me the truth about their abilities.

"Luca Romano was hunting her," one of them said. "That's all we know."

Hearing my father's name out loud was unnerving. "Why?"

"We don't know. She told us he'd send the Phoenix after her eventually. That's why she trained us."

"I'm not wanting to kill you," I said. "But I will if you so much as take one step toward me."

They nodded once more. Like they were a couple of bobble-heads. My body hurt. I was bleeding across my belly and I hadn't learned shit here. And I'd killed Mary-Ellen.

I should have felt bad about that last bit, but my training was thorough regarding that. If someone tried to kill me, they died first. End of story.

"Boys, this has been lovely, but I'm leaving now." Announcing my departure was a test. Were they going to let me go, or force my guns on them?

They looked at each other and I knew the answer before they even turned their heads back.

Guns it was.

CHAPTER NINE

Behind me, Mary-Ellen's home burned in bright blazing streaks that lit the afternoon sky. Gasoline was an excellent accelerant, but nothing burned like blood full of magic. Not that abnormals were any more combustible than the average Joe, but once they were dead something in their blood changed and it was like liquid fire.

I glanced in the rearview mirror only once to make sure the place was indeed engulfed and then continued on my way back to the ranch.

As I drove, I tried to figure out what the whole point of that visit had been. Just a test of my skills against an abnormal? Zee wasn't wasteful like that, so I didn't think that was the case.

But I'd found nothing other than the connection to my father, something that unfortunately many abnormals had. They went to him for money, for jobs, and when they tried to screw him over, I was sent in to deal with them.

"Did you enjoy that, Dinah?" I asked. I'd killed both Kagusta with her.

"Yeah, it was good. Thanks, Nix."

I flinched, not because she called me by my name, but because the two guns rarely spoke to me using my name at all.

At least not until just before I'd had to put them away. Right before I'd met Justin.

"No," I said. "Don't go there, Dinah."

"Calling you by your name isn't . . . bad," Eleanor said, her voice carefully emotionless. "We never called her by her name and she still died."

Her. Bianca, my sister.

I shook my head, and clenched the steering wheel. This was not the time to think about Bianca killing herself. From what I could gather from Dinah and Eleanor, one of them had done it at her request. "Zee doesn't want me to get too comfortable with you two, and I know why. I was at my darkest hour when you spoke to me like that before."

"Are you not at your darkest hour again?" Eleanor asked.

I didn't answer her, because she wasn't far off. The two guns would see me through this as no one else could, and all three of us knew it.

An hour later, I was back at the house. Walking up the front steps, I could feel every ache, every jarring motion to my back and the skin on my belly.

I was going to look like I'd gotten the shit kicked out of me. Which I hadn't. But also, I kind of had.

I let myself into the house and went straight to my room and the master bath. I ran a steaming hot tub full of water and put in a large amount of Epsom salts and Himalayan pink salt. Both would draw out the soreness and any potential leftover toxicity from Mary-Ellen's talons.

I laid Dinah and Eleanor onto the side of the tub, stripped and slid into the blistering hot water with a hiss of air. Leaning back, I let my head rest against the edge, thinking.

I went over the scene with Mary-Ellen again and again.

The only thing that made sense was that Zee was trying to prove to me that I'd lost my edge. That I wasn't as aware as I'd been even ten years ago. I rubbed a hand over my face and let my mind go to a blank space. White noise, emptiness.

It was a refuge from a world filled with emotions.

I soaked in the tub until the water cooled. With effort, I pulled myself out, and thought the salts had helped with the pain through my body. I wasn't a fool. This was not going to be an easy bounce back.

"Shit." I couldn't afford for Zee to be right. I could not afford to not be at the level I needed to be in order to find justice for my boys.

I dressed, strapped the two guns onto my lower back and made my way through the house once more. Abe was sound asleep on the couch, snoring. I snapped my fingers at him and he flipped over, his head whipping around before he saw me.

"Come on, let's go find Zee."

With Abe at my side we headed out back. I could see Zee down at the barn, mucking out the paddocks.

I reached the fence around the enclosures and leaned on it, raising a foot and setting it on the bottom rail. "I killed her. Is that what you wanted? Or you got something else for me?"

Zee stopped with the motion of manure fork to wheelbarrow and leaned on it, mimicking me.

"Did you have to kill her?"

I grimaced. "She attacked me, tried to kill me. You know it's a hard line on that."

"I do. What did you learn?" His eyes were on my face, watching for the nuances that would give away my thoughts. I closed my face down.

"That you don't think I'm capable," I said. "That you think I don't realize how hard this is going to be, that I'm not ready for it."

He snorted. "Yes and no. You've got to understand you aren't that kid anymore, whose whole life has been death and fighting and magic. You aren't that hardened bitch, Phoenix. I'm not sure that you ever truly were."

I stared at him. "She was a Kagusta. That mean anything to you?"

He frowned. "Kind of bird-lizard shifter?"

"Bingo. She knew my father. Thought he'd sent me after her."

"Not an uncommon story."

I narrowed my eyes. "But maybe that's the thing. Not uncommon, but how strange that I would end up in the same place she did?" I shook my head. "Don't answer that. I'm ready to go to New York, and I know you are, too, so let's go. Neither of us needs more training—"

"I'm not going," he said and I froze mid step. Sore, aching, and tired through to my bones, I was sure I heard him wrong. I had to have heard him wrong. There was no way he'd back down from this fight.

"What do you mean?"

"I'm not going. To Hide us both at this point would be too much for my magic," he gestured at the deep scars on his arms and face, "and I'm slower, too. I'll end up getting you killed."

I frowned. "That wasn't the plan. And since when have you been slower than me?"

"You got Abe, take him. He's better, and you and I both know he'd die for you. You've got the ladies."

Dinah laughed softly and Eleanor joined her. "Ladies? That's the nicest thing he's ever called us."

"That's not the point." I took a step closer, ignoring my guns. "What do you mean it's too much for your magic? What's really going on, Zee?"

"I got the shakes." He held his hand out flat and it was

shaking. "Doctor says it's progressing faster than normal, probably because I've had so many head injuries. He doesn't understand what I am."

I stared at him, freezing rain pouring down around us. The shakes were common with Hiders who used their ability too freely. Like a conduit whose wiring starts to short. "The shakes. You're sure?"

He gave me a quick nod. "Besides. You need someone here to take care of the horses."

His words were slow to sink in, because to me he'd always been invincible.

I held my hand up, stopping him. "I've already lined up sales for all of them. The house is next."

He shrugged. "No need to sell the house, not yet. The life insurance from Justin will cover things for a while. I can manage all that while you're gone."

I knew he wouldn't want comfort, but I didn't know how to react to this news of his. So, I bulled forward. "The house is going. The realtor knows I won't be around. She will stage it if necessary."

He shook his head. "That's a mistake. You don't need the money."

That much, he was right about. I did not need the money from the house.

I just knew I couldn't live there with the memories that followed me. The whisper of my boy's feet on the hardwood, the sound of Justin's laughter, the love and family I'd finally found was *here*. I couldn't live with the ghosts of what could have been.

No, the house had to go.

"You're running again," Zee said. "You aren't a child anymore, Nix. Don't run just because this scares you. This is your home. Bear would want you to stay."

Zee frowned. "I'm done here. We can go back to the house and talk."

I waited for him to put the wheelbarrow and fork away. He would not want help, and I wasn't about to cross that line. He stepped out of the barn and together we started up the slight slope toward the house. I kept up with him easily, for the first time noticing how careful he was with each step, with each movement. How he was doing everything he could to control the muscle tremors through his body.

Damn it, I'd been so wrapped up in my own preparations, in my own anger, I'd not seen his decline. A decline that probably had started far before the accident if I was honest with myself, and pushed the instant guilt away. While he'd Hidden Bear and I, he'd been worked nearly to death by my father, and whoever it was he'd worked for before that. A Hider's abilities were at a premium, but the cost was high. Eventually the kick back from the magic would kill him, but not before it ate away at his body bit by bit.

"Any luck with the coding on the papers?" The question from him was not unwarranted. I'd been trying to break the code every night since I'd found the damn papers, but with the glyphs and letters moving and shifting, it had been near impossible. I'd work at it until the pages blurred. I'd just start to make strides forward—or think I was—only to find there was another language thrown in, and the pattern I'd been following was gone once more. Code breaking was not a strong point of mine.

Particularly when magic was involved.

"No."

"Unbreakable?"

I shook my head. "No, I've got someone in mind. You remember little Mick? He's a genius at shit like this." I opened the back door and let Zee in first. So, when he didn't take a step forward, I knew something was wrong.

Beside me, Abe let out a snarl and lunged forward. I caught him by the collar at the last second.

Zee carefully stepped into the house. "Who are you, and what are you doing here?"

I kept my hand on Abe, and slid the other to Eleanor.

Slowly, I stepped to the left of Zee. "Abe, *platz*." I gave him the command and he dropped to the floor beside me. I kept my eyes on the man in front of us. He was wearing black from head to foot, gloves covered his hands, and the lower half of his face was covered with a black bandana. But his eyes . . . I knew them. From where was the only question.

His voice was muffled, but I heard his words just fine. "I came to give you a warning . . . Phoenix."

Nothing else he could have said would have set me off like that. He knew who I was. I had Eleanor out and pointed at him in a flash.

"You'd better talk fast, my fingers are twitchy," I said.

I got the impression he smiled under his facial covering. "I know who you are. I know you've been hiding all these years. I could have told your father, but I didn't. I let you live in peace, remember that."

This was not the man who'd tossed the house. He was too thin. His feet too small.

Abe continued his low snarling, the sound echoing through the room.

"Bully for you," I said, my words icy. "Why are you here?"

"A warning. Like I said. Do not step back into your old world. They don't know you're alive, but if you go after them, I won't have a choice but to tell them where you hid to save my own life. Burning Mary-Ellen's house like that was a perfect beacon to them. You shouldn't have done it."

He spread his hands wide and dropped a flash bang that exploded with a burst of light, the sound blinding me even as the smoke filled the room. I flattened myself to the floor to try and see through the smoke and Abe lay beside me, shaking hard.

"Abe, *fass*!" The words were inside my head with the ringing in my ears from the flash bang, and I hoped he heard me.

He hesitated, and I repeated the command. Finally, on the third shout from me, he left my side which meant he'd indeed heard me. But he would be as blind as me, and I wasn't sure he'd be able to find anything with his nose through the heavy smoke.

"Fucking goddamn it!" Zee roared, slammed into something and went down. My eyes watered and I fought to clear them.

"Who was it?" I spit the words out as Abe made his way back to me. I crept to the back door and pushed it open. The breeze cleared the smoke in a matter of minutes, but Zee hadn't answered me.

"Zee, did you know him?"

"It's my fault he's here." He sat on the floor with his back against the island. "I called in a favor and asked around. Tried to see if there was anything big going down with Mancini."

I shook my head. "He slipped in here. There's only one airport in and out." I grabbed the keys off the counter, my shoulder holster still holding Eleanor and Dinah, and slid them over my shoulders. "You coming?"

Zee nodded. "Yeah, I am."

I tossed him the keys. "I'm a better shot."

He grunted. "Only because I taught you."

"How about us?" Dinah whined. "We help."

Seconds later we were in the truck, Abe with us in the backseat. His eyes were intent as Zee hit the gas, chasing down the asshole who'd walked into my house and tried to intimidate me. He might know who I was in theory, but he was about to get a lesson in practice on who not to mess with.

Phoenix Romano Stark was not someone you crossed and survived.

CHAPTER TEN

The rain cutting through the sky turned the thawing spring roads into a slush mud pit full of potholes and spots so slick that if you didn't know how to drive, you ended up in the ditch within minutes.

Zee wrestled with the wheel of the truck as we took a curve in the road, mud spitting out so hard, it peppered the side panels of the truck. We weren't that far behind the man who'd walked into my house, and tried to *warn* me. His warning had also held enough of a threat that there was no way he was going to get far.

"What are you going to do when we catch up to him?" Zee didn't look at me.

"He's going to tell me everything he knows." I kept my eyes locked on the road ahead of us. Whoever had walked into my house thinking he knew how to deal with me would not have gotten that far in this slushy mud. The tire tracks told me he was driving a car, low slung and more likely to bottom out on one of the deep ruts that showed up without fail in the Wyoming spring.

The gun rack in the backseat held a single gun, Zee's

Winchester thirty ought six. A hunting rifle that could take down a grizzly bear or even a bison at a distance with the right ammo. I leaned back and grabbed it off the rack, opened the dash, and found the ammo. Bolt action, I slid a round in, flipped off the safety and waited with the gun cradled in my arm, pointing toward the side window. We went up a hill and as we started down the other side, the car in front of us that I'd been expecting finally came into view.

The two guns resting on my lower back grumbled about not being used, but Zee was right. Where I could, I needed to find a way to use them less, or more accurately, not get so chatty with them. Magic could warp you, and the guns were most definitively imbued with magic. I could feel it if I focused when I held them. Their desire for blood quite literally infected me, and I saw it at the end of my career. Justin's belief that I had killed a bunch of children for kicks was not correct. But I had ended up staring down the barrels of the guns at a pair of siblings that stepped in front of their father I'd been brought in to deal with. I hadn't squeezed the triggers.

But I'd wanted to.

I didn't need further warping, I was enough of a killer as it was.

"Did he really think we'd just let him walk away?" I asked as I rolled down the window.

"You've been gone a long time, Nix. People start to talk away the truth when they haven't seen it in years. You aren't the bogeyman you once were."

I snorted softly and leaned out the window, sighting through the scope. The rear left tire was the first to go, followed quickly by the right. Rear wheel drive did shit when your tires were blown. The thump of the butt of the gun into my shoulder was a reassurance that warmed me, but it was also the shoulder Mary-Ellen had injured and the pain was no small thing. I gritted my teeth through it even as sweat dripped down the sides of my face.

The car slid to the side of the road and the man in black jumped out, a gun raised at us. What a tool. I shot him in the left knee with the Winchester, a blow that could almost take his leg off if I hadn't aimed to the side. He went down, clutching at it, a scream erupting from his mouth. He raised his gun and I shot him through the elbow, again, making sure I just zinged him. I'd blow his limbs off later if I had to.

"Just like the little ducks at the fair," I said as Zee put the truck in park and I stepped out. I left the bigger hunting rifle behind and pulled Dinah from my holster. Abe stalked along beside me, pinned to my side as if I'd glued him there.

The man no longer had his face covered and when I reached him, his eyes were wide. "I tried to warn you, and you'd kill me for it?"

"Who am I?" I whispered the words, the words I'd intoned before every person I'd brought under my thumb, under my father's rule.

He swallowed hard. "The Phoenix."

"That's right. Which means we can do this the easy way and you can tell me everything you know, and I'll let you go with only the wounds you have. Or we can do this the fun way." I smiled at him, let him see the darkness I carried inside. Let him catch a glimpse of the violence as it welled up through my body. "They killed my son. If you thought I was dangerous before," I leaned in and pressed the muzzle of Dinah to his lower jaw, "it's nothing to what I've become."

He was shaking, his blue eyes wide as he struggled to breathe. "What . . . what do you want to know?"

"Oh, he's smarter than he looks," I murmured.

Zee laughed. "Doubt that. He's been watching you and tried to warn you. Which means he has a thing for you. It's the only reason he wouldn't have turned you in."

I raised my eyebrows. "That right?"

He blanched. "I . . . I was sent to look for you. The more I looked, the more I realized you'd outsmarted everyone. I could respect that. I only found you last year."

Eleven years he'd been looking. "My father sent you after me?"

"Yes, he expected me to find you. I kept looking even after he pulled me off. Someone . . . someone else is looking for you now. A new guy."

My eyes narrowed. "My father gave up on you, but you kept looking."

He blanched further, rain sliding down his face making him look like he was crying. Or maybe he was crying. Hard to say. I kept a hold on him as the rain poured down around us. Eleven years . . . and his face slowly came into real focus.

"I know you." I stood, pulling him with me though he wobbled on his one good leg. He was only a little taller than my five nine, but I recalled him being thinner, the gangly arms and legs of a youth who sprouted too fast. Younger than me in more than years.

He nodded. "I just came into your father's business, not long before you left."

"Bradley," I said his name and he smiled. I did not return it. "Knowing your name isn't going to save you from me."

He closed his eyes and a breath slid out of him. "The man coming for you, he's not going to let you see him. He's better than I am at this."

"No shit, Sherlock. His name," Zee growled. "A name and we'll let you go."

Bradley laughed, bitter and sad. "I am not a fool to think she'll let me go. Not now. His name is Simon, that's all I know."

He had a point. I started walking back to the truck, dragging him with me as he flailed. "Phoenix, please! I could have turned you over to your father and I didn't. I could see you were happy!" His begging did nothing. I didn't feel a thing. Because that was the best way to handle this.

I opened the tailgate and shoved him up and onto the bed of the truck.

He sat there, like a well-trained dog. Which he was, only trained to someone else. I was going to take his allegiance and make it my own. "You abnormal?"

He shook his head. "No."

Well, at least there was that, and when I took a quick breath and looked over him, he wasn't lying. He was a normal.

"What are you doing, Nix?" Zee slid into the driver's side as Abe and I got into the cab.

"Making use of the tools at hand." I twisted in the seat and leveled Dinah at Bradley. Even from where I was, I could see him swallow hard.

"It makes no sense, Zee. Why would my father send an untrained boy after me?"

"He's had *some* training," Zee countered.

"Nothing close to what it would take to bring me down." There was no ego in my words, just the truth.

"What are you going to do with him?"

"I need another set of eyes. I'm going to take him with me," I said.

"Are you out of your damn mind?" He slapped the seat between us.

I shook my head. "You pointed it out yourself. He's got a thing for me. I'll use that. It won't take much for me to force him to transfer his allegiance from one Romano to another."

Anger radiated off Zee. I didn't have to look at him to know he was pissed. "You aren't one of your father's dancing girls, Nix. You never went for the easy out with men—"

"I will do what I have to do." The words were hard and cold.

He changed tactics. "There is still no explanation for why Bradley, and not someone more experienced like this Simon guy, until now." Zee pointed out the niggling question to me again.

I closed my eyes, thinking about my father, doing what I could to get into his head. He had a way about him. How he liked to do things.

"My father is cheap," I said. "If he sent an untrained man, he did it to use him as bait. If he showed up dead, my father would know where I was. Send in someone more experienced for a shorter period of time. Saves him big bucks that way."

"That means Bradley has some sort of tracer on him then?" Zee asked. We stared hard at each other for a good ten seconds.

"I'll check him when we get back to the house. He's been there, so if he's got a tracer in him, they'll already know."

Zee grunted. "Or he had no plans of actually finding you. Sending Bradley back there could have been a front to keep Mancini happy. You may hate your father, but he's not a dumb-ass. He knows you know how to hide. He knows I'm with you, helping you hide."

"You think the new guy, this Simon, he's been sent by Mancini?" I asked.

"Fuck, I don't know," Zee grumbled.

I frowned as I stared out the front window, what I was seeing taking me from our conversation. "Is that smoke above the trees?"

"Son of a bitch." Zee hit the gas.

The house came into view . . . and it was burning.

My first thought was that Mary-Ellen had somehow risen from the dead and exacted revenge on my home. But that was impossible when I'd lit her feathers on fire myself.

I leapt from the truck and winced as my body shot

through with pain from my shoulder all the way down my spine.

Abe was right behind me as I bolted not for the front door but the big pane window that led into Justin's office. I pulled my gun and let off two shots, shattering the glass seconds before I jumped forward.

Smoke billowed out, the sharp acrid scent of gasoline biting the inside of my nose and mouth.

"*Legen*." I gave him the command as I did the same thing, dropping to my belly and creeping forward as I kept close to the ground. I needed to get to Bear's Christmas gift. Everything else could burn, everything else of value was in the barn.

I slid toward the door as it was booted open, and a big man with a face mask stepped into the room. I didn't hesitate. I lashed out with my right leg, sweeping it across the floor and into his legs, knocking him to the ground. Keeping my body pinned low, I raced up his legs and sat up on his hips as I pulled a knife from my thigh. I wanted him alive, and that meant keeping Dinah and Eleanor out of this at least for now.

I whipped the blade down and he jerked out of the way, blocking me, forearm against forearm.

"*Fass!*" I yelled.

The body below me jerked as Abe bit into his legs and started to shake the intruder.

I slammed a fist into his solar plexus, putting all my weight into it. My lungs burned with the smoke and growing heat, but I would not slow down. Whoever this shit was, he would have answers.

The bastard below me whipped his arms up and grabbed my elbows, and pinned them to my side.

I think not.

I jerked my legs up under me and drove my knees into his

belly. His hold loosened and we rolled to the side until he was on top of me.

The cooler air against the floor was a welcome breath. I sucked it in as I wrapped my legs around the bastard's waist and jerked him close to me. I still had my knife in my right hand and I twisted it, slashing upward, catching him under the chin, slashing through the mask.

He reeled backward, kicked Abe in the face, and was up and running, far faster than I would have thought a man his size could. Abnormal? I didn't think so.

Before I could see his face, the smoke covered him more completely than any mask.

Abe whined. "*Hinaus!*" I sent him back through the window with the command and stumbled after the intruder. Smoke filled the hallway and I dropped once more to my belly. Better air, and a safer place with that asshole in here somewhere.

I crawled across the floors as they heated rapidly, my knife in my right hand. My bedroom door was open only a crack, and I pushed through it. Eyes watering, lungs burning, I struggled not to start coughing. That would give my position away like a damn homing beacon.

I made it to the dresser, reached up and fumbled until I found the still-wrapped Christmas present from Bear. I shoved it into my shirt and headed straight for the French doors that led onto the back deck. I pushed to my feet and ran for the door, hitting the handle and twisting it at the same time.

I spilled into the fresh air, went to my knees, and sucked in a big breath.

The crackling of the flames filled the air as the timber house went up like a roman candle. The man who'd started the fire, I had no doubt that he wasn't done and I needed to find him fast. I pushed to my feet once more, and ran around the side of the house.

Zee had moved the truck back and he leaned over the back of it. I didn't slow, but didn't hurry my pace either. A part of me already suspected what had happened. "Shot Bradley, didn't he?"

"Yeah, he came out the front door, picked the kid off first, then went for me."

I looked Zee over. Didn't see anything, no bullet wounds. "No return fire?"

He nodded. "I did, but the shakes. I missed him."

I looked around for tracks, finding the ones I searched for finally. "Four-wheeler. Smart man, but human." There was no way we'd catch up to him, not by the time I saddled up one of the horses. Even then, there was no way to truly catch him. Smarter than Bradley, anyway. Was it the mysterious Simon, though?

I had a feeling it wasn't. Something about this man, the way he moved, led me to believe I knew him somehow. I just couldn't put my finger on how, but I would. And when I did, we'd have a nice long chat.

Sirens lit up in the distance. Not the fire department, but the police from the sounds of it. Fuck it all. I wasn't surprised they'd been called in. What could make it harder for me to move forward looking for Justin and Bear's killers?

Being in jail would slow me down.

"Goddamn it." I shook my head. "Zee, it's a setup."

This whole thing had been a goddamn setup. Bradley, the house, the man inside. A way to get me out of the way and stop me from poking my nose into the reasons behind Justin's and Bear's deaths.

"We've got to get rid of Bradley," I said, "and fast."

Zee nodded. "I'll take him out back to my place, bury him

in the compost. I'll be back, wait for me here and don't say anything to them."

He got into the truck, started it up and was gone in a matter of seconds, leaving Abe and me to face the police.

I shook my head, a rush of adrenaline sliding through me, making my fingers tingle.

No, Zee was wrong. It was time for me and Abe to leave, I could feel it in my gut.

Zee would understand.

I jogged around the side of the house and down to the barn. At a rapid speed, I opened the secret room behind the saddle rack and grabbed my already prepped pack. Filled with cash, IDs, the coded papers, ammo and several weapons, I slung the backpack over my shoulder.

I took one last look at the sleepy horse heads hanging over their stall doors, watching. Big eyes blinked at me, and one mare cracked a wide, toothy yawn, flipping her tongue.

"I'll be back," I whispered and then shook my head.

Well, shit, it looked like Zee was right about me after all.

With my bag on my back, and Abe at my side, I hurried up to the main—and still violently burning—house.

As I stepped around to the front, the lone cop car pulled in. The fact that it was just one cop car, and no fire truck backing it up, said it all. They had come to make sure the job was finished. To finish me off.

Luckily, it was Officers Ryan and Schmidt.

Schmidt lifted his gun at me. "Put your weapons down!"

I raised my eyebrows and my hands, palm out. "No weapons here, Officer."

Abe gave a low growl.

"*Nein.*" I held my hand out over his head, keeping him where he was.

"I said, put your weapons down!" Schmidt flicked the

safety off his gun. So that's how it was going to be. I was not a cop killer, but it looked like that was about to change.

I flexed my fingers. The weight of Eleanor and Dinah in my holster called to me. The weapons weren't clearly visible, of that I was sure. I wasn't holding them, not yet anyway. I didn't want Zee to hear the gunshots and come running.

The moment slowed, stretched, as I dropped my left hand to my thigh and knife instead of Eleanor. I pulled and threw the knife in a single smooth motion that buried the blade into Schmidt's forehead. His gun went off, but I didn't flinch. The direction of the muzzle was off the second I nailed him. I started toward Officer Ryan. He pulled his gun but it got caught in his holster as I strode toward him.

"*Fass!*"

Abe shot forward and tackled the officer, grabbing him by the gun arm and dragging him away from the cop car.

Abe's growls were no competition for the crackling of the flames, but I heard them as I drew closer. Deep and guttural, his dark eyes were locked on the young officer. Abe was not the sweet farm dog he'd once been, any more than I was the sweet ranch wife.

Officer Ryan got his second gun out with his opposite hand just as I reached him. I slammed my foot into his wrist, pinning it to the ground.

"Everyone is in on this? Taking me down?"

He spit up at me; the spit hovered, fell and landed on his own face. I frowned at him, though the frown turned into a half-smirk. "Not exactly the effect you were going for, was it?"

I twisted my foot, and his hand opened. Leaning over, I picked up the gun. "*Aus.*"

Abe unlocked his jaw and backed off, panting hard with excitement.

The house burned behind me, the last of my life disappearing in smoke and flames.

I cocked the gun and pressed it to Officer Ryan's temple. "Talk to me, or get ready to have a chat with God about your sins."

His face drained of blood and his Adam's apple bobbed violently. "Orders came down that . . . that you were to be watched. That there was a suspicion you were a violent offender in hiding. That's all I knew. Schmidt had the details, not me. I swear, that's all I knew!"

That much I could believe. Schmidt would be close to retirement, looking for a sweet payout that would pad a better lifestyle than a mere pension. I rolled the gun in my hand and slammed the butt of it into his head. His eyes rolled back and his body slumped into the mud. I grabbed his arm and dragged him to Schmidt's body. I wiped the handle of the blade still in Schmidt's forehead and then wrapped Ryan's hand over it, pressing his fingertips over it tightly.

For good measure, I took Schmidt's hand that still held the gun and wrapped my hand around his, put the muzzle to Ryan's right shoulder, deep in the soft flesh, and pulled the trigger. Let them figure this shit out with the forensics lab.

I stood and went to the cop car. "Abe, let's go, buddy."

He leapt in the passenger side and I shut the door behind him. I took off my bag and flipped it into the back, then slid into the driver's seat. I backed the car up as Zee drove back into the yard with the truck. He lifted a hand to me, and our eyes met. He gave me a nod.

I knew he would understand.

Time to truly begin the hunt, to bring down the predators who'd come to my door, thinking to find a shivering little mouse.

Time to show them the real monster they'd woken.

CHAPTER ELEVEN

The drive into town was tense in the growing dark as the day faded, mostly because I knew more than ever, I was on the wrong side of the law. I'd never killed a cop before. Bad guys, that had been my job. Men who'd fucked over my father and tried to steal from him, or our family. I'd never killed anyone before that would have been labeled a 'good guy' and that had made what I did acceptable in my own mind.

My legs rattled with excess energy.

"Phoenix," Eleanor spoke, "why did you use the knife and not one of us? We could have killed him much faster."

"Zee is right. I rely on you ladies too much. I need to be better prepared if you get taken away. Or if I am facing a beast that can't be killed with a simple bullet." And then there was the connection to them that was almost too strong. Zee was looking out for me, and he would know being an abnormal himself.

Dinah snorted. "No such thing."

I knew she was wrong, there were a few beasts out there

that were immune to bullets, hell my father had three of them at his side. I had to hope I wouldn't end up dealing with any of them.

"Abe, you ready for this?" I glanced at him. He tipped his head to the side and gave me a woof. Good enough.

As we neared town, firetrucks passed us at top speed, headed the other way, their lights shattering the night. I wasn't going to have much time to switch out the police cruiser for another vehicle. And it wasn't like town was big enough that another missing vehicle would go unnoticed.

Unless . . . unless it was Noah's.

Noah wasn't here. He'd left as he'd said he would a short time after the funeral. But he had a cheap overseas-model car he left parked at the airport for when he came to visit. I'd never questioned it before, thinking he just didn't want to be a burden on Justin. Now I wondered if it was so he could move around without people knowing he was here.

I took the turn that would lead us to the airport. Only seven miles out of town, it was a busy airport, surprisingly enough. Again, not so busy that I wouldn't be noticed, stinking of smoke and covered in soot as I was. I looked down at my body, taking in my appearance as I drove.

My clothes were torn from the fight, and they were splattered with mud from grabbing Bradley and dragging him around. Abe wasn't looking much better, his fawn-colored fur tipped in mud. He blinked his dark eyes at me, as if he couldn't believe how dirty we were too.

I patted his head. "We need to get cleaned up, buddy."

I pulled the cruiser onto a secondary street, parking it to the side of the road, and stepped out, sweeping the area with my eyes. There was a row of houses, three of which I knew were rentals.

I grabbed my bag from the backseat and Abe heeled to my left without being asked. We jogged to the townhouse that Noah used without being seen. I waited for a solid five minutes, watching the windows in the rental house, but no lights came on, there was no movement of someone walking around. I walked up the stairs as if I belonged there, put my hand on the doorknob and tried it once. Locked, of course.

There was a window right next to the door. Perfect. I pulled off the long-sleeved shirt I wore, leaving me in nothing but a camisole, and wrapped my hand in the muddy shirt. A quick punch and I was through the glass, and the deadbolt was flicked open. I stepped through and into the dark house. "Abe."

He didn't need a lot of encouragement, hurrying in with me. I locked the door behind me for what it was worth.

I turned, letting my eyes adjust to the dark main living space. Couch and recliner, TV, a nice coffee table. I walked past them to the back of the house where the master bedroom and bathroom were. I could get cleaned up, then Abe and I could run the last few miles to the airport to pick up Noah's car . . . my thoughts stuttered, trailing off as I flicked on the small bedside lamp.

The room . . . it was not empty as a rental should be, not by a long shot.

The walls were covered with paper clippings, maps, lists. At first I thought I was seeing things wrong. Yet here it was, evidence of what Justin and Noah had been neck deep in.

I put a hand on one of the paper clippings and read it through.

Business tycoon Luca Romano is showing no signs in slowing down the expansion of his multinational company. With his most recent bride at his side, he opens the newest of his businesses, a Hollywood studio dedicated to helping struggling actors find the limelight.

The news clipping was dated almost a full year before. In Justin's hand.

Justin's sharp, angled scrawl had written the date on the

paper, the same angled scrawl that had been on the coded papers here and there as they danced around. I pulled the papers out of my bag and held them up to the clippings. Justin's scrawl, and the neater printing.

The neater printing that was on the wall was also on the coded papers.

"Noah, you lying bastard." I struggled not to rip the news clipping from the wall.

They both knew who my father was . . . and they'd been tracking his movements.

I skimmed the remaining papers, looking for a thread other than my father. But they were all tied to him, all tied to his business and what he was doing, who he was with. My heart picked up speed as I skimmed article after article.

A slow pattern began to emerge. I looked at the cities where my father was doing business. I closed my eyes, thinking about the cities Justin and Noah had been traveling to the last few years.

Boulder. New York. Los Angeles. Salt Lake.

They matched.

"What have you two done?" I whispered, pressing my hand against the wall. I didn't care that I was leaving a muddy print. Noah would know someone broke in the second he saw the window. I backed away from the wall and went to the kitchen.

There was food on the counter, and a coffee pot still half full of black sludge. I frowned and went to it, put the back of my hand to the pot.

Still warm.

Noah was in town, then.

My heart picked up speed.

The man at the house . . . he'd been looking in Justin's office. He'd seemed familiar. Noah at the door after the funeral. The Gore-Tex material in Abigail's mouth.

"Mother fucker."

I wanted to sit and cover my face with my hands, because he'd been right there in front of me at the funeral. At my house. And now he'd set my world on fire.

I had no doubt he was on an ATV somewhere out in the woods. It would take him time to get back here. I had a choice. I could wait for him, and force information. I could wait and kill him. Or I could go, and leave him to roam, knowing he would show back up, knowing that if I tried to force info from him, it would likely come out as more lies.

I clenched my fist, struggling with my decision.

I headed to the bathroom, stripping my clothes off as I went.

I found dark gray sweatpants, white socks, and a stack of T-shirts in the one dresser in his bedroom. I pulled what I needed and went to the shower. I scrubbed off as fast as I could, then beckoned Abe into the tub.

He jumped in and I washed the worst of the mud off, and towel-dried him. He took the opportunity to shake several times, spraying the room with the last flickers of mud and water that smelled lightly of dog. My lips twitched, a smile almost happening because I knew that Noah disliked the smell of dogs. More than once he'd commented on not ever being able to live in a place with animals like we did.

"Abe, come here." I pointed at Noah's bed. Abe jumped up and immediately began to roll around, drying himself on the nice clean sheets. Though it wasn't exactly torture, it was a small dig. And it made me feel better for a moment.

I rinsed off once more to remove the dog hair and Abe's mud from my arms, then dried myself and dressed in Noah's clothes. Warm and loose, they would allow for easy movement and the ability to hide my weapons. I had the shoulder holster on over the white T-shirt, then found a windbreaker in the closet. Not exactly warm but it would do.

Dinah grumbled. "I want to be cleaned too. I feel sticky."

"Later," I said. "We're on a tight schedule here."

I twisted my hair into a tight bun at the back of my head, grabbed my clothes from the floor and went into the kitchen. Digging around, I found a black garbage bag I put my wet clothes in.

"There is still time," I spoke out loud, more to myself than Abe or my guns. "Still time to find out what we can."

Abe woofed at me from the bed with a big dog grin on his face and wagged his tail.

Time to toss the house. Whatever Noah had hidden here, I was going to find it.

And find it I did.

There were several standard issue guns, a couple of pieces of fake ID . . . and an FBI badge with the name Lancaster on it. I'd known him as Noah Black. I frowned and tossed them to the side. Double crossing a double crosser? Had Justin known Noah was FBI? I shook my head. Too many lies, there was no easy way to untangle them.

More than all that, though, I searched for the family bible that had been stolen, sure that it was Noah who had taken it, that it would be key in breaking the codes.

But there was no bible in the apartment.

I checked the time. Half an hour, we'd been here long enough.

"Time to go, Abe."

I slung the bag over my shoulder, not caring that I looked exactly like what I was doing. Robbing his house.

I let Abe out the back door first, and then followed him through grass yards to the wooded areas, rather than using the road to get to the airport. Even though I was sure Noah had his vehicle with him, the airport was still a good place to pick up a car that wouldn't be missed for at least a day or so. Lots of long term parking there.

We crossed open fields in the dark. I talked while we walked. Despite what Zee thought, Dinah and Eleanor were excellent to bounce ideas off.

"Noah and Justin were tracking my father for some reason. Maybe . . . maybe they thought they could blackmail him? Because they knew about me."

Dinah snorted. "No, that seems too simple."

"Did they know you weren't your sister?" Eleanor asked.

I shook my head. "No, I let him believe I was Bianca and that I'd faked my death. Zee masked my tattoo with his Hiding abilities. They never knew." The Hiding he'd done was broken now, which meant I could be found if anyone was looking.

A very large part of me wanted to be found.

I thought for a moment. "Then there's Tank; the brake lines were tampered with his signature style, but there was no way he could have fit under the truck unless he's lost a shit ton of weight in the last ten years."

"Someone he trained?" Dinah offered.

"Yeah, probably. But he'd be the place to start."

My mind worked to put the pieces together, to find the commonality. And that was the problem as far as I could see. There was no real commonality.

I adjusted the bag on my back. "Bradley was sent to look for me, but was really being used for bait, I think Zee was right about that. But I feel like there's something I'm missing. What the hell is it?"

Abe gave me a soft woof, but otherwise was quiet. Neither of my guns spoke.

I shook my head. "Looks like we're going to pay Tank a visit first then. He's the only thing I know for sure. And he's in New York. Or he was the last time I saw him."

Tank's boss was the head of the Mancini family. Magical mobsters, if you will. Most were hardened criminals, and most had never been caught in large part because of that magic.

One piece that stuck out to me was that if Tank had been brought in to deal with whatever it was Justin had dabbled in, then my husband had been dealing in high-level shit.

It didn't matter to me that Justin had been doing something illegal. Reality was, illegal practices had been what I'd spent most of my early life doing, so there was no judgment from me. Except that it had cost our son his life too.

If I was honest, it wouldn't have mattered as much to me if it had just been him that had died in the accident. I would have grieved, but I would have gone on.

If Bear had survived, I would have gone on with the life I'd created for myself and our boy. I would have looked for the killers. I would have bumped up security around the farm. But I wouldn't have gone after them, not like this. I would have had Bear with me to take care of, to love still. There would not have been this fury that was propelling me forward.

The blinking lights of the airport called me out of my thoughts.

I circled around to the long-term pay parking.

I settled on a dark blue mid-sized truck that had a time stamp on the window ticket for two weeks from the current date. Two weeks before it was officially missing. Perfect.

I broke a back window with the flick of a baton from my bag. Unlocking the doors, I let Abe into the front seat passenger spot. From the driver's seat, I ripped off the paneling under the steering wheel, cut the wires, and jump-started the engine in under a minute.

The engine growled to life and I checked the gas gauge. Right full, and according to the meter beside it, that would probably give us close to four hundred miles. Four hundred miles.

I pulled out of the parking space and headed toward the exit, taking the only road out of town leading east. East to the coast, to Tank and the mob.

CHAPTER TWELVE

Thirteen hundred miles between Wyoming and New York was a blur of cheap fast food, dirty truck stops and thirty minutes of sleep snatched here and there. Not a single abnormal, not a single person who so much as looked at me sideways.

New York was as I'd left it, what felt like a hundred years ago. Busy, bustling, full of people, smells, energy and music. That was the side most people saw. The other side was . . . not so pretty.

Dirty, dangerous, broken down, full of death and very bad things like abnormals and magic. Here and there, I saw them, the abnormals. A flicker of movement on the peripheral of my vision that drew my eyes time and again.

The thing with abnormals was when you weren't looking for them, that's when you saw them. The energy around them was different. People naturally gave them more space, side-long glances. They moved in a circle of their own; even when they fit in, they stood out. This was not a skill easy to learn as a human and it had taken me years to perfect it.

I stopped at a local secondhand store that was still in

business and picked up clothes. Things that would work in multiple situations. I didn't want to advertise I was back in town, so I grabbed a frilly dress and thigh-high boots far more suited to a stripper. My mother would have loved them both. Along with the dress-up clothes, I grabbed several wigs, and a few other types of outfits from casual to business.

From there, I headed to the heart of Manhattan in the Garment District. Known for the violence here, I was less likely to be noticed. The cheap-ass motel room I rented smelled like bug spray and whiskey.

I stared into the partially fogged mirror of the bathroom, my body wrapped in a thin towel.

Phoenix Romano had been barely a woman when she'd run from her father. Her long dark hair and matching eyes were stamps of her family as surely as her attitude and penchant for violence. She'd worn clothes that matched that blackness, to the point where people mocked her behind her back.

Now, I was Nix, and with my white-blonde hair and a pair of green contacts in, I was nothing like that girl from my past. The frilly pink dress kissed the tops of my knees, covering the height of the thigh-high boots, which covered the fact I was carrying knives on my upper legs.

At least on the outside, I didn't resemble Phoenix.

A long loose trench coat covered the dress all the way to my calves. A thick pink belt made of strips of leather wrapped around my waist, and allowed for a holster to be set in my lower back. There was no way I'd leave Eleanor or Dinah out of this. I ran my hands over the variety of weapons I had, counting them. Three guns besides Dinah and Eleanor, three knives, and two sedative darts tucked into a case in the trench coat pocket. Just in case.

A girl can never be too prepared.

"Where are we going tonight?" Eleanor asked.

"Finding an old friend," I said as I put her into her holster.

Abe was passed out on the crappy queen sized bed, and I gave him a pat before I left. "Abe, *bewache*."

He sat up, his ears perked as he watched me leave the room. Asking him to guard would mean that if anyone who wasn't me tried to enter the room, he'd attack and go for the kill.

I locked the door behind me and headed down the stairs. The boots were snug, comfortable, and gave me an extra three inches, also adding to my disguise.

On the street, I hailed a cab.

"The Lounge on 36th Street," I said, accenting my voice ever so slightly to come across as a touch Southern. The cabbie nodded and pulled into traffic.

The stop and start of the cab through Manhattan lulled me, and for a moment, I let myself think about Bear. His birthday was coming up. He'd have turned eleven in May, and I'd promised him this year we'd do a week-long camping trip in the mountains, just the three of us with the dogs and roasting marshmallows and hot dogs over an open fire . . . I swallowed the sudden lump in my throat and the dreams of the future that would never be now.

I looked out at the city as it passed by in a weak attempt to distract myself.

I never thought I'd come back here, to this life and the death it afforded the world. My father would have something to say about it, I was sure. Something stupid like "birds always come home to roost."

There would be no mention by my father about how alike we were. Because I knew now, more than ever, I was more like him than my other siblings. I could hate the fact all I liked, but the truth stared me in the face.

Like him, if it meant finding my boys' killers, I would

make a deal with the devil. Mind you, my father made that deal for money and power, not for something like saving one of his kids.

My jaw tightened at the thought of Tommy, Daniel, and Gabe. The three boys were the oldest, in that order. And while they were the heads of various departments of my father's business, they didn't have his killer instinct. They were mean bastards who loved to torment others, especially those smaller and weaker. They were womanizers and gamblers and stupid as a bag of rocks as far as I was concerned. It wasn't just the killer instinct they didn't have, it was the intelligence. They floated along on Daddy's money and they thought they'd earned their places in his business.

I snorted to myself softly.

No, the intelligence and killer instinct had come through in Luca's two daughters. I frowned as I thought about Bianca. Older than me by almost six years, we had not been friends, not by a long shot. She'd been the beauty queen, working hard to take over our father's empire at some point. I was the ugly duckling she looked down on. But as I'd finished my training with Zee, and I'd grown into my looks, there had been an understanding that grew between us. It was us against the boys, and it was only after her death that I'd realized I had no choice if I wanted to live any sort of a life. I had to walk away from everything I'd ever known.

I had to try to be normal and re-write the future that waited for me.

That had been her one and only gift to me.

Her death had opened my eyes.

My four siblings had belonged to our father's first wife. I was the only one my mother, Sophie, had. I kept my breathing slow and even as the thoughts and memories played through my mind. All the years of self-analysis had taught me a few things. I was something of a sociopath, and there was no denying it. No one who did what I did and slept soundly at night without remorse for the deaths I caused could be anything but.

My brothers and father all fell into the severe narcissist category, and my sister . . . well, she was somewhere in between.

Not that it mattered what she'd been. I struggled to get my thoughts off my family and back onto the task at hand.

My only plan at the moment was to have a nice, long chat with Tank Follietta, and then from there I would take my next step. Tank was one of the few men on Mancini's roster who wasn't an abnormal.

After my run-in with Mary-Ellen, I wanted to keep my interaction with the magical community limited.

From Tank, I would start breaking down exactly who had called in the hit on Justin, and just what I was going to do to them.

Sure, I had my ideas, but I liked to personalize things when it came to people dying. I blinked and looked out the side window, taking note of where we were as the cab slowed.

The Lounge rose from the underground like a beast climbing out of a cavernous lair. There was only one level on par with the street, the rest of the building was sunk below. Dirty and gritty, it was a hotbed for both Mancini's men and those looking to deal with the Mancini. On the outside, it looked a bit like a seedy, nondescript strip bar. Which was the front of it.

"You sure this is the Lounge you want?" The cabbie looked over his shoulder at me. "I know so much better clubs in cleaner areas. Nice girl like you shouldn't get mixed up with places like this."

I handed him a fifty-dollar bill. "Who said I was a nice girl, old man?"

The cabbie's mouth tightened. "Get out."

Yeah, that was about right. Soon as you claimed bitch status, the guys thought you weren't worth protecting anymore. I clenched my mouth into a smile, and blew him a kiss before I stepped onto the sidewalk. Adjusting my trench coat, I tucked my hands into my pockets, fingering the box with the sedative darts in the right side. I walked up to the entrance, keeping my senses on high alert. The sign above the building was bright neon-red looping letters that sagged a little as though their weight was slowly tearing them down.

I didn't knock on the door, just let myself in. There were two large burly men standing side by side with arms the size of chopped firewood between me and the interior door. Bouncers in every sense of the word. I turned my head to the side, letting my eyes unfocus. There was nothing around them that made me think they were abnormals.

I loosened my smile and gave them a wink.

"Hello, boys."

They didn't smile back, but that was no surprise. "We're full tonight. No more dancers needed."

I laughed softly and flicked a hand through my hair, tossing the long, loose blonde curls. "I have a private with Tank."

They exchanged a look. "Tank ain't here yet."

I shrugged. "You want me to wait here for him?" I gestured at the dank space they stood in. "I don't mind. You two can keep me company." I slid one hand down my upper body to settle onto the crook of my waist.

The one on the left shrugged. "Fine. Tank lets you in, then so be it."

"No, the boss said no more tonight." This from the one on the right.

I held up both hands slowly and wiggled my fingers. "I don't want to cause trouble. I'm just here to make a living, you know? I'll wait for Tank out front." I turned and let myself out.

Calculated risk, that was what I was doing. Tank had come here every night as long as I'd known him, and it looked like that much hadn't changed at least. I settled in for what I hoped was not a long wait, leaning up against the building, keeping myself partially in the shadows.

Minutes later three men strolled up the sidewalk from the north side of the street. Laughing, talking, two smoking, the other not. Dark suits and ties, two in ankle length trenches. I narrowed my eyes, watching them, noting their laughter because one of them sounded familiar.

"Gabe, your father is going to let that merger go through, isn't he? Mancini has a lot riding on that." The one on the far right spoke loudly, already inebriated by the way his words were soft on the edges. But that wasn't what I was focusing on. I wasn't sure if luck was on my side or not.

Gabe. The youngest of my three brothers, and the one who'd tormented me the most. The one who'd set me up for a beating and whatever else happened.

He'd be in his early thirties now, a few years older than me. His dark hair was slicked back in the latest style, and he was the only one of the men not wearing a trench. He grinned and my heart tightened seeing the whisper of what Bear would have looked like if he'd made it to adulthood. Charming, handsome, the strong bones of his face edged with stubble. My father made pretty babies, I'd give him that. But Bear would never have Gabe's mean streak. Bear would have been a good man. His heart was too kind to be the asshole my brother was.

"Of course the merger is going through, Johnny boy. As long as the money is there." He slapped Johnny on the shoulder and gave him a strong look. One that said it all, at least to me. As long as Mancini coughed up the money, and whatever else the deal entailed, Luca Romano would make sure John and his boss got what they wanted.

I kept my back against the wall for a split second before making a decision that was probably wrong. I did it anyway. I had to know if I could slide by my family, and there was no time like the present.

I pushed off the wall and took a step into the light. "Hello, boys. Which one of you is Tank?"

The three men stopped, one of them swayed and they slowly took me in with three almost identical looks that started at my feet and slid up my body. I had to grit my teeth to keep the smile plastered on my face.

Gabe grinned as his gaze slid from my face down my body and back up a second time.

"Tank is your date tonight? Poor girl, you should come with us. Not only are we ten times as good-looking, we're loaded." Gabe held a hand out to me, a ring set with a large ruby on the middle finger of his right hand. The same kind of ring my father wore. The rings that gave them access to three very big, bad guardians from the demon world.

"We'll pay you well. Big tips." He winked, and my stomach rolled with disgust.

John laughed. "And you'll like the look of us better than that asshole Tank."

I pouted my lips and cocked a hip. "But he's *already* paid me. I don't welch on my business deals. That goes poorly, you know, for girls in my position."

Gabe's eyes narrowed suddenly and I kept my face open, free of emotion even while I longed to snap a fist out and punch him in the face. I wanted to pull Eleanor and show him just what a bitch she could be. Almost as if sensing my thoughts, Eleanor shifted on my back.

I let him take my hand and pull me close even as sweat dribbled down my spine and hatred filled me. If he recognized me I would have to kill him right here. But this was the test I wanted. Could I slip by? Would I be just another stripper to take advantage of?

"You smell far too nice for the usual ladies Tank employs." He smiled again, and whatever wariness was in his eyes was gone.

"Tank likes the best," I said.

"I do, do I?" A rough, gravel-filled voice cut through. I spun away from Gabe and all but fell into Tank's arms, letting my ankles buckle in the high heels, forcing him to catch me. His massive hands gripped my upper arms and steadied me. I flashed my long false eyelashes up at him.

"There you are. I've been waiting on you. Can't pay a girl top dollar and then make her wait. It's rude, you know." I looked up at him from under my lashes. His hands tightened on me. Tank was easy to manipulate. Big and having been beaten with the ugly stick repeatedly as a child, he had a hard time coming by women honestly. That and the fact he worked for the Mancini family, which made him known as a danger . . . none of that added up in his favor.

He all but lifted me around so I was at his side. "I didn't pay for you."

Gabe, John, and their friend went still. I ran a hand over Tank's neck. "Mr. Mancini said you haven't taken enough time off lately. He sent me over as a surprise."

Tank's face lit up with a smile, showing more than one missing tooth. "Well, Mr. Mancini is right about that shit. Come on, baby, it's cold out here."

I had to give it to Tank. He was about as strong as they came, hence the nickname. He lifted me as though picking up a child, his arm around my upper back and away from my guns, thank God. He carried me with one arm so my feet barely brushed the ground all the way into the Lounge.

The two bouncers gave him a nod and didn't even look at

me. I kept my eyes and ears open as Tank walked us through the bar. A few drinks on the tables fizzed and popped with an energy that was all potions. In the corner of the room, there was a soft growl that could only belong to a shifter of some sort.

No matter how hard I looked, I saw nothing out of place, all the way to the only elevator. Tank hit the button, looked me over a couple of times and shook his head.

"Must have spent a fortune on you. You look too fresh to have been doing this long."

"I'm worth it," I whispered in his ear. "Best you'll ever find in the business. The very, very best."

He grunted and put his lips to my neck, in an attempt at foreplay. I let him, as I wrapped my arms around his thick neck. We stepped into the elevator and he had me against the back wall which pressed Dinah into my right kidney. She gave a grunt.

I could see past him to Gabe and John watching us. I gave them a wave as the doors slid shut.

"Tell me there's no cameras in here," I whispered.

"Nope, not here. Just in case someone gets lucky." Tank slid his hand down the front of my coat, plucking at the ties of the trench.

Again, I let him. My coat fell open, showing thick leather straps around my waist holding the dress to my body.

"Kinky." He grinned up at me.

I smiled back, and let the darkness swell in me. "Useful, too."

I shot my hand around to my back and pulled Eleanor out at a speed that left him still smiling even though I had her pressed her to his already-hard dick. With the other hand, I hit the stop button. No one would think anything of it. They'd seen us making out on the way in. I was betting on having five minutes, tops.

"We need to have a chat, Tank. Your mark was left on a brake line in Jackson Hole, Wyoming. Recall it?"

His eyes were wide and the smile slowly slid from his doughy, pockmarked face. "Who the hell are you?"

I pressed Eleanor harder against his dick. "If you want to continue enjoying the pleasure of the women you hire, I suggest you answer my question first."

"I ain't never been to Wyoming." His eyes didn't leave mine. He was an accomplished liar, but I didn't think he was lying right then. Hard to lie when your dick is being shoved up the barrel of a half-cocked gun.

I kept the pressure on him. "Then who else uses the puncture clamp technique?"

"I taught one guy. Let him use my tools."

"Why?"

He shook his head slowly. "I'm not a young guy anymore, and too damn big to fit under most of these new-fangled low chassis cars. 'Sides, I don't like to travel, and the boss is bringing in fresh blood. I only have to train them, and I get to keep my job."

I leaned into him a little harder and he flinched, and swallowed hard.

"His name, and I'm gone."

He blew out a breath before answering. "Stephen Demetris. Young guy, like I said. Handsome asshole. Abnormal." He frowned at that.

"Where will I find him and what kind of abnormal is he?" The thing with the Mancini crew was they all liked their particular clubs or bars. That was where they could be found, where people knew to go to hire them for their dirty business.

"Avalanche, it's across the bridge out in Brooklyn. He's a ghoster. Sometimes you see him, sometimes you don't. Depends on his mood."

Ghoster. I'd dealt with them before. The trick was to make sure they never saw you coming before they had a chance to disappear.

I reached over and hit the stop button, releasing it, and the elevator slid downward.

"You . . . are you still coming with me?" His eyes were just a tad too hopeful.

"Like it rough, do you?" I arched an eyebrow. That hadn't been a side of Tank I needed to know.

"Yeah, I kinda do." As the door to the elevator slid open, I put Eleanor away and turned. "After you . . . my friend."

He spun as he stepped out and stared at me, his eyes widening again. "Only one girl ever called me that. She's been gone a long time."

Damn, he was smarter than I thought under all that dumb.

"And that's the only reason you aren't splattered all over the wall, because she once thought of you as a friend." I hit the button for the first level and the doors slid shut. He knew who I was but no one would believe him. Again, a calculated risk.

Tank was a gossip, always telling stories. More than once, he claimed to have seen a UFO that turned out to be a plane landing at JFK.

The elevator ticked upward and I adjusted my coat over my dress. The doors slid open and I stepped out, starting across the open floor of the upper bar.

"Well, I'm not all that surprised Tank blew his load so fucking fast." Gabe laughed as I walked by him and his arm snaked out around my waist, brushing against my guns. I spun with his pull, and slammed my elbow into his nose. The crunch of cartilage was immediate and he hollered, let me go, and grabbed for his nose.

"You weren't invited to touch me, little shit. I suggest you think about that the next time you try to grab a woman without being asked." I turned on my heel and walked away. I still had work to do tonight, much as I wanted to continue to pound my brother into the ground.

"You bitch!" Johnny boy's slurred words were more than enough of a warning.

The elevator dinged and Tank stepped out. Shit, what did he want?

I did not want to kill them all, but at the same time, the urge to wipe the floor with them was strong.

That would be a big-ass mess to clean up and hard to keep quiet that I was back in town.

Johnny grabbed my shoulders from behind, tugging me to his chest. I swung my head back, and caught him on the bridge of his nose. He let me go and I swung a leg out, driving the heel of my boot into his belly and sending him across several tables, people, and a variety of drinks. The spell drinks fell, and three exploded, sending people screaming every which way.

Tank hurried to my side and motioned for me to move. "Outside, quick, I've got more to say to you."

He didn't touch me, which told me he remembered the rules I had. Smart man. I let him walk beside me, curious as to just what was going on.

Gabe and his buddies didn't get up from where I'd laid them out. My brothers and their friends weren't all that brave. They only took on people they thought they could hurt easily. People they thought they would have no problem controlling. In other words, they didn't like strong women.

Tank walked with me down the street two blocks before he spoke.

"That really you, Phoenix?"

I gave him a sharp nod. "I'd rather no one knew I was back in town yet."

"Well, shit, you could have just told me it was you!"

I turned to him. "If you'd been the one to do the job in Wyoming, you wouldn't be alive right now."

He blinked his tiny eyes at me. "Who'd they whack?"

I debated lying to him, debated if it mattered. Tank was . . . in his own way, dependable. "My son. He was ten."

"Fuck me sideways. Tried to get you and got the boy instead?"

I didn't correct him. Enough that he knew why I was here. "You going after the guy who did the brakes, going after Stephen?"

"To start. Unless you know why the job was called in, whose name is at the top of the sheet?" I glanced at him when we got to a corner, the lights red for crossing. This time of night, the human traffic was slower, more drunken, but otherwise oblivious to the world and to Tank and me standing on the corner talking about a hit job.

He shook his head and looked me right in the eye. "Your father keeps tabs on Mr. Mancini and what he does better than we do ourselves."

I nodded. "That's my next stop if Stephen doesn't know anything."

He frowned. "Why are you telling me all this?"

I laughed at him as I hailed a cab. "Who is going to believe you, Tank the gossip boy, that I showed back up? Anyone? How many sightings has my father gotten over the years about me?"

His tiny eyes blinked rapidly. "Lots, from all over the city here."

"And how many panned out?" I opened the cab door.

"None."

"Exactly. He won't have to know I was here. I'm not looking to reconcile."

Tank grunted. "Gabe didn't even recognize you."

I slid into the cab. "If I hear that he suddenly thinks of me, Tank, I'll know who to thank for it. If Stephen is warned, I'll know who to thank for it. You don't want my gratitude."

He shut the door for me and gave me a mock salute. "You would have made a wicked-ass wife for Mancini's boy Bruce. You should have taken him up on his offer."

Another burst of laughter slid out of me. "I'd have killed him in his sleep and fed him to the dogs, then blamed it on his girlfriend he was fucking on the side."

Tank didn't laugh. He knew as well as anyone those words were no joke.

CHAPTER THIRTEEN

Avalanche was indeed an upscale bar, one that had music pounding out of it so loud, the neighboring shop windows rattled and thumped in time with the bass.

Stephen Demetris, Tank's protégé, was not only easy to find, but his friends at the door pointed him out to me.

"That big bastard in the corner there, surrounded by his guys."

He was young, maybe in his mid-twenties at best. Obviously he worked out, by the way his high-end suit fit, and he'd not been drinking all night if the way his eyes scanned the room was any indication. His hair was buzzed short, so I was guessing brown, and I couldn't see his eye color. The details always mattered; you never knew when you might need them.

It was his size, though, that made me stare. He was the same height as the Santa that had loitered outside the Christmas party. He turned to the side, took a step, and his body swayed the same way even, as though he still held the Santa's sack on his back.

As a ghoster, he could have slipped in and out without

being caught. Ghosters were able to bend light around them, creating the illusion they were just gone. Shadows and light were their tools. It made sense to me now that he had been there that night. Ghosters were one of the hardest abnormals to find.

But not tonight.

My heart rate slipped up a notch. A real fight, then, if his ability to stay sober when his friends were plying him with drinks was any indication. He was keeping his head on straight in case of business. Smart. Which meant this was going to be interesting if what I saw in his body position was correct. He had his back to the wall, watching everyone who came through the door, and I was no exception. I paused, twisting my body as I undid the straps of the coat. The thick leather strap belt around my waist and the short dress peeked out.

I wasn't the most beautiful woman in the room, but I knew how to use what I had to my advantage. And the short skirt, tall boots and leather straps accentuated what I had. A body made to be stared at and hair to be grabbed in the throes of passion.

I took long strides across the room, going straight up to him without any hesitation because there would be no subtlety here. If I were too cautious, he'd be gone before I could get near him.

I slid my hand around his upper thigh to the inside of his leg and then cupped his package.

"I hear you like a good time. Tank sent me over as a thank you." I purred the words into his ear, made myself bite the lobe and tug him from the bar. His friends hooted and hollered and Stephen let me lead him away, his eyes already fogged with lust.

Disappointment whispered through me. Perhaps he wasn't the fight I'd hoped for. He might not be drunk, but he wasn't any smarter than Tank as he followed me into one of the private back rooms.

As soon as the door was shut, he pushed me against the wall and kissed me hard. I let him get into it before I put my hands on his chest and put some space between us. His mouth tasted like rum and coke.

He stared down at me. "I don't know you, do I?"

I looked up at him from under my eyelashes. "Oh, we know each other, intimately, you might say."

He frowned a little. "We do?"

"We had a close call in Jackson Hole when you were there on business." I had my hand in the right pocket of my trench. I flipped open the box and slid one of the darts out, feeling the edge of it. Truth serum.

He tipped his head to the side and I slammed the dart into his neck.

His hand slapped at the dart, his eyes went to me and he slowly slid to his knees. "What?"

I didn't waste time. While he moaned on the floor, I slid the thick strapped belt off my waist, and separated the strands of the leather. I flipped him over, tied his hands behind his back and then tied that to his feet.

I dragged him to the door and propped him on his knees, with his back against the faux wood. I lowered myself in front of him with my knees together. He slowly came around, and by the time he did, I had two of my knives out of their sheaths on my upper thighs.

I tapped the edge of one to the side of his head. "Jackson Hole. You were there, you tampered with some brakes, shot out a few tires. Pretended to be Santa to get close to your mark. Who was the mark?" I knew the answer to the question, but this was the way to get him spilling his secrets and making sure I was getting truth.

He groaned and shook his head. "What the hell are you talking about, you crazy bitch?"

"Stephen, Stephen, can I call you Steve?" I leaned in and laid the flat of my knife to the soft skin at the top of his cheek, pressing the razor edge into his lower eyelid and the point into the corner of his eye. The truth serum needed a little more time, but I wanted my answers now.

At least tied up, he couldn't ghost away from me.

"I suggest you don't so much as squeeze out a silent fart, Steve. In fact, I suggest you don't speak unless I give you the okay. One twitch, and you could lose an eye. Terrible thing, losing an eye. Can you imagine being a ghoster that is blind in one eye? Would you lose business? I'm thinking so."

His breathing slowed as he stared up at me. I smiled back. "These are the questions you're going to answer, slowly, one at a time. Who was the mark in Jackson?"

His mouth barely moved as he spoke, his eyes finally showing me the truth serum was kicking in as they dilated.

"Justin Stark."

"Why?"

He shifted as if he were going to shake his head, and I tssked at him. "No moving."

"Don't know," Stephen whispered. "Just a job."

Just a job.

"Who called it in?"

"Don't know, it came through the usual means."

"Which is?"

"Email. On my phone."

"You still got the email on your phone?"

His throat bobbed. "Yes."

I smiled. "That's very good news for you."

I pulled a pair of latex gloves from a pocket, then reached to his side, and checked his pockets until I found the right one with his phone. I slid my finger over it. "Code?"

"776521," he whispered.

With one eye on him, I put the numbers into the phone and pulled up the email.

I scanned the page.

RE: Wyoming Business Visit

JUSTIN STARK IS your contact there. Please be advised that his friend Noah Lancaster will not be in town until later that week. Do not forget to contact Mr. Lancaster as well. We will be disappointed if both men do not understand the depth of our concern for the current business situation.

HERRINGTON GROUP

"WHO IS THE HERRINGTON GROUP?"

"They . . . work for Mancini. They are a contractor." His words were soft, slurring.

I pressed the tip of the blade into the corner of his eye until a prick of blood welled up. He whimpered, and there was a sudden tang of urine in the air. I raised an eyebrow. "Already?"

A tear slid down his face, over the edge of the blade.

I let out a sigh, but didn't ease back on the knife tip. "A little boy died that night in Wyoming. You killed a child. The mother has hired me to find out who did it."

He closed his eyes. "Didn't know."

I didn't doubt that. "But you still pulled the trigger, didn't you? You put the holes in the lines and you were one of the shooters. Who set the death myst magic on the truck?"

"Peters. He's dead. Died last week."

I frowned. "The other shooter died last week? How?"

"Gunshot. Long distance hit."

If I could have frowned harder I would have. Someone else had killed Peters.

I changed directions. "You knew Stark had a family?"

There was a long pause before he answered. "Yes."

"Didn't you take that into account when you set up the hit?"

I knew the answer to this. Of course, Stephen had considered that Justin had a family. The reality was, it didn't matter to him as long as his mark was dead and he got a paycheck for it. Collateral damage was a hard truth in this world, and a large part of why I'd left it.

I shifted my weight and removed the knife from his face. He let out an audible sigh. Before he could so much as squeak out a word, I grabbed the last strip of my leather belts and a wad of cloth, shoved the cloth inside his mouth and wrapped the leather around his face. He bucked and fought.

"No use now. You see, I can't have you going back to your boss and telling him the questions I asked, can I? That would ruin the surprises I have planned." I patted his cheek as I pulled Dinah from the now-uncovered holster in my lower back. She gave a shimmy in my hands.

"Oh, he's handsome. You sure you want to shoot him?" she asked.

I stood, checked the chamber, and flicked off the safety. From my outer thigh at the top of my boot, I took the silencer and attached it to the tip of Dinah's muzzle.

"I hate this," she muttered, her words muting as I twisted the silencer on.

Stephen whimpered and shook his head, tears leaking from his eyes. He tried to drag himself away from me. I grabbed him by the foot and pulled him to the center of the room. I leaned down and put my mouth to his ear.

"You killed my son. You killed him knowing he was in the truck and you are going to get a far cleaner death than you deserve only because you weren't the one who called it in. This is the price you pay for being here, for being a killer."

I had learned from Mary-Ellen. No giving them a chance.

I leaned away, put the gun to his temple, and pulled the trigger. The reverberation of the shot up my arm created a rush of adrenaline.

His body jumped and spasmed as the nerve endings fired one last time. I took the silencer off, wiped the tip of it on his coat, and then put it back in its pocket. I put Dinah back into her holster as she sighed with what could only be described as pleasure.

Blood pooled around Stephen's head as I leaned down and went through his pockets. I took his phone again and popped out the SIM card and dropped the phone onto his chest. He had no other information on him, no cards, some cash, a silver chromed lighter, and that was it. I took the cash. Not because I needed it, but it would allow whoever investigated to think this was a simple robbery gone wrong. Or at the very least, it would give them pause.

I stood and stepped over his body, careful not to step in the blood as I peeled the gloves off and tucked them back into my coat pocket.

From there, I wrapped myself in my trench coat and slipped out the door. I paused, thinking about the club, and the people in it. A lot of Mancini's crew, men and abnormals who'd killed and hurt so many families, who thought nothing of violence and the ripple effect it caused.

I shook my head against the altruistic thought. I was not here to make things right for anyone but Bear. That didn't mean I couldn't do a little extra damage, though. Mancini was somehow involved in this, of that much I was sure. At the very least it would piss him off, and that made me smile.

I stepped back into the room with Stephen's cooling body, and the blood pooling around him. Putting my back to the door, I bent once more to Stephen and took the lighter from his pocket. I flicked it open, and set it against the line of blood on the floor closest to me. The flames licked up immediately, red, blue and green as they spread across the room, the ghoster's blood setting the room on fire in rapid time.

I tucked the lighter into my pocket and stepped out of the room and shut the door tight. I leaned against it for a moment, taking stock of where I was in the building.

To the left would take me through the front of the club with all those bodies and eyes watching. Stephen's friends would recognize me, of that I had no doubt. I turned to the right and made my way deeper into the back of the club. There was the sound of laughter from many of the closed doors, and even the grunt of bodies fucking hard if the sounds were any indication.

A low voice barked at me. "Hey, you aren't supposed to be back here."

I didn't turn around, just kept walking as if I'd heard nothing.

"Get back to the front of the club, bitch!" A hand dropped onto my shoulder and I spun, driving the heel of my hand into his solar plexus, stopping him in his tracks. He gaped at me like a fish on the line, his mouth flapping open and shut as he struggled to breathe.

The silence was broken by the sudden scream of fire alarms bursting around us along with the spray of water from the sprinkler system. Water would not help cool the magically induced flames.

I turned from the would-be bouncer as he fought for air, and jogged down the hall. At the next intersection, the exit sign was clearly marked above a broad steel door. Behind me, the clatter of people climbed over the sound of the alarms, as those gambling and fucking scrambled to get out of the now-burning building. I smiled to myself as I hit the bar of the emergency exit door and let myself out into the alley behind the club. Straightening my coat, I settled into a ground-eating stride, not quite a run, as I headed for an open street where I could get a cab.

Sirens erupted in the distance and I didn't change my pace. The worst thing besides being seen at the scene of a crime was to be seen *fleeing* the scene of a crime. Something all those Mancini men from the back rooms would be doing, whether they realized it or not.

Four blocks over, I hailed a cab and had him take me to a diner that was a ten-minute walk from the motel room I'd rented.

More than that, though, was the mobile store next to the diner. I went in, bought a cheap phone that had been unlocked and slipped the SIM card into it, using Steven's cash to pay for it. I didn't turn the phone on, just slipped it into my pocket, then headed into the diner.

I ordered two large steak and eggs, french fries and a double slice of apple pie with the last of his money which made me smile. The cashier taking my order looked me over. "Wish I could get away eating like that and looking like you."

I smiled. "This is for my man, Abe. He's a big boy and can pack away all of this and then some."

She laughed and gave me an exaggerated wink. "Is he any fun in the bedroom? That's the most important part."

"He's got a toe fetish." I smiled again and she looked away, flushing all the way to the roots of her hair. So much for making friends. Anyway, it was true. Abe had a thing for licking toes, which was why I always kept my socks on.

I took my order and walked back to the motel. I paused

outside, checking the tells I'd set in place. A few trip wires, a small amount of sand set on the door step that was still smooth. No one had followed me home, and no one had touched the back door that led up the stairs to the room. I let myself in, and headed up the stairs, two at a time. I paused again at my door listening.

"Abe?" I whispered his name and he was at the door, digging to get out. I opened the door and he shoved his nose against the plastic bags holding all the food.

We ate, and I changed out of my club clothes so I could take him for a walk out back to do his business.

Once more inside, I lay on the bed and looked at the only pictures I had left of Bear. Of him and Justin in the newspaper clipping that talked about their deaths and the accident. My name was mentioned, but otherwise there was no picture of me. No pictures of Bear and me together.

I flipped open the shitty little mobile phone and turned it on. I went straight to the contacts that were mine to exploit. Number and names of a bunch of Mancini men, their thugs and . . . an old friend of mine.

"Seriously, Barron?" I stared at the name and shook my head. "I didn't think you'd have the balls to still dabble with Mancini."

He'd been a guy I'd slept with a few times out on the West Coast. A thief and procurer of stolen and hard-to-find goods. Good at what he did, but he was a bit of a coward.

After scribbling down all the names and numbers, all the information I could, I snapped the SIM card in half and tossed it out the window. Two of the names on my scribbled list had been tagged with Harrington. That was the group Stephen said contracted him out for Mancini. The question was why? Always before, Mancini had contracted things himself. I shook my head. Not my problem.

The newspaper clipping stared up at me from the bed. I

folded the picture and put it on the side table. I was not able to see Bear's smiling face without tears prickling at the backs of my exhausted eyes. Fatigue rolled over me and I finally let myself fall into a deep sleep. I was going to need the rest.

Tomorrow was going to be a busy day.

CHAPTER FOURTEEN

Abe woke me the next morning, not whining to go relieve himself, but with a low, rumbling, growl. I rolled off the bed and grabbed Eleanor from the nightstand in the same movement. A soft knock on the door.

"Who is it?"

"Mrs. Chang. I have letter for you."

The owner of the motel had a letter for me . . . not even Zee knew where I was. Trepidation tripped down my spine as I moved to the door and pressed myself to the side. I held Eleanor ready and opened the door just a crack. Mrs. Chang stood there in her bright blue pants and even brighter yellow top. She smiled and held out a letter. I took it through the crack.

"Thanks."

"Oh, good, good. Have good day!" She waved over her head as she walked away.

I closed the door and looked at the envelope. No writing on it. I held it up to the light, doing what I could to see into it without opening it.

The dark lines of words on another piece of paper were all I saw.

I tucked Eleanor into the back of my jeans and took a knife from my stash to open the letter. I spilled the contents onto the night stand. Still using the knife, I flipped the letter open.

I know who you are.

THAT WAS IT, five little words, and yet they said a whole fucking lot. A sharp snap of irritation cut through me. Who knew who I truly was? And more important than that, how did they know where to find me?

I was sure I'd been covering my tracks.

I sat on the edge of my bed. Who had I spoken to? I went through the list. Zee, even if he knew where I was exactly, would never turn me in. Tank wasn't bright enough to find me even if I gave him directions. Then there was Bradley. He'd been looking for me, and he'd warned me there was someone else looking for me, too. Someone who'd found me and wouldn't be as nice as Bradley was.

Someone named Simon, if he could be believed.

Was it the man who'd set the fire on the ranch house? No, I was almost certain that had been Noah. And Noah, while a liar and possibly even FBI, was not the kind to leave notes.

I glanced at Abe. He needed a walk, and apparently, I needed to figure out just who this was. This was a complication I did not need to deal with.

Whoever was following me was trying to spook me, that much was clear.

"Not going to work, asshole," I muttered. I slipped on my

holster and put both Dinah and Eleanor into their spots. I'd mixed them up once and they'd both made sure I missed my marks for days after that.

I didn't mix them up anymore.

I added knives into the tops of both boots and additional ammo into the straps of the holster for the guns that weren't like Eleanor and Dinah.

"What's happening?" Eleanor asked.

"Someone has found me. I have to decide what I'm going to do about it."

"Shoot the fucker," Dinah said. "That always works well."

"Yes, well, I would, but he just left a note." Or a her. It could be a her.

I checked that my stash under the floor board of the cupboard was covered with a decoy—a garbage bag of clothes with two Berettas I used for backup on top, and a small wad of cash peeking out the edge. An easy grab for anyone looking.

I slid on a zip-up sweater with a hoodie, then snapped the long leather leash to Abe's collar.

We headed down the back stairs in a matter of minutes. I didn't go out the back door, but headed through the common area where Mrs. Chang's apartment door was. I knocked, and a moment later, she opened the door. Seeing me, she gave a broad smile.

"Yes?"

"The man who gave you the letter, what did he look like?"

"Oh, not a man. Little girl. Tiny girl. Big pink hair, spiked collar." She touched her neck and wrinkled her nose. "Not a nice girl like you." She smiled again.

"How long?"

"Maybe ten minutes?" She spread her hands wide and pursed her lips. Good enough for me.

I hurried Abe out the back door, took the letter from my

pocket and pressed it to his nose. "*Such*." The German word for *seek* came out with a *z* at the front of it, so it sounded like *zukh*.

He pulled hard on the leash and I let him go to the end of it, running to keep up with him. We raced out around the side of the building and down the extra-wide sidewalk. I swept the area, doing all I could to see pink hair in the crowd. But it was Abe I was depending on to help me find what I thought would be a messenger girl.

He kept his nose to the ground, following the smell only he could pick up. The leash was taut in my hands, even though I ran flat out. He pulled me along, weaving between bodies. He took a sudden right turn down an alley and there she was, right in front of us.

Pink hair, spiked collar and black grunge clothes topped with half-laced army boots. A weird mix of punk and goth.

I dropped Abe's leash. "*Fuss*." Heel.

He dropped back to my side and I pulled Dinah from my lower back, holding her steady with both hands. "Freeze. Police!"

The girl in front of me stuttered to a stop and raised her hands over her head. Her back was still to us. "I didn't steal nothing! I haven't done anything wrong!"

"You delivered a letter."

"I got paid to do it! I didn't hurt no one," she cried out.

"On your knees!" I closed the distance between us, and booted her in the back of the knees, forcing her down to the rough pavement. I shoved her hands to the top of her head and when she tried to look around at me, I pressed the gun to the side of her face.

"Eyes closed."

She cried softly and closed her eyes tightly. "He paid me good. I swear I didn't steal nothing."

"When did you take the letter from him?"

"This morning, early. He gave me the address on a slip of paper and the letter. He, he gave me a hundred dollars to do it."

I kept the gun on her and quickly frisked her top half. In her left pocket, I found the slip of paper with my address on it. Precise handwriting, all in capital letters. Just like the letter in the motel room.

"Did he have a name?"

"No." Her head was bowed and her chest heaved between sobs.

"What did he look like?"

"I'd just woken up. I don't remember."

I glanced over my shoulder to the open street. No one had noticed us yet. I grabbed her by the back of her jacket and hauled her to her feet. "Get walking."

She stumbled and I kept at her until we were far enough into the alley that I was satisfied. I moved her so we stood between two large dumpsters.

"You aren't a cop." She tried again to look over her shoulder. I smacked her face with the back of my hand.

"Eyes forward. And no, I'm not a cop. Which means you are in far more trouble than you realize."

Another whimper.

"Tell me everything you remember." I kept one hand on her shoulder, and the other kept the gun laid against her cheek so she could see the tip of the muzzle.

Abe sat beside me, content to wait now.

"He was well dressed. I think the suit was Gucci, and . . . he had brown eyes."

That didn't eliminate many people. "Anything stand out about him?"

"He had a lisp," she said.

"Age?"

"Maybe thirty?"

A lisp was something I could work with. I needed to get into my father's database to find out just who he'd set on me, and to see if there was anything on Mancini's hits.

So much for keeping things simple.

I pulled two hundred-dollar bills out of my pocket. I shoved them into her coat. "If he comes to you again, take the job. See if you can get his name."

I let her turn around, let her see me. "He's a very bad man. He helped to kill my son." A lie, but close enough to the truth that she believed it.

"You thought . . . I was working with him?"

I took a step back. "You know where I am if he comes to you again."

"Will he try to kill me?"

I shrugged. "I don't know."

I left her in the alley, shaking from the top of her pink hair down to her army-boot-covered feet.

He'd been kind to her and I'd been a bitch, yet I knew she would help me over him. Gut instinct and all that. Reading people was important in this business. It was why I'd trusted Tank as far as I had while most people wouldn't have.

My plans for the day shifted. As Zee said right at the beginning, Mancini could wait, he would always be there, and while I hadn't found exactly the person who'd called in the hit on Justin, it would come.

I needed to eliminate Mr. Lisp first, or I was going to get caught somewhere with my pants down in the middle of a situation where I needed them on.

Once more at the apartment, I went through my clothes, picking out suitable business attire. Black pencil skirt, a demure white top, low heels. I laid them out. They would do for getting into Blink Management. Blink—as my father had always called it—was the central hub of his business. All branches of his empire stretched out from there, and it was the place where his databases on Mancini and all his contractors could be found.

Mr. Lisp didn't know me all that well if he thought I would be overly bothered by him knowing where I was. To be fair, that knowledge worked in my favor because it meant at some point he would come for me here, thinking I was asleep, or letting my guard down. I'd be waiting for him.

From my closet, I pulled out a light brown wig with long curls. That would be best. Not my natural black hair and not the blonde locks I currently sported.

I styled the wig, twisting it into a soft bun that would sit at the nape of my neck, a few strands escaping the edges. A pair of black-rimmed glasses set with plain glass, and that would do the trick.

I shook my head. "Abe, it's time to cut my hair."

He didn't even lift his head from his paws as I took one of my smaller knives and headed to the bathroom. This was not the first time I'd done my own hack job of my hair. When I was twelve, I'd done a similar thing.

Harder to be grabbed by a ponytail that no longer existed.

I worked on the cut for half an hour, angling it so there was a longer swath at the front and the back was super short. I brushed a hand through the poorly done pixie cut. Good enough for me and even better for dealing with wigs.

I spent the rest of the day getting my ID ready, printing a picture of myself and my new name "Beth Andrew" with a small, portable printer, and set the picture and information onto an ID card. The mocked-up barcode wouldn't work, but that was often the case when my father's employees turned over as fast as his did.

When you were an asshole, people didn't stick around long to see if your shit was going to stick to them. When you were an asshole with freaky fucking demon guards, the turnover was astronomical.

Preparations took me into the afternoon and then into the evening. Darkness clothed the city and the moon rose high above the tall buildings, giving a sliver of light through my one window.

Time to walk back into the place I'd run from, the place I'd sworn I would never return to.

But I had no real choice. I had to deal with the man gunning for me, Mr. Lisp, if I was going to revenge my boys. The last thing I needed was whoever was hunting me to show up when I was otherwise occupied killing my boy's killers.

Distractions in the middle of a fight did not tend to go well.

Now it was just a matter of waiting.

The next day couldn't come soon enough.

CHAPTER FIFTEEN

Blink Management LTD was situated in the Financial District not far from Wall Street, which meant a long commute from the Garment District if I wanted to make it there early enough to put my plan into place. I took the subway and was inside the glittering glass building by 7:30 a.m. Long before most employees had shown up for work. Even so, there were still a few go-getters that were hurrying through the main doors and toward the elevators.

Wearing my wig, glasses, pencil skirt and white top, I walked through the sliding doors and right up to the check-in desk and the sleepy guard there. He was from the night shift, still waiting for his replacement at eight.

I slid my homemade card through the scanner, it beeped red. The guard looked up and I shrugged. "It's new. Today's my first day."

I scanned it again. Red. I bit my lower lip and sucked in a sharp breath. "I can't be late. I'm temping for Mr. Romano. Can you help me, please?" I pushed my glasses up with one hand and offered him my card with a fake shaking hand. The guard shook his head and waved me through.

"Probably will work by lunch. Go on up and keep your head down."

"Thank you, and for the advice, too." I gave him a smile, tried to keep it demure. My father's security had fallen since I'd left. I would never have let anyone through without at least taking their name, or putting them down on a list to be checked at some point. The guard wasn't even trying.

His sloppiness worked in my favor.

I hurried to the elevators and stepped on with several other employees.

I hit the button for the twenty-fifth floor and waited quietly in the corner, listening to the chatter.

"Did you hear that the Japanese merger is going through? Apparently, it's being headed up by Gabriel."

"Yeah, but who is he going to pick to oversee it?"

"Does it matter?"

"Kind of, yeah. The pay raise should be substantial. And they'll be spending a good deal of time in Tokyo. It would be nice to see Gabe there."

In other words, it would be nice for Gabe to be as far away as possible.

That was interesting. The only business my father had in Tokyo in the past had been to try and woo the Yakuza to work with him. They had the money, power, and no small amount of magic, and he wanted in on it. He was the smartest fool I'd ever met.

The talk went like that back and forth between the employees, ebbing and flowing as they got off on their various levels and new people came on. The ride up took a long time because of all the stops.

Finally, the doors binged open on the top level. Nothing in the layout had changed. My father's office was the entire side of this floor with his top executives in their own offices around him, and the secretaries that looked after them scattered in front of the various doors.

There was a secretary bent over the desk in front of my father's glass office. He wasn't there yet. I'd be surprised if he showed up before ten, which gave me a couple of hours to work. Not that I should need that much time.

I went straight to his secretary.

"Excuse me, but I've been sent in to replace you." I put my one hand on the edge of the desk. The woman—she looked to be in her forties—snapped her head up.

"What did you say?"

I smiled at her. "The temp agency got a call this morning." I pulled a sheet of paper out with my father's letterhead on it, briefly terminating her job with a simple 'to whom it may concern' at the top. Although it might seem strange in another business, my father liked to have the person coming into a position fire the one going out.

Her face blanched. "He said I was doing a good job just yesterday."

I frowned. "I'm sorry, I was sent in with the letter and told to be here before eight. You have all the information I need to get started?"

She was shaking and started to cry as she wrote down the passwords for getting into the system. Truly, this was far too easy, and I almost felt bad for her.

"He's a right bastard," she bit the words out as she gathered her stuff. "A right damn bastard to work for, and now to fire me like this after so many years?"

Shit, maybe things had changed around here if he'd kept her on that long. I shrugged again. "I probably won't be here long either then."

She looked me over and a glare settled on her face.

"You're pretty enough, he'll keep you around until you say no."

Didn't I know the truth of those words.

With that, she stomped off, and I settled into her chair. I wasted no time in pulling open the most recent files she had on the desktop. Business, business, that wasn't what I was looking for. My father had always kept his shadier side of things under a hidden file. Again, one that I suggested he change regularly. But again, he refused. And now I was banking on his stubbornness to help me.

Bullet Point is what he called the file, thinking he was being so smart with the double entendre. I'd told him repeatedly that criminals were not as dumb as he thought. The problem was he had so much faith in his deal with the devil, he believed he was untouchable. Maybe he was, what did I know?

I did a search for the file, and there it was.

I glanced up as the elevator opened and several people came in, my brother Gabe amongst them. Damn it, what was he doing in so early? Something must have gone very wrong to get him here before ten.

I locked my eyes on the computer screen and began to scan through the file as fast as I could. I needed to find the sub-list of contractors and jobs they were put out on. That should give me both the guy with the lisp looking for me, and the person who called in the hit on Justin.

Looking over the top of the computer, I kept half my attention on Gabe. He had two black eyes he'd tried to cover with a shitty makeup job, and his nose still looked more than a little swollen. I had to bite the inside of my mouth to keep from smiling.

"When my father gets here, tell him I'm in his office." He barked the words with barely a glance in my direction.

It took all I had not to point out that the entire front of

his father's office was glass, and unless he planned on hiding behind the desk, his father would see him clearly the moment he walked off the elevator.

"Of course, sir" is what I managed to answer with.

Gabe paused at the edge of my desk. "Your voice is very familiar. Have we met?"

Shit, fuck, damn.

I shook my head and made sure to keep my eyes lowered. I made sure my tones were crisp and clipped, as different from the Southern charm I'd affected the other night as possible.

"I've worked in other parts of the building, sir. Perhaps you heard me speaking then?"

He didn't answer, just started once more for our father's office, dismissing me without another thought. Or so I thought.

"I changed my mind. We'll need you to take notes, so you should come with me." Gabe snapped his fingers at me. Snapped his fucking fingers like I was a dog that needed to heel to his side.

I swallowed the anger that coated my mouth, and made myself open the desk drawer. I found a folder with some blank sheets in it, a pen, and followed him into the glass office.

"Something very familiar about you," Gabe said again. "I'll figure it out soon enough."

"I think I'd remember a man like you, if we'd met before." I was careful with my wording. The last thing I wanted was for him to try and kiss me, or worse.

He picked up a small remote from the desk and hit a button. The glass walls darkened until . . . shit, two-way glass. My heart rate jacked up more than a few notches.

"I can wait outside until your father—"

"No, I think you can wait here with me. If you like your job, that is." His tone implied more than waiting.

I didn't have a choice. I lifted my eyes to his and glared. "I am not that kind of woman, *sir*. And if you think I won't report you, you will be sorely mistaken."

"You'll lose your job." He smiled as he closed the distance between us.

Shit.

"There are other jobs." I backed away from him around the big desk. I knew that even if the glass was visible so other people could see what was happening, they wouldn't believe it. The Romano family was far too well connected for anyone to believe ill of them. Even when it was right in front of their faces. Or maybe they also knew that their jobs were on the line. People tended to let things slide.

"Mr. Romano, I suggest you back the fuck off." I snapped the words, hoping to get through to him.

"Oh, there's a spit-fire in there. I like it." He took a few quick steps, his hands outstretched and—

The door opened and our father stepped through. "Gabe, stop bothering her." My father, Luca Romano, glanced over me. "Who is she, your new secretary?"

My father hadn't aged a day since I'd left. Jet-black hair and matching eyes, skin that looked perpetually tanned and a mouth that was often drawn in a hard frown just like now. The flicker of an aura around him made me suck a sharp breath. The ruby ring on his middle finger drew my eyes. Which one of the guardians would he call if he knew it was me here, standing in front of him?

"No, she's yours." Gabe straightened his suit and gave me a wink that made me want to vomit.

I clutched the notepad to my chest as I fought the feeling of being a teenager again, of being the little girl who wanted her father to love her the best. To be the golden child for a little while. Of course, I knew now it would never happen. Not only was I born from the second wife, I was a girl. Two strikes, and I was out of the running for the golden child.

"The temp agency sent me in. They said your secretary quit." I kept the words low.

He grunted, and his eyes flicked over me. "Too bad, she was good and just ugly enough to keep me from being interested. You're going to be a problem for me."

He had no idea just how true that statement was going to be. Just not the way he thought.

Gabe laughed and I said nothing.

"Gabe, I assume you have a strong reason for being here this early in the morning." Luca glanced over at him as he took the remote away and hit the button that cleared the glass once more. I was thinking the same thing about them both. My father looked like he had not gone to bed the night before, so something was up.

No one on the outside of the office even looked up as the glass cleared.

"Fannin is causing problems again out in LA. And the merger with the Yaku—Japanese and Mancini has a hitch," Gabe said. "Killian Fannin is trying to cut into our profits by undercutting us on the . . . products. I don't know where he's getting his base ingredients, but they are higher quality than ours at half the cost."

"And distribution?" Luca looked straight at Gabe, ignoring me. "Who are they using?"

"Bellamy."

"Fuck."

Ingredients, distribution, and Bellamy, a known abnormal who also happened to run a trucking company . . . I had a feeling they weren't talking about a new food product. The longer I was in the room with them, the better chance my cover would be blown, but also the better chance I could learn something useful. My father, though stupid in some ways, was dangerously smart in others. He'd paid for all my training, brought in Zee, had even overseen some of my disguises. I needed to get out of here now and back to the desk and the file I'd come for. I opened my mouth to speak but my father beat me to it.

"Mancini believes he's running the show, correct?" My father stared hard at Gabe, and tapped that ruby ring of his which made sweat bead up all the way down my spine.

Gabe nodded. "Of course. I made sure of it. He won't see the blindside coming."

I cleared my throat. "Should I be taking notes?"

My father glanced at me, then at Gabe. "No, go back to your desk. Clear my schedule for the morning."

I bobbed my head and did a half-curtsy, then hurried out of the office.

"She's cute, and she's got a mouth on her," Gabe said as I shut the door.

"She's my secretary. You don't get first dibs, I do," my father said.

I leaned against the door breathing hard; not from fear, but revulsion as I fought the urge to vomit where I stood.

Back at my desk once more, I opened the Bullet Point file and continued to skim through it. Nowhere could I find the list of contacts and their current jobs.

My cursor froze over a name I knew all too well.

Justin Stark. Jackson Hole, Wyoming.

What . . . was Justin doing in my father's files? This wasn't just a job on Justin, but a whole file. Had he found me after all? I opened the file and hit print as I began to read. Beside me the printer started spitting out papers.

Working for the mob.

Double crossing.

Informant.

Working with the FBI.

The words began to blur.

I let my mind go back to what Gabe and my father had been talking about. The merger would bring Mancini, the Yakuza, and the Romano families together, but then Mancini was being blindsided, but how? Damn . . . that was some powerful shit.

The door to the office opened. I heard it but couldn't respond fast enough. "What are you doing?" Gabe growled, the sound of papers being crinkled up in his hands.

I looked up. He was right at the printer and held all the papers I'd just printed out. I had no choice now, I had to run.

He tapped his ruby ring and it glittered to life.

Oh shit, this was going down faster than an avalanche.

My hand was still on the folder I'd taken into the office with me. I tightened my hold on it and bolted around the desk, kicking my heels off as I went. I ran past the elevator doors to the emergency exit that led into the stairwell.

"Stop her!"

There was a cracking noise like logs being shattered by a cold so deep it exploded the wood. That was the noise of the Stick Man coming to life.

Fear chased me, herding me more than anything else could have.

Gabe was behind me, his long legs eating up the distance between us, second after second. I hit the stairwell door hard, threw it open, and took the first step down the stairs.

I was grabbed from behind, just my one arm, and jerked to a sudden stop.

Gabe still had the papers in one hand. "Who the fuck are you?"

The Stick Man filled up the space behind him and all I could do was stare.

Arms, legs, and body made of thin, dark brown sticks,

right down to his grasping fingers, the Stick Man was one of the three guardians my father had been given. Bullets did not hurt the Stick Man.

Which was a raw deal for me.

I used the momentum of my body to twist around and slam my knee into Gabe's belly. A whoosh of air flew out of him and I grabbed at the papers in his hands, yanking them away before I bolted once more, this time down the stairs.

The Stick Man clattered after me, using the railing to pull himself along at top speed.

I didn't waste time on words, though a steady stream of profanities raced through my mind.

This scene was going to go badly, if I didn't make it to at least the second floor before Gabe called the front desk on me. I tried not to think about what would happen if the Stick Man caught me and hauled me back up to my father.

I raced down the stairwell, the claws of the Stick Man snatching at my wig.

I all but skidded onto the landing for the twentieth floor. I shoved my way out of the stairwell and threw the lock on it for what it was worth. Last time I was here there had been bathrooms close to the emergency exit and the stairwell and I was hoping that hadn't changed. Damn it, I should have checked the building layout again.

The Stick Man slammed into the door, rattling it. I had minutes, maybe less.

A few people stared at me. I smiled back.

"I wouldn't open that if I were you. Abnormal gone nuts." I huffed out the words.

The two women covered their mouths and the fat older man grunted at me.

"The women's toilets?" I tried to straighten my hair, feeling the wig coming loose.

One of the women pointed down the hall. "To the left, around the corner."

I nodded my thanks and hurried down to the bathroom. I let myself in, ran past the mirrors to the stall at the far end.

The Stick Man had no sense of smell, but he'd start checking rooms. If nothing else, he was thorough.

I put the folder and the papers I'd taken from Gabe on the back of the toilet, and pulled off the wig as soon as the door was shut. This was going to get dicey. I had a camisole under the demure white button-down shirt. I yanked the shirt off, and tied it around my waist. I was still barefoot, nothing I could do about that. I pulled one of my knives out and put a slit up either side of the skirt, and then took the blade to the hem. I cut the skirt so it almost skimmed the knife sheath on my thigh. I grabbed the stack of papers, stuffing them all into the folder.

That was going to have to be good enough. I left the wig behind the toilet and let myself out. I threw the glasses into the garbage and leaned into the mirror to pop the contacts out. I looked more like me, and that wasn't a good thing either, but the short blonde pixie cut was nothing like the big curly wig, and the dark eyes were the opposite of the green contacts.

A deep breath and I headed to the elevators once more. I walked on with a bunch of women just as the Stick Man burst out of the stairwell. They all screamed, and I added my voice to theirs as I hammered the close door button.

The Stick Man's head swept side to side. I wouldn't say he had eyes, but he was looking for me with whatever senses the guardian had. He let out a crackling growl and started toward the elevator.

The women screamed and shrank from him and I continued to hammer the button. "Come on, come on!"

The doors slid shut, slow as molasses in February, but they were closing.

Until the Stick Man got his fingers through. I grabbed my knife and swept it up, driving it into his hand. Sap oozed out and he let out a god-awful screech that made the hair on the back of my neck stand up. I tried to get my knife back for another blow but it stuck in a knot of wood. The claws raked at me, driving splinters into my skin, deep and with a violence that would make them hard—if not impossible—to get out. They moved under my skin like worms.

That could not be good.

The group of women behind me suddenly came to my defense, shocking me. Three of them ran to my sides and began beating on the Stick Man's hands with their purses and even a shoe, cracking the thin fingers until he was forced to let go and the doors shut. The elevator began to go downward once more.

I stared at my hands and the squirming slivers under my skin. "This cannot be good."

An older black woman with gray shot through her hair put a hand on my arm. "Honey, you come with me to my office. I've got tweezers for those."

At the fifteenth floor, she pulled me out with her, not allowing me any room for argument. Mostly because I could feel the magic weaving around me, forcing my feet forward, the smell that could mean only one thing.

This kindly, grandmotherly woman was an abnormal.

And she'd caught me.

CHAPTER SIXTEEN

"I don't think tweezers are going to get these out." I turned my arms outward so the woman at my side could see the wriggling slivers. I tried to do more than that, tried to get my feet to obey me while I did what I could to distract her from her hold on me.

"That won't work on me, Nix. I know you. I know who you are. Your Hider can't keep you safe from eyes that know here." Her dark brown eyes flicked over me in a way that felt like a dismissal. She ushered me into an office that was big enough for a single desk, two chairs, and a large filing cabinet. Her words were reminiscent of the note left in my dive of a rental room, but I doubted that she was the one who'd left it.

"Sit."

My legs bent without any instruction on my part. "What are you?"

"Abnormal," she said without looking back at me. Her hands were inside the cabinet and I could hear the clinking of glass on metal.

She lifted three vials with thick cork stoppers out, and a pair of shimmery silver tweezers.

"What you got, Rose?"

"Your *tweezers* speak?" I arched an eyebrow.

"You should be one to talk," the woman I assumed was Rose said.

She smiled kindly at me. "Your guns are a tool, and tools can be used for good, Nix." She tapped the desk and my arms shot forward, palms up and showing the squirming slivers. They were past the crook of my elbow now, headed for my shoulder.

"Shit." I whispered.

"Yes, that is quicker than I thought too. Linx, get to work." She held her hand out, palm up, and Linx flicked through the air, floating above my arms. The sharp points of the tweezers grew and lengthened until they were needle sharp, and one side had a slight curve to it.

My stomach rolled with what I knew was coming. "Do it."

I made myself watch as the tweezers shot down, not unlike Mary-Ellen's beak, and cut through the skin to the sliver that was furthest up my arm. Blood welled up around the tips, but Linx was sure in his dive and a squirming sliver came out in his grasp.

"Got it," he said like a kid with his mouth full of macaroni. He dropped the sliver into a tin bucket with a sharp ting of wood on metal. I looked to Rose.

"Convenient that you have all this here."

She gave me a wink. "For you, it surely is."

My mouth tightened. "Why are you helping me?"

"My calling is one of healing, and help," she said. "It's why I chose to work here. Your father is dabbling in things he shouldn't be and good people are put in his path every day. I'm doing what I can to stem the injuries from here."

Linx kept at my arms, moving from one to the other, depending on the slivers and how far up they were. I glanced down. One sliver was at the top of my shoulder and starting its way across my chest. The pain was sharp and piercing as the tweezers dove into my skin.

"They're going for my heart," I said softly.

Rose nodded and lifted both eyebrows. "That they are. Good way to finish you off and not even have to face you, don't you think?"

The squirming in my arms was gone with one last piercing from Linx. "That's it."

"Good job." She held out her hand and he floated down to her. She dipped him into the narrow bottle of bright purple solution.

"Not that I don't appreciate this, but again, why are you helping me? You know who I am, you know what I've done to your kind of people." I wanted to understand her motives, because they made no sense to me.

Rose sighed. "Nix, you were a child, a pawn of your father's. You may have killed many abnormals for him, and humans too for that matter, but I believe that wasn't you. It's not your heart to be a killer." Her eyes were soft and all I could think was how wrong she was. How very, very wrong.

"Thanks for your help." I slid off the chair and stood.

"The Stick Man, he's going to keep coming for you," she said.

"I know." I had my back to her, the file folder clutched in my arms. Once one of my father's guardians were set on a prey, there was no stopping them.

"You want to know how to kill him?" she asked, and I whipped around to stare at her.

"You know a way to kill the Stick Man?"

She grinned. "I do. But it's not easy, and it's not pretty."

"I don't do pretty or easy, so tell me." I heard the edge in my voice. Rose's eyes crinkled at the edges as she smiled.

"Blood fire."

I frowned at her. "What?"

A thump behind us stilled me. The scratch of branches across the door. Rose hissed and threw a vial of red fluid into the bucket with the still-dancing slivers, struck a match and dropped it in.

The flame that burst out of the tiny tin bucket reached the ceiling. Blood fire; that vial had been the blood of an abnormal, I could smell it. I glanced at Rose.

The door behind me shuddered and Rose gave me a nod. "I can hold him for maybe a few minutes. Is that enough time for you to get out?"

I frowned at her. I still didn't understand why she was helping me, but I nodded. "I'll take it. Thanks."

I positioned myself behind the door and waited for Rose to give me a nod. Her gray curls bobbed and I yanked the door open.

The Stick Man spilled through the door, filling up the space even though his limbs were scrawny.

He froze in mid-swipe toward Rose. She skirted around the edge of the desk, her eyes on him.

"Go, Nix. Go and find your boy."

I'd taken a few steps but I stopped where I was. "What?"

"Go, I can't hold him." The Stick Man roared and twisted out of her hold, driving its arms through her upper body and lifting her above her head before she could strike her lighter. She was dead; I knew it.

I turned to go as she dropped Linx. I grabbed the tweezers from the air and clutched them against the folder in my arms as I ran for the elevator.

I hit the button, frantic. The idea of more of those creepy-ass slivers sliding through my skin and working toward my heart was too much.

The elevator opened and I stepped in, grateful for the

crowd of women in it once more. "Are they evacuating?" one of them asked me, and I nodded. Unable for the first time in a long time to find the words I wanted.

It had been a long time since I'd seen an abnormal attack another abnormal, and even longer since I'd seen any of the guardians.

Pull your shit together, Phoenix, I thought.

I ran a hand through my hair, knowing it would stand up more. But that was the goal. I would stand out as I left. And would have to hope it would be enough to keep the guards on the main floor from stopping me.

"Forgot your shoes?" one of the women asked with her eyebrows raised.

I managed a forced laugh. "Something like that."

Miraculously, she handed me a pair of flats she had folded up in her purse. "These have saved me more than once. I suggest you get yourself a pair."

"You are amazing, thank you," I whispered as I balanced on one foot and then the other to get the thin black flats on.

She sniffed. "You're too pretty to be this dumb. Get yourself some smarts, girlfriend. This company eats pretty girls like you for lunch."

I nodded. "Yeah, I figured that much out already." I stuffed the folder and papers I'd taken off Gabe into the back of my skirt, under the ties of the shirt around my waist. I held Linx so he was flush against my arms. My bleeding, punctured arms. More than a few of the women were giving me looks. Shit, I was going to stand out in the worst way.

The doors of the elevator opened and there waiting were the guards . . . and Gabe.

I tucked in behind one of the women, using her as cover as I walked out with the group of women.

"Brown hair, black-rimmed glasses, heels," Gabe snapped. "Where the hell is she? Did the Stick Man get her?"

He pushed through the women and there were gasps all around, of which I joined in. His gaze flicked over me, sliding off me like I was nothing. I turned so I was further into the group, my hands on my arms as if I were cold.

I picked up the pace, hurrying to the front door.

A guard stood there, his arms over his chest. "Sorry, we're on lockdown."

"Well, shit, that isn't going to fly." I snugged up close to him, whipped my one leg between his and shoved him off balance. He went skating backward, his arms windmilling as he yelled.

I didn't wait to see who noticed. I just walked on out the doors.

"Stop her!"

That was my cue to move.

I bolted, more thankful for those damn flats than I ever could have imagined. I squeezed Linx tightly.

"Oh yeah, I like you already," he said.

Down the sidewalk, I ran, weaving my way through the crowds of men and women on their way to work. I knew Gabe wouldn't give up easily. I knew he was going to look for the woman who'd taken the papers, but for how long? It wasn't money, so I was banking on a week or two at the most. But the Stick Man, he'd come for me. He'd keep looking. Rose was right about that.

Shit, like I needed a second killer coming for me.

I made it all the way to my motel room, up the stairs and had the door closed behind me before I dared to so much as glance at the papers. And when I did . . . I slid to the floor, my entire body shaking as the words that stared up at me shattered everything I thought I knew. Everything I thought I'd understood.

Job on File
Place: Jackson Hole, Wyoming

Mark: Justin Stark.
Called in by: Luca Romano

CHAPTER SEVENTEEN

The papers I'd printed at my father's business, that I'd taken from Gabe before bolting out of the Blink Management building, rattled in my fingers. They shook so hard, I had a difficult time reading them at all. Abe pushed against me, desperate for attention as always. I pushed him away. "Not now, buddy." I whispered the words.

"What is it? Let me see," Linx grumbled from the floor where I'd dropped him.

"Who is that?" Dinah barked. Their voices faded, white noise all around me.

I'd taken the papers from my father's office, thinking I would find out who was still looking for me; that I'd find out which bogeyman was on my trail to punish me for stealing from my father and the mob all those years ago.

What I didn't expect to find was the exact information on who had called in the hit on my husband. I had all of three sheets of paper, two of which were nothing but Justin's statistics— known aliases: Justin Black, Joseph Donald, JJ Gray—and his most recent jobs. But that wasn't what had me on my knees. No, that was much, much worse.

The person who'd called the hit in on my husband, who'd called in the mob to do his dirty work, was Luca Romano.

My father.

Less than an hour before, I'd been two feet from the man who'd had my husband killed. The man who'd put a hit on my family, and in doing so, had killed my son. Abe whined softly, his warmth against my leg the only thing holding me together as the last of my world shattered.

Rage did not begin to cover the hatred swirling through me, spilling upward like a blizzard that iced over the last of the warmth my body held. My father had made me what I was. He'd made me a killer to use against those who he thought had done him wrong, to hunt the abnormals that had cheated him in his mind.

He'd created me, let me develop into the boogeyman he'd used to threaten his rivals.

Now that boogeyman was about to come home to roost.

I sat on the floor until the shakes left me entirely, and my body was once more under my control.

I forced myself to look at the rest of the papers from the folder.

There was talk of the new studio in Hollywood Romano had started, of the money flowing in and out. Millions every month. Another scam, another scheme. I didn't care. None of that mattered now. Magic and money went together like ham and cheese, and I had no doubt he was dabbling in the latter still.

I closed my eyes. Rose had told me to find my boy. My boy, she had to mean . . . who? Not Bear, of course, not Bear. But who then? What boy was mine?

I stood, stripped out of the business attire and slid into casual clothes. I slipped Dinah and Eleanor onto my back, grateful they were quiet.

"Abe, come." I slipped a leash onto his collar.

We didn't have far to go to get to a payphone, one of the reasons I'd chosen this motel. I could have grabbed a cell phone, but I didn't trust them. I knew they could be traced.

Taking coins from my pocket, I slid them into the metal slot and dialed Zee's number.

He picked up on the first ring. "Nix?"

"It was my father who called in the hit, Zee. Justin was doing something that involved my father, as we suspected, but it was Romano who called it in."

"Justin knew who you were," Zee said, his voice thoughtful. "He could have been using it against your dad. We suspected that."

"Does it matter?" I realized then it really didn't. I didn't care about the reasons why Justin had been dealing with my father. What mattered was that he was gone. Bear was gone, and I knew who to blame.

"Nix. I'll leave right now. I can be there in—"

"No," I cut him off, "I'll be done by then, so don't bother coming."

He was quiet a moment. "What about your tail? Simon?"

I snorted and turned in the phone booth so I could see up and down the street. "He thinks he's a big bad ugly. I'll deal with him when he shows up. He's trying to frighten me with street kids." I didn't mention that I had the Stick Man looking for me. For the first time, I didn't want Zee here. I wanted him to stay where he was and let me do this on my own.

"You sure about that?"

"He won't be able to stop me, not now," I said.

"You sure, Nix? You need to be sure."

Those few words held a wealth of understanding of who I was, and where my mind had gone. Was I sure that killing my father would fix the harm he'd done to me? I wasn't. But I didn't know how else to handle this. I didn't know how else to make things right. There had to be something that would allow me to make my father pay, and his life seemed like a measly pittance against my sweet Bear's.

"I've got to go, Zee. If I don't phone you by tomorrow morning, you know why."

"Nix, wait . . ."

I was hanging up the phone, but I could still hear him.

"Phoenix, there are better ways—"

I shook my head and held the receiver down hard. I glanced at Abe. He would have to come with me. His fate was tangled with mine, and if I died doing what I planned, he would at least be with me and Bear, too.

I rubbed a hand over his head. "Come on, Abe."

"Who are we hunting now?" Eleanor asked, always the more perceptive of the two guns.

"Forget that, who was the talking tool back at the room?" Dinah snapped.

It was a struggle to speak, but I knew it would help if I told them what I was doing. If nothing else, they always backed up my violence.

"Luca Romano killed my husband and son. His life is forfeit. The tool's name is Linx and he was given to me by a woman who saved my life."

"An abnormal saved your life?" Eleanor asked.

"Yes." I didn't say more than that. I needed a place where I didn't have to worry about my next step, a place where I could just walk and walk and let my mind settle into my plans.

Walking—or running—had always been the place where my mind had found the threads I needed to splice together in order to make a complicated plan work.

I scanned the area we walked constantly as Abe sniffed plants and bushes. A park with a trail that looped around the edges was perfect and I set my feet on autopilot.

My father in the past frequented La Bella Cuisina after work, like a king taking the time to eat with his subjects. He always had a few business people with him, at least one of my brothers and very often whatever girlfriend he had on his arm at the time.

Run by abnormals that owed him, he ate and drank for free. Of course, that put the owners at a loss, which forced them to go to him for more money. By now if Romano didn't own it outright, I'd be surprised.

Getting to him would be difficult if he'd changed his routine, but like so much about my father, I doubted he ever thought about how someone might try to kill him. That had been part of my job, and I'd thwarted two attempts on his life that he didn't even realize happened.

We were on our second loop around the park before the itch in my shoulder blades announced someone following me. I stopped and bent down to Abe, picked up his front left paw and inspected it as though he'd gotten a thorn. From the corner of my eye, a figure picked up speed.

A broad daylight attack would be something ballsy. I had to give whoever was coming at me that.

I stood and twisted, my right hand diving to my lower back to Dinah's handle. The man coming at me didn't slow, not for a second. In fact, he picked up speed, smiling. Mid-thirties, trim, average face and coloring. Nothing about him stood out, nothing about him would make you look twice. Brown eyes.

"Hello, Phoenix."

I didn't take my hand from Dinah, but I didn't bring her out either. "You have me at a disadvantage. You know my name."

He smiled, but did not hold his hand out. "Simon."

"Simon," I said softly, "so you are the one tracking me?"

"Ah, not exactly." His smile faltered. "You see, I *was* working for your father, but he decided not to pay me."

I couldn't help the laugh that burst out of me. "You aren't getting a paycheck from me."

He tipped his head to one side, and his eyes glittered. Eyes that spoke of more than a trickle of magic.

My father had sent an abnormal after me.

"Ah, but I have an offer. You see, between you and me, we could do some serious damage to your father, and convince him to give us large sums of money." His smile was back now.

"The girl you sent to me with the note?" I arched an eyebrow.

"Aptly named, Pink. She works for me. You gave her a bit of a scare, but she was impressed that not only did you pay her, you weren't the psycho we thought you were." He waved a hand forward, suggesting we walk together.

Abe didn't growl at him as he stepped up beside us.

That was interesting. Abe was trained to essentially warn me if an abnormal was close.

I didn't get even a single growl from him. "Traitor," I muttered.

Dinah sniffed. "He's a dog, not a gun."

Simon slowed and looked to my back. "Who was that?"

"Someone you don't want to meet," I said. Talking about Dinah and Eleanor, even to an abnormal who would understand the concept of an inanimate object being able to speak and think, was not something I did.

"No lisp?" I arched an eyebrow at him.

"Ah, no. Just trying to throw you off."

"Smart." I'd give him that much.

Simon tucked his hands into the pockets of his slacks, his coat tucked behind his arms. He looked like a casual businessman on a lunch break. "You see, your father . . . well, you know how little he likes to pay out his precious cash."

I didn't respond. If Simon was going to talk, and dish on my father, then I would listen and learn what I could.

He glanced at me. "You stole a great deal of money from him and lived away from him for a long time, using Zee's magic to hide you. I think we could do it again."

I took a shot in the dark, one that I was sure to miss but I took it anyway. "You burned my house down, and now you want me to work with you?"

He didn't even blink. "No arson from me. I was on my way to find you because your father stopped paying me months ago."

"And the kid, Bradley?"

He shrugged. "What about him? He was meant as bait. Your father thought he'd find you, and you'd kill him, and we'd have you then."

"Obviously, it didn't work," I pointed out.

"Well, obviously. Long as little Bradley doesn't show up and spill the beans, we should be good. He had quite the crush on you." Simon rolled his eyes. Like we were old friends talking about a mutual acquaintance.

"Bradley is dead."

He grunted. "Pity, kid had potential, even if he was obsessed with you." Simon squinted into the distance. "So, what do you say to my proposition?"

"I'll think about it." I had no intention of doing any such thing. I just needed to get him out of my way, and now that he'd pointed out he wasn't interested in killing me, all the better.

Mind you, there was still the Stick Man to deal with.

The trees around us suddenly seemed to loom in close. "I have to go," I said. I was a fool. What had I been thinking, coming to a damn park?

There was a creak of branches behind us, and Abe's ears perked up, a low growl slipping through his teeth.

Simon pulled one hand out of his pocket slow enough that I knew he was being careful on purpose as he handed me a card. "I'm very good at finding people, Phoenix. That's part of my abilities. You're good at killing people, and from what I understand, you have some other rather... unique... skills for a normal." His eyes darted to my lower back. "I think we'd make a good team."

I took the card and glanced at it. No name, nothing but a number.

I flicked it once with my middle finger, and tucked it into my back pocket. "Like I said, I'll think about it."

"Do that." There was more than a hint of warning in those two words. I raised my eyebrows and let a smile slide over my lips. A very not nice smile.

"Let me be clear, *Simon*. Threatening me in any way will make it so you are no longer doing your job. It will ensure you not being able to breathe anymore. Abnormal or not, capiche?"

"And threatening me is no more of a better idea, Phoenix." He smiled back at me, and I saw the darkness in him. I saw the way he'd dressed down, deliberately blending into the world around us. A pair of killers out in the open, having a nice chat about killing each other.

"I'll call you tomorrow with my answer." I deliberately turned my back on him.

"Why tomorrow?"

I kept walking, forcing him to keep up if he wanted to hear my words. A power play on my part. "I like to sleep on business deals. And I am not the only one you'd be dealing with."

Half-truths, but they would keep him from guessing what I was up to. Because if he knew I was going to kill my father, there would be no way he'd be okay with it. Not when he wanted money out of the miserable bastard.

I could see the cement walkway that swept out of the park when the branches creaking above my head turned into the snap of wood pulling away from tree trunks. I broke into a run, not daring to even look behind me.

That sound of wood being ripped apart followed, and I turned on the speed, arms pumping and heart pounding with adrenaline.

The Stick Man slid from the trees ahead of us, spread his arms wide and opened his mouth impossibly wide. Teeth made of sharp spikes of wood pointed at me and Abe. The Stick Man drew in a breath, his body widening, prepping for what?

"I suggest you move." A hand touched my arm and I spun on my foot, rolling my body as if I were playing basketball with Bear and he'd tried to put a pick on me.

Abe went with me. Simon lost his hold on me, and the Stick Man breathed out, shooting his wicked slivers through the air where I'd been.

I pulled Dinah and Eleanor as I planted my opposite foot and spun back to face the Stick Man. I had the girls up and firing before I was fully stopped, the bullets ripping through the Stick Man's head.

The wood splintered and exploded with each successive hit, but his body repaired itself, closing over the metal.

"Dinah, switch it out. Detonating rounds!" I yelled as I kept moving around the Stick Man, keeping out of reach, but keeping the bullets going.

Beauty of magic weapons was, these two didn't run out of ammo.

"On it!" She shivered and her inner chambers twisted, rumbling against my palm.

The next time I shot with her, she bucked so hard I fought the momentum to be thrown back.

Her bullet hit the Stick Man in his belly and exploded on impact, blowing his top half away from his bottom.

He screeched and clawed across the ground toward me and I squeezed Dinah again, much to her delight. The second bullet exploded between his eyes and his upper body stopped its clawing crawl toward me. That would slow him down, though not for long. While I hoped that the Stick Man was dead, I doubted it. Rose said I needed blood fire to finish him off. Exploding was all well and good, but not the final blow. I was sure of it.

My hearing came back slowly.

Simon was gone.

Abe and I were alone.

Sirens were coming.

Time to go.

CHAPTER EIGHTEEN

I took a cab back to our motel room, but not right away. I needed to catch my breath, and I didn't want to lead the Stick Man back to my motel room.

I ran my hands over Abe, checking to make sure he hadn't picked up any stray slivers. He trembled from the tip of his nose to the tip of his tail. That had been the first really bad abnormal he'd ever dealt with.

And the Stick Man was one of the worst.

I patted my lap and he dropped his head onto it and I rubbed his ears.

"Where you headed?" the cabbie asked, the air around him shifting, for lack of a better word. Damn it, abnormals everywhere. When I'd been hunting them, there had seemed so few. And now every other person seemed to have magic in their blood.

"Just take us for a tour of the city. I've not been here in a long time," I said. Time. I needed time and yet I could feel it ticking down.

The cabbie gave me a nod and pulled into traffic. He

didn't say a word about Abe, or the whimpering that slid through him.

When my heart finally started to slow in its wild adrenaline-filled pace, I gave the cabbie directions back to the motel room.

He pulled over to the curb and I handed him cash with a heavy tip. "Thanks."

He gave me thumbs up. "Anytime."

Banter that covered up the fact that I smelled like gunpowder and my eyes were wild when I'd gotten into the cab. As an abnormal, maybe he was better at blocking out the weird of the world.

As I stepped into the narrow alley between the building where we were staying and the one next to it, I froze.

The back door that opened to the rickety stairs had been kicked open, the deadbolt and hinges hanging limply, the sand I'd placed and smoothed disturbed. I bent and unleashed Abe. "*Fuss.*"

He glued himself to my leg, his body tense with only the slightest tremor of leftover fear from the Stick Man, as he picked up on my energy.

I pulled Eleanor from my back, and settled into a crouch as we crept up the stairs. She was quiet, as I knew she would be. Dinah would have been whispering questions.

There was no doubt which room would be burglarized. I was no fool. Simon might have made himself known to me for his own reasons. But that still left the arsonist, who was also Bradley's killer, who I strongly suspected was Noah.

A man I'd once called a friend, a man who I would probably end up killing at some point.

Abe crouched lower and lower until his belly scraped along the staircase and I kept my back to the wall, creeping up sideways. We neared the top and I put one hand out, signaling for Abe to wait. I went up the last couple of steps myself, peering into my room. The door had also been kicked in. This guy was not going for subtle. I waited where I was, listening. There was no sound of rustling papers, or the crackle of another fire being started.

There was no creak of wood, no sign that somehow the Stick Man had not only put himself back together, but had found us too.

Not that it meant the arsonist wasn't still in the room. He could be waiting behind the door, or in the tiny bathroom. I took a breath, held it, let it out slowly and prepped myself.

I lunged forward, hip checking the door to fling it wide. I sidestepped with the gun held high, scanning the room in a matter of seconds. "Abe."

The dog shot into the room, but there was no low growling from him, and no indication that anyone else was with us.

I shivered and lowered Eleanor. This was not going as I'd planned, not at all. I didn't put Eleanor away, but kept her out as I checked the bathroom. The closet too, even though I knew it was too small to hide someone, but there was no chance I wasn't going to make very sure of things. The black bag with my obvious stash was gone.

I flipped open the hiding spot in the closet. Still full, and the coded papers were right on top. A smile slid over my lips. If it was Noah, and he was FBI, I doubted he worked for the feds anymore.

"Pretty fucking sloppy, Noah." I shook my head.

I took stock of the room. The bed sheets had been flipped off, and my clothes had been rustled through, but my hiding spot for my weapons, money, and information hadn't been found.

I propped my door closed with a chair—the best I could do for now, but it didn't matter. No matter what tonight brought, I wasn't staying here any longer than it took to get ready for this job. It was far too compromised.

I'd been found by Simon. I'd been found by Noah, and the Stick Man was hot on my ass. Time to move.

I went to the tiny closet and popped the floor open again.

"Time to get to work, Abe."

I pulled out everything I had and laid it on the bed. The guns I put from smallest to largest, all seven, one after the other with their respective ammunition.

Two HK 45 (.45ACP) tactical handguns.

My third Beretta.

A double-barreled shotgun with under-barrel grenade launcher.

Ruger precision rifle .243.

And of course, Eleanor and Dinah.

Next came the different clothing I had to choose from.

From business causal to jeans, sweat pants, and a goth rocker outfit, not to mention my frilly party dress from the other night, I'd covered most possibilities. But it was the skin-tight black pants made of Lycra and spandex along with the matching black top that I found myself staring at. I'd stuffed the outfit into the bottom of my bag, hiding it under my weapons before I left the ranch.

There were two spots stitched into it, one in the belly of the shirt, and one in the right thigh of the pants legs. The two shots that had brought me to fully understand how bad my family was.

"One more time," I whispered as I set the clothes aside and threw the rest except for a pair of jeans and T-shirt into the closet.

I took a box of hair dye from my stash—jet black—and went to the bathroom. The dye job was a tedious thing, but I wanted my father to know exactly who killed him. I wanted him to see my face and know without a doubt that I had come for him.

And why I'd come for him.

There could be no doubt on his part that it was his daughter on the other end of the gun.

The fucker was going to have a heart attack right before I put a bullet between his eyes. The thought made me smile, which set me to laughing. My head was upside down in the tub as I laughed till I cried. Cried until there was nothing left in me once more.

The emotions floored me and I struggled to put them once more into the tiny box where they belonged.

I'd killed Stephen Demetris, the man who'd pulled the hit off and done the dirty work of killing Justin and Bear. Someone else . . . perhaps Noah? . . . had killed Peters who'd set the death myst magic under the truck.

Now, I would kill the man who'd called it in—the man who'd decided that my life would be torn apart again.

The miserable bastard was never going to see this coming.

CHAPTER NINETEEN

I waited quietly in the room while the day faded and darkness slowly crept over the city that never slept. I sat on the edge of the bed, going through my slow breathing meditations that helped me stay calm. A job was never a simple thing, and there was always some element of excitement and adrenaline.

This one more so than any other. Death of a tyrant. Death of a father.

Shortly before five, I went down to the payphone and dialed up La Bella Cuisina.

"Hello, this is Luca Romano's secretary. He asked me to check his reservation for tonight?"

"Ah, yes, of course! It's here, set for an even dozen for nine 'o'clock."

"Wonderful," I said. "Thank you."

I hung up before he could say anything else. I'd confirmed my father's appearance, and that was all I needed. This was coming together smoothly, which was a good sign. And which also made me nervous.

I had never had a single job go off without some sort of hitch. That was the truth of dealing with people. People were animals, and animals were unpredictable.

I went to a local food mart after I used the payphone. I grabbed some hot dogs for Abe, and a small bottle of tequila for me. It caught my eye, and made me think of Justin. He'd wanted to take me to Mexico for our honeymoon. I'd refused, afraid someone in the airlines would tip off my father.

Instead, Justin had bought tequila in a rather large quantity, bags of tortilla chips, an extra hot salsa, and a sombrero. We'd gotten roaring drunk, and ended up making love on a bed covered in the chips. I tightened my hold on the tequila bottle, my throat tightening.

Damn you, Justin. You should have trusted me. You should have told me what you were up to and I would have . . . I would have stopped this before we lost our boy. Then again, maybe if I'd trusted him with my secret of who I really was, we wouldn't have lost each other, or our boy. Shit, I didn't not need this train of thought right now.

I rubbed my hands over my face, went to the front and paid the bill.

Once more back in my room, I fed Abe the hot dogs which he happily gulped down in two bites each.

I held a glass of tequila up to the light. "To you, Justin. You pissed off the wrong man, and it cost more than you probably could ever have imagined. But I still love you, and you stood by me through the years. I love you, even if you were an idiot." I threw the shot back in a single gulp.

The alcohol burned all the way down and made me gasp, made my eyes water, set fire to the inside of my chest. The flames licked up my throat and I held the heat as long as I could inside me. I was the Phoenix, meant to burn from the inside out.

Coughing, I wiped away the tears.

Not enough alcohol that it would affect my aim, but enough to burn off some of the nerves. Besides, Dinah and Eleanor corrected what off moments I had with my aim.

For the first time in years, my nerves were acting up. As if this were my first hit instead my one hundredth. I suppose that's what I got for going after Luca Romano. Never again would I call him my father, he lost that title. I didn't care that he'd had no idea that it was my son, that it was me whose life he destroyed when he set a mark on Justin's back. The reality was, it could have been any family. Any mother who lost her child.

That didn't make what had happened any better. The difference was I had the ability and the means to make it right. To call him to account for his actions.

I stood and gathered my bag of weapons, leaving behind all the clothes except the extra pair of jeans and T-shirt stuffed in the bottom of my bag. On the off chance I made it through this alive, I would want to change out of the black cat suit.

Where would I go if I succeeded and *did* make it out alive? The thought bounced around in my head, a question I had no answer for. The last few months had been all about finding my boys' killer or killers, taking my revenge on them and having that closure. Now that I was this close to it, the reality was I had not thought past this moment.

Nor did I want to.

Maybe I would go back to Wyoming, to the farm. Maybe I would rebuild.

Maybe I'd keep running.

I shook my head as if that alone would clear my mind. Down the steps, out the back, and around the corner to where the truck I'd stolen from the airport in Jackson Hole waited for me still. I had another week before the time stamp was up. Plenty of time to dump it and get something else. Again, that was assuming I would make it out of this alive.

I wore my black suit, tall black boots that rose to my knees, and a loose dark blue sweater over the black skin-tight top. The sweater had been one of Noah's I'd taken from his apartment and it held a whiff of his cologne, the same cologne Justin had always worn. For a moment, I could believe he was with me, the scent of him just on the edge of my peripheral.

I shook it off. This was not the time for emotional reruns.

Abe lay across the bench seat of the truck and put his muzzle on my thigh as I drove us to what I would use as our drop-off point. Two blocks from La Bella Cuisina, I parked on a side street that had far too many streetlights for my liking, but that could be easily handled.

I pulled Dinah out, the silencer already on her, muffling her voice as she grumbled about only being used for grunt work.

I stepped out of the truck and went to a crouch, taking out the four streetlights around my parking spot in a matter of seconds. No dogs barked, no alarms went off. I let myself back into the truck and checked the time. Nine thirty, which meant my father would be well into his cups by now, his senses dulled.

I needed his senses dulled. He was not an abnormal, but he'd made a deal with the devil, and that had given him abilities that even I didn't fully understand.

I looked at myself in the rearview mirror. The dye job had taken me quite literally back to my roots. I slid a hand over my hair. There was no way he wouldn't recognize me.

Perfect.

I slipped out of the blue sweater and folded it up on the

seat. I rolled both windows all the way down, enough that Abe would be able to get out if he had to. As it was, I wanted to make sure he wasn't trapped in the truck if I didn't come back. I pitied anyone who tried to take the truck with him in it.

I wrapped an arm around his neck and gave him a tight hug, breathing in his scent, and then kissing him on the nose. "Be good."

I stepped out once more, and grabbed my bag of gear. I slung it over my back and rubbed Abe's ears, then pointed at the truck. "*Bewache*."

He gave me a soft woof. I leaned in and made sure the wires were set to go under the wheel. A quick escape is what I'd need if I made this thing happen.

Shutting the door behind me, I walked away and down the side street, weaving my way between buildings until I was behind the restaurant. Standing next to the ground floor office window, I checked to either side of me before I pulled a baton from my bag. A quick thump against the glass and my hand was through the narrow opening, and I unlocked the window latch.

I pushed up the old frame and climbed through easily.

How many times had I warned my father about this place? That this restaurant was too easily accessible, that he was too predictable going here as much as he did?

The abnormals who ran it were not high powered. Their gifts lay in their ability to manipulate food and flavor. A few could create magic. Not one of them could protect worth shit.

His lack of care, his belief that he was above being truly targeted, was something I was grateful for now. The office was dark and I crept through, avoiding the chairs. I put my bag on the desk and opened it. I pulled out two flash bangs first. Then I set my weapons of choice into their holsters on my thighs for easy access. Dinah and Eleanor were silent as I slid them in.

"Like a gunslinger," I said softly, repeating my father's words to me the first time he'd seen me heading out on a job. All in black, holsters on my thighs, black lace mask covering the upper half of my face leaving nothing but shadows of my eyes and mouth visible.

I pulled a similar mask up and adjusted it. I didn't really care if it came off, but it was the initial shock value I was going for as much as anything.

I wanted him to be afraid the way I'd been afraid for Bear.

I wanted him to know he was about to die, the way I'd known Bear was dying in front of me.

I wanted him to feel every one of his last breaths and know that his daughter, the one he'd thought would come to nothing, the one he'd been the cruelest to, would be the one to end his life.

A knife went into each of the sheaths inside the tops of my boots. I attached the two flash bangs to my waist, then adjusted my shoulders. The feeling of anticipation grew in my belly with each passing second.

The sensation was the same no matter what job, no matter who, I'd been set on.

I turned to the wall behind me. The electrical paneling for the restaurant was here in the office, one more strike against this place. Flipping the panel open, I stared at it, then opted for making sure it didn't come back on. I flicked the breakers off; the restaurant went up in a bunch of shouting. I pulled Dinah and put two silent rounds into the panel to be safe.

I walked to the door and waited for whomever would come and check on the panel. I didn't have to wait long.

The manager Tony, a chubby little abnormal with a flair for pastries, who had his head so far up my father's ass I was surprised he could even see, waddled in. He took two steps, and I shot him in the side of the head.

He crumpled and I stepped into the darkened Hallway. My father's voice was above everyone else's.

"Tony's got this, everyone just calm yourselves. Bambi, come here, darling, and sit with me."

I strode through the hall and into the restaurant where the light coming in from the street outlined people. All those around my father were his friends, those who were on the fringes of society. Some abnormal, some human.

People I'd killed for in the past as my father handed my skills around.

I pulled up both guns and started firing. Five of the twelve were head shots, down before anyone else realized what was happening.

The rest woke up through their alcoholic haze and dove under tables, no doubt going for their own guns. I stood, silhouetted, waiting for the gunfire.

"Luca Romano," I said, "you killed my husband and son."

A weird urge to tell him 'prepare to die' came over me but I bit it back. *The Princess Bride* had been one of Bear's favorite movies. He would have loved if I'd spit that at his killer.

"Phoenix?" He sat up, clearly not understanding I was going to kill him. "Phoenix, you . . . what the fuck did you do with Dad's money?"

Always the money, it would never be about lives, or death, or pain. Just money.

Wait . . . I stared hard at him, really seeing him. Realizing my mistake. "Dad's money?" Worse, though, was I was taking too much time.

One of his men popped up on my left with a gun raised, and I spun, let off a shot that slammed into his shoulder and flipped him over his table. I strode forward, kicking a chair out of my way. No one else had shot at me.

Distantly, I wondered why, and then I knew.

They thought I was still being controlled by my father, that I was here on his orders.

I started to laugh. "I'll give you ten seconds to clear out. After that, I'm killing you all, regardless of who and what you are."

The scramble was instant. I saw the man I'd thought was my father going with them. I pulled a knife from my boot top and threw it, hitting him in the shoulder. "Not you. You and I are going to talk."

He went to his knees as he cried out, clutching at the knife. His date screamed and bolted, stumbling in her six-inch high heels.

Seven seconds passed and the room was indeed clear. My brother was on his knees. He glared up at me. "You turned out to be quite a faithless bitch. You think you're going to get more money out of Dad? He'll kill you now, for sure."

Fury rippled through me. "Tommy, why isn't he here? Where is he?"

He spit a gob of saliva at me that landed near my boots as he touched the ruby ring on his finger, no doubt calling the Stick Man to him.

Time was ticking, but I needed answers.

I lifted a foot and pressed it against the hilt of the knife as his face paled and he gasped. "Don't. Piss. Me. Off," I said softly.

I stared at him, at my oldest brother who looked and sounded so like my father that I'd mistaken one for the other. Luca wasn't here. I couldn't kill him and end this as I'd planned.

My brain ticked over what Simon had said in the park that afternoon. That we could work together to take things from my father, to take money from him.

Zee had said something similar on the call. That there

were other ways to make things right. Other ways of hurting my father. My jaw clenched and the mother bear in me roared with frustration, with anger and hurt. He was so close, he was so close somewhere in this city, and if I found him, I knew I could kill him and walk out without looking back.

But that wouldn't hurt him like I'd been hurt.

Tommy stared up at me and began to laugh. "You can't do it, can you? You never had the ability to kill. I knew it was someone else doing the dirty work, and you were just taking the fame."

I crouched down to him as I put Eleanor's muzzle against his temple. "Oh, Tommy, Tommy. You have no idea, do you?" I tightened my hand, my finger itching to squeeze the trigger.

Even now, he thought I was weak, that I was a little girl to be pushed around. "What will make Luca bleed, do you think? Will he care if I kill you, or will he just fill your spot with another bastard child of his?" I tipped my head. "One day, I'm sure I'm going to kill you, Tommy. You'll cross me and force my hand. But for now, I'm going to let you live because I want you to deliver a message for me."

I sat back on my heels but didn't put Eleanor away.

"And what's that, cunt?"

I shot him in the kneecap, hardly moving to do it. He screamed and grabbed at his knee. I pushed his hands away and jammed a thumb into the bullet wound.

"Tell Luca I'm going to make him suffer for killing my husband and son. I'm going to make him pay the highest cost that he will understand."

"You stupid little bitch! You shot me!"

I dug my thumb in harder and he screamed again. "Did you hear me? Repeat it."

He tried to push my hand off but I put Eleanor to his belly. "Really, I can find another messenger if I have to."

"You're going to make him suffer." Tommy glared at me,

his mouth twisted with pain as he spit the words at me. I couldn't see his eyes but I knew what look they would hold. One of disdain, one of distaste, one of condescension.

I took a step back. "I am going to be this family's worst nightmare, Romano."

I squeezed the trigger, hitting the table behind him. He screamed and fell sideways, covering his head. I wanted nothing more than to put him over my shoulder and take him somewhere I could make him truly suffer. Where I could show him how very ugly I could be.

But Zee was right. There were other ways.

That my father would know it was me coming for him, causing him pain and costing him money, that would have to be enough.

For now.

I let myself out of the restaurant through the kitchen. The staff cowered and I ignored them. The abnormals glimmered with a light all their own, but none tried to stop me.

The night air was cool on my skin as I walked away from the restaurant.

Sirens bellowed in the distance.

Breaking into a jog once I was clear of the restaurant, I made it to Abe and the truck in no time. He saw me when I was still half a block away, leapt from the truck and met me with his tongue hanging out and his tail wagging hard.

"Come on, Abe. We've got work to do."

I let him back into the truck and started the engine. I didn't know exactly where I was going, but I needed to move. My father knew I was here. He knew I was after him.

He would be sending all three of his guardians after me.

A smile slid over my face. I was going to make him pay, make him suffer like he could never have imagined, and I knew just how I was going to do it.

While I sat at a stoplight, I fished around in my bag until

I found my jeans and in the back pocket, a card with a single number on it.

It looked like it was time to give Simon a call to see what he had to say.

And just what kind of skills the abnormal had.

CHAPTER TWENTY

The idea of working with an abnormal, who'd been hired to track me down and kill me if he couldn't drag me back to my father, would bother most people. In my mind, if Simon had skills Luca Romano thought were comparable to my own, then he could be an asset. Especially if he had intel on my father. Intel would be crucial not only to getting Simon his money, but for cutting the legs out from under Romano and making him bleed. Making Romano suffer was the new goal, and Simon was going to be key to that happening.

I stopped at a box store and bought another new cell phone and a SIM card with a stack of minutes. I'd have to switch phones again later to be safe, but for now this would work.

Simon answered my call on the fourth ring. "Hello?" His voice was thick and groggy with either sleep or booze.

"You better not be drunk," I said.

There was the rustle of material. "Phoenix?"

"We need to discuss how we are going to get you your money." I kept my voice even. "Meet me at the Lounge in thirty minutes or I will assume you no longer want to get paid. Ask for Nix at the bar."

I clicked *End* on the mobile phone and then dialed Zee.

He picked up, not groggy in the least. "Talk to me, Nix."

"You were right." I paused and let those words I said very seldom sink in. "There are better ways."

A sigh slid out of him. "What are you going to do then?"

"There is one city that keeps coming up, Zee. Over and over. Hollywood. That's where Justin and Noah were going for their big score. That's where a new merger is happening between Romano and Mancini, that's where a new acting studio is opening for Romano. We know there is money flowing if Mancini is involved." I thought about Barron. He had been my friend, and he had good connections there. Or he had connections. I wasn't even sure he'd still be alive.

"Mancini is beyond dangerous. He is the king of the abnormals, Nix. Avoid him if you can." Zee cleared his throat. "You want me to come?"

I smiled to myself. "No. Stay in Wyoming. I've got a potential helper."

"Who?" There was no jealousy in his voice, which gave me a surprising amount of relief.

"The guy Romano paid to find me. Didn't get paid and wants his money."

"Can you trust him?"

"I don't trust anyone but you and Abe. But this possible help . . .he's an abnormal and he's got skills." I put a hand on Abe's back as I said his name and his tail thumped against the far door of the truck.

"Smart, doll face. You think you can bust up Romano's business then, make him bleed out in more ways than one?"

I was grateful he didn't call him my father.

"Yes. Based on what Gabe and Romano discussed, I think there are spells being created and sold, perhaps on the black market to normals. The amount of money flowing through, what else could it be?"

He barked a laugh. "A few things, if I remember Romano's business right. Could be weapons. Could be other kinds of trafficking in death magic that's been twisted."

I gritted my teeth. The reason I'd left my father's business employ was simple. I'd seen just how twisted he was. I saw the underbelly of the underbelly. Death was one thing, torture another, and trafficking people was a level of ugly I couldn't—and never would—understand. Especially when those being trafficked were kids, even if they were abnormals.

I tapped a hand on the steering wheel. "I faced Tommy down, Zee. Gave him a message for Romano. He knows I'm coming for him."

There was a heartbeat of silence before he exploded. "Goddamn it. Why would you do that?"

I shrugged even though he couldn't see me. "I was going to kill Tommy. I thought it was Luca Romano. But I realized that you were right. To make him suffer is a far better thing, to make him bleed out until there is nothing left."

"Nix, be careful. If he knows you're alive and coming for him, he'll send the guardians. The demon gave him—"

"He'll think I'm in New York. I'm going to hit him where he least expects it."

A sigh slid through the connection. "Just . . . be careful. He may be a psychopath, but he's a smart psychopath, and that deal was no small thing."

I laughed softly. "They didn't call me Flaky Phoenix, Zee," I pointed out and he laughed, the reaction I'd been hoping for.

"Damn it, just . . . do what you do best, then. And stay alive."

"That much I think I can manage. See you later." I hit the end button a second time, then turned the phone off. Ten minutes later, I pulled into the parking lot for the Lounge and shimmied out of my killing clothes. On went my jeans and long-sleeved shirt over which I settled my leather holsters on my upper thighs once more, and knives back into the tops of my boots. I didn't bother to hide the weapons on me, but left my coat off so the holster and guns were clearly visible.

"Phoenix," Eleanor said my name for the second time maybe ever, "your father's contract with the devil prevents him from losing his power and money. You could take one thing from him, and another would fill its place."

I dropped my hand to her holster. "What I'm doing is going to piss him off, Eleanor. He'll make a mistake. The contract was about power and money, not life and death. This will draw him out. This will make him come to me." It would put fear into him and make him sloppy. "I'm going for suffering, not a quick death."

"I see," she said and fell silent.

I let Abe out of the truck. "*Fuss*, Abe. And don't stray."

He gave me a woof and I dropped a hand to his head, taking a small amount of reassurance from him just being there, from the connection to the life I'd lost.

With ground-eating strides, I headed to the front door. The bouncer saw me coming, and his eyes widened.

"No weapons!" That was the standard deal. If you knew you belonged in the Lounge, you walked right in with weapons showing. If you didn't belong, you handed them over to the bouncers.

I pulled Dinah on him before he could so much as twitch. "One way or another, I'm going in with my weapons." I flicked the safety off with my thumb. He swallowed hard but otherwise didn't move.

"No dogs," he said.

"Fuck off." I lowered the gun and shouldered past him.

Though he was twice my size, by his reaction he'd never had a gun pulled on him. He was literally shaking in his boots.

Pussy.

Abe and I walked through the upper part of the Lounge. I half-hoped Gabe would be there. He'd recognize me now, and I wanted another shot at his face with my fists.

But luck was not on my side and my brother was nowhere to be found. The weight of so many pairs of eyes on me didn't bother me. This was my world. This was where I knew my way in the dark.

I went straight to the elevator and hit the button. Over my shoulder, I spoke. "Tank in tonight?"

The bartender continued to clean a glass. "Just got here."

"Excellent. I have a friend coming. He'll ask for Nix. Send him down."

"You got it."

I wasn't worried about the bartender calling me in. This place was used for Mancini's crew. People and abnormals came through all the time with weapons, and attitudes, on full display. And I wasn't hiding what I was, or what I was packing. Which in a weird way meant I wasn't the threat I could be. By their codes, I had been more dangerous when I'd come in before, hiding what I was behind the frilly dress.

I stepped onto the elevator and Abe kept tightly to me. The doors slid shut and we rode down to the third basement level where Tank had taken me only a few days before.

The doors opened and I stepped out into the hush of a room. Hushed except for the audible clicks of several guns.

I laughed. "Please. You think that would stop me from wiping the room with all of you?"

"Phoenix?" Tank stepped forward.

I nodded. "I have a guest coming to speak to me."

Tank's tiny eyes opened about as wide as they could,

which meant they looked almost normal in size. "You want a room?"

"Yes. And then you and I are going to have a chat." I stepped forward and dropped a hand on his shoulder, pulling him forward so my mouth was close to his ear, no easy feat with his size against my own. "You talked about me to the wrong person, Tank. I thought we were friends."

A shudder slid through him. "We are friends."

"Friends don't rat on each other. Especially when we are some of the few normals here." I gave him a little push away from me as the elevator dinged behind me. Abe gave a woof of recognition and I half-turned to see Simon step out. Apparently, Abe liked Simon. I wasn't sure how I felt about that.

For now, I would take it as a sign to go forward with my plan. I crooked a finger for Simon to follow me deeper into the basement level.

"Third door on the left is open," Tank called after me.

I followed his instructions, flicked on the light as I went into the room and Simon walked through after me.

"You friends with Mancini?" His eyebrows went up. "That wasn't in your dossier."

"Luca Romano didn't care how I made things happen, only that I did it well and quickly. He was buddy-buddy with those who ran business in line with his. I took that as a nod to use those I could."

"Why are you telling me so much?" He frowned at me.

I smiled back. "Because you want money from Romano. And I want to make him suffer."

His eyebrows shot up. "A partnership then?"

"Temporary. One job only, enough to get you the money owed to you."

"And what do you get out of it?" He circled around the

one table in the center of the room and pulled up a folding chair.

I sat across from him in a similar chair. Abe sat beside me, his eyes locked onto Simon. Though he might like the tracker, he wasn't trusting him.

Good boy, Abe, I thought.

"I make him hurt." I said. "I'm going to make him bleed, Simon. The offshoot of that is I'll be taking what is most important to him. Money and standing with the Collective."

His eyes were thoughtful.

"What are you thinking in terms of a plan?" Simon spread his hands on the table. "I have some information—"

"Romano is running a new business in California." I slid one of the papers I'd taken from the office in the folder across the table. "From what I can see, it's bringing in a couple million a month. What I've heard makes me suspect some sort of magical drug running." He didn't need to know about the merger with Mancini. I would keep that tight to me and use it if I had to.

Simon took the paper and looked it over. "Where did you get this?"

"Doesn't matter," I said. "What matters is if we can find where this setup is, we both get what we want. You get money, and I get to make Romano pay for what he did to me."

Simon pushed the paper back to me. "What exactly did he do?"

My eyebrows shot up. "You don't know?"

He shook his head. "Nope, I was just to find you. Not an easy task, if I may say so. Took me twelve months, longer than any other job. Your Hider did an excellent job. Why did he quit?"

"He didn't." I frowned. "You know a guy named Peters?"

Simon's eyes widened. "Peters? Death magic Peters?"

I nodded. "He broke the Hiding on my home, and that rippled outward." I changed the subject. "How much per month does Romano owe you?"

"Hundred grand."

"And he paid you none of it?"

He shrugged. "Just enough to keep going for twelve months, a tenth of what was owed, but when I went for my final paycheck this last week, and told him you were in Jackson Hole, well, he pulled a gun on me, and had me escorted out by the Shadow."

I fought a shudder. The Shadow was the second of my father's guardians, and while the Stick Man was deadly and freaked me right the fuck out, the Shadow was one that truly scared me. I'd never met the third of the guardians.

I pulled my shit together. "That sounds about right."

Where Luca could, he made sure his money stayed with him, no matter what contract he had. I mulled over his words a minute. "He knew I was in Jackson Hole?"

"As of a few days ago he did, that's when I went in to get my pay day."

I schooled my face as I asked my next question. "Did you give him my new name? Did he know I was Bea Stark, married to Justin, mother of Bear?"

Simon nodded. "Yes, I gave him all of the info. That was my job."

That burning rage that had fueled my life since Bear was killed arced through me in a sharp shot like lightning. There was no way Romano wouldn't have fed that information to my brothers. Which meant Tommy had known when I'd faced him in the restaurant why I was there. He'd known that Luca had killed my husband and son.

And he'd not been sorry even a little that his nephew was dead.

I closed my eyes and placed my hands flat on the table as

I struggled to breathe around this new truth. A miniscule part of me had thought that perhaps, just perhaps, if my family had known that it had been my boy, my husband, who had been killed, that there might be some remorse. That maybe there would be some reflection that striking down a child was not a smart thing for so many reasons.

The words came from me slow and measured. "He had my husband and son killed, and he knows it now, even if he didn't when it happened."

"Holy shit." Simon breathed the words softly. "Your boy was just a kid?"

"Yes." I opened my eyes, letting the rage fill them, letting it flood through my veins until I felt nothing but the anger burning a path through my every nerve ending. "Now you know why I want to make him suffer."

"Why not just kill him?" Simon lifted an eyebrow, looked me over in a way that was all too thorough. He frowned. "Wait, you went to kill him tonight, didn't you?"

I nodded. "He wasn't where he should have been. So be glad about that." I was shaking with fury. "Death won't hurt him enough. What will hurt him is if I wipe out his business. If I take all his money. He doesn't attach to people, Simon. He attaches to money."

He was quiet a moment, then went back to our previous part of the discussion. "He doesn't ever cheat Mancini?"

"That's just suicide."

"Which is why he was so pissed at you taking that cool million." Simon glanced at me, and I didn't correct him that it had been five million I'd taken. "He still paid Mancini his cut, which meant he was out double the amount."

I smiled and couldn't help the laugh. "Good. He damn well deserves to be ass-fucked until he bleeds out his mouth."

Simon barked a laugh and pointed a finger at me. "You're subtle. I like it."

"Don't get used to it. I'm headed to Cali right now. You coming with me?"

"Plan along the way?"

I nodded. "Yes. I'll drive."

The thing was, I was too keyed up to do anything but stay awake. I felt like I'd had an IV placed in me with a steady intense drip of caffeine. I was no longer shaking, and everything was clear, bright, and sure in my head.

The intense desire for revenge was still there, but I didn't want Luca Romano to die, not until he saw his empire crushed under my heel, not until he realized I took away everything he held dear, that the revenge was complete and as sweet as it could be before I cut his still-beating heart out of his chest.

CHAPTER TWENTY-ONE

Taking on a partner—other than Abe and my girls—was not something I would have ever considered even twenty-four hours ago. In the past, I'd worked alone. I'd done my jobs solo because there was less mess, less concern that someone else would fuck up the mark. I'd never even taken Zee with me. He'd been my mentor, one I planned with. But he'd kept his hands clean.

I glanced at the sleeping Simon. Abe had his face on my lap, and his tail on the abnormal's. Driving across country would take a few days, less if we took shifts like this. By then, we'd be forced to get another vehicle. That would give me time to find out what Simon was capable of.

From the backseat inside my bag came a muffled grumble. Not Dinah nor Eleanor.

Linx.

I reached back and pulled the silver tool out. Linx shivered in my hands, and took on the form of a small silver hammer. "Whack me on his knees. I'll wake him up."

"Linx, what can you turn into exactly?"

I laid him on the dashboard in front of me. Without Rose, there was no levitation.

He shimmered and started shifting between shapes as he spoke. "Anything that is a tool. Key. Tweezers. Hammer. Plyers. Ice pick. Whatever."

"And if I ask you to shift into something you've not done before?" I flexed my hands on the steering wheel, thinking.

"Like what, sweet cheeks?"

Oh, God. Another smart-mouthed inanimate object. "Like a knife?"

He flickered and shimmered, lengthening to a knife in only seconds. "What else?"

"Throwing star?"

"Done. Listen. Rose wanted me to come with you and that's cool," Linx said, "but the deal is really this. Any tool, anything you can think of, I can become within a size parameter. Like if you ask for an axe, I can do it but it'll be smaller than what you want."

"Got it." I reached up and pulled him from the dash, setting him against my thigh.

Fatigue was finally catching up to me as the first rays of the new day cut through the clouds. "Simon."

"I'm awake." He grunted the words. "You got some fucked-up weapons, Phoenix."

I ignored the unspoken question of where I got them from. "We'll stop to eat, then you can take over driving for a bit."

He rubbed at his face and nodded. The next truck stop appeared in the distance and I headed for it, pulling off the interstate.

After taking Abe for a quick walk on the minimal amount of grass, getting him water and breakfast, I went inside to where Simon had already dug into a huge platter of flapjacks, sausage, eggs, hash browns and toast. I wrinkled my nose and ordered my own breakfast from the waitress.

"Steak and eggs, steak rare, coffee with two cream and sugar."

The waitress was gone a second later and I leaned over, taking a slice of toast off Simon's plate. His eyebrows shot up. "That seems rather familiar considering we just met."

I slathered the slice of toast with peanut butter and took a bite. "You won't be able to finish that anyway." I motioned at the plate. Small talk was not something I was good at. I hoped he picked up on that and just stayed quiet—

"What did you do in Jackson Hole all those years?"

I had to fight to unclench my jaw and take another bite of the toast. I spoke around it. Maybe that would drive the point home that I wasn't interested in talking. "Horses."

"Horses?"

"Raised and sold them. Arabians for the most part, sport models, not the show lines. Did you not look that up when you found me?"

He shook his head. "Nope. Found you, that was my job."

"Sloppy. Devil's in the details," I said.

He frowned over a bite of eggs halfway to his mouth. "Sloppy?"

"You're looking for a known killer, and you don't research what's going on around her? You don't know that her son and husband were killed by the man who sent *you* looking for her? You don't know who else is there on the ranch?"

"None of that mattered." He waved his fork at me, then shoved the food into his mouth. I snorted and shook my head.

"Zee is a Hider. It would have mattered."

"I can handle a Hider."

I frowned over my toast. "What are you then? You look

for people, you're a killer, you're abnormal. But what is your designation?"

"Shit, I haven't heard it put that way for years." He dug into his eggs, scooping several bites into his mouth. He swallowed and pointed his fork at me. "Designation dangerous."

I rolled my eyes. "You would have been in trouble if you'd run into Zee, I'm telling you that now."

Justin wouldn't have killed Simon on sight; shit, he'd have invited him in for dinner. But Zee . . . Zee would have killed him and buried the body out back in the shit pile. He might not have ever told me either so I wouldn't worry.

"What are you smiling about?"

"Thinking about you being killed by my uncle."

"That's not very nice." He didn't seem overly bothered as he continued to shovel food into his mouth, which impressed me. I laughed and shrugged.

"Don't ask me a question if you aren't prepared for an honest answer," I pointed out.

The waitress came back and plopped my steak and eggs in front of me. I dug in, eating fast, catching up to Simon in no time. When I realized he was no longer eating, I looked up and found him staring at me with wide eyes.

"You do speed eating competitions in your spare time?"

I grunted and kept shoveling. Food was fuel, and I needed it to keep going, which was why I went straight to the protein. The more, the better.

I was finished before Simon, even though he had a head start on me.

"You going to spill yet?" It was my turn to point my fork at him.

"You'd call me a chameleon. My magic gives me the ability to blend in with my surroundings. Different than a Hider who just disappears." He looked to his food. "Chameleon with a penchant for speed."

"A blended abnormal then, a parent of each kind?" I asked.

"Far as I know." His face closed off. I knew the end of a conversation when I saw it.

I flipped some money onto the table and glanced out the window to see two police officers approaching my truck. Well, my stolen truck.

Abe paced side to side in the truck, and his jaw flapped open as he barked.

"We've got company." I'd thought I'd have longer before we'd have to switch out vehicles. The time stamp said I still had two days. Apparently, it was off.

I was out the door and moving fast toward the truck. I had both guns on a shoulder holster hidden under my light coat.

"Officer," I called out when I was still twenty feet away, "is there a problem?"

The two cops swung around and faced me, their bodies and faces tense. "This your truck?"

I nodded. "It is. And that's my dog you're upsetting."

The first officer put his hand on his belt. "We're looking for a truck that fits this description. Driven by a woman with her dog."

"What for?" I blinked my eyes as wide as I could, hoping I could talk my way out of this. Broad daylight out in the public was not the best place to start pulling guns out.

"You entered a club with weapons out in New York last night?" the second officer said.

"Did you get a license plate number? Because I haven't been in New York."

"Where are you headed?"

Shit. I knew where this was going. They would detain me here with questions long enough that either they would get backup here, or I would be forced to go into the local police station for questioning. Neither of which could happen. All of which meant Romano was using his connections to Mancini to hunt me down faster now that there had been a legit sighting, and Zee was obviously not with me.

Of course, it probably hadn't helped that I threatened Romano and his money.

Simon stepped up beside me and slid an arm around my waist. "Honey, are you ready to go? My mother is going to be seriously pissed if we are late again."

I glanced at him. "These two officers think I was in a night club in New York last night."

He burst out laughing and there was a tingle over my skin. Simon was doing something with his magic. I had to fight not to push him off me.

"We were in a hotel down the road here. Couple miles back," Simon said.

The second officer opened a notebook and took a pen out. "What hotel is that?"

Simon didn't hesitate. "Easy Inn Motel. On the cheaper end, but you know how it is being newlyweds."

He could spin a story fast, I'd give him that. While the officers wrote down the information Simon gave them—including a phone number and home residence—we worked our way to the truck. I handed him the keys. "You should drive now, you're a better driver, honey, 'cause all this has gotten me shook up."

The one cop made a sad face, the other narrowed his eyes. Apparently, my skill at lying had gotten rusty.

We were back in the truck and pulling onto the interstate before I dared a look over my shoulder. "We need a new vehicle."

"Yeah, I picked up on that." Simon glanced in the mirror. "I can try cloaking us, but it will still be a truck."

In the far distance, the flicker of red and blue lights lit up the morning sky.

Shit. "Faster, Simon. They've already called the motel."

He hit the gas and the truck raced down the highway. We hit the next exit at top speed, almost sliding down the offramp.

So much for sleeping while Simon drove.

We were under the offramp and heading into the suburbs around the highway when the red and blue lights went across the interstate behind us.

"How long before they figure out we took the exit?" Simon asked.

"Ten minutes max before they turn around and realize we aren't on the highway." I kept my eyes on the road, looking for a place to ditch the truck and find something else. The "something else" would be a problem. A stolen car would be reported within hours . . . a flashing sign for a rental place popped up. That had possibility.

"There. You go in on your own and rent a vehicle. I'll meet you back at the underpass."

"Done." He hopped out and leaned in. "See you later, *honey*."

I rolled my eyes and slid across over Abe—not as easy as it sounds—and took the wheel. I waited until Simon jogged into the parking lot of the rental place, then steered the truck to the left, spinning around until I was headed back the way we'd come.

Which was how I passed the cops as they came flying into the suburbs. I gave them a wave and hit the gas.

Whoever said a killer wasn't allowed to have any fun when on the hunt for revenge was truly wrong. I kept my foot jammed to the floor, the engine roaring as the truck gave me all it had. Abe panted excitedly beside me and I hit the power window button, rolling both down so the rush of air whipped up my hair and his fur.

There was the pop of a gun going off at the same time the back window of the truck shattered.

"They are not playing today, are they, Abe?"

"Can we help please?" Dinah yelled. "I smell bullets!"

I pulled Dinah out and shifted my weight so I could point her out the now-shattered window. I couldn't aim much, so I pointed as best I could toward the hood and let Dinah do the rest. If I could take the engine out, that would buy me the time I needed. I squeezed the trigger and the sound of a bullet hitting the flat of the hood made me smile.

"Good job, Dinah."

The cops veered off to the left and I took a hard right and found what I was looking for at the far end of the street, a dead end with an alley running between two houses.

I hit the gas hard and cranked the wheel, straightening the truck out. The truck all but flew down the narrow street.

I slammed on the brakes as the truck slid into the alley, grabbed my backpack and leapt out before the wheels had fully stopped moving. Abe was right behind me as we ran between the two houses.

The cop car screeched to a stop and two car doors slammed. Good. They were on foot, which gave me the edge.

I circled around the first house and back to the street. I spun on the silencer to Dinah's muzzle and shot out the tires in the cop car and my truck in quick succession while Dinah giggled.

Hiking my small pack onto my back, I ran across the street, heading toward the interstate. I wasn't sure Simon would be waiting for me, and if he decided to leave me out high and dry, then I would have to come up with Plan B in record time. Hitchhiking was always a possibility, but getting someone to pick me and Abe up would take time.

Time was not something I would have if Simon ditched us.

Abe and I wove our way through the small subdivision until we were on the main road that would take us to the highway. There was heavy bush on either side of the road, and if I cut through it we would shave time off and keep out of sight. With a sigh, I checked my wrist watch for the compass, making sure we headed the right way, and slid down the embankment that took me into the thicker bush.

Abe leapt ahead of me, bouncing through the long grass.

Ten minutes into the bushwhacking, I checked my wrist compass again and made a slight adjustment. The interstate was a bit more to the east, and I angled us that way. Sweat ran down my face and my hands and legs were covered in scratches, but I didn't dare slow.

The cops back there may have been fat and slow, but it wouldn't take them long to get back involved.

The growing sound of traffic on the interstate was like music to my ears as it began to filter through the underbrush.

I picked up my pace. Seconds later, the trees and undergrowth thinned and I was on the edge of another embankment that led up to the road directly under the interstate. I crouched for ten seconds.

No sirens yet. Which meant it was now or never. I bolted up the slope and looked down one direction of the road and then the other.

No Simon. "Son of a bitch." I bit the words out and hiked my pack on my shoulders a little higher. Even if I could get a disguise going for me, Abe wasn't going to be able to go incognito.

I started toward the onramp to the interstate. My best bet would be to get up there and see if I could get a trucker to pick me up.

If I ever ran into Simon again, I was going to kill him.

I broke into a jog, even while I slid a leash back onto Abe. "Let's move, buddy."

He gave me a woof and paced himself beside me.

Halfway up the onramp, the sound of an engine behind us slowed me. A dark blue sedan flicked its lights, then slowed as it drew close. The side window rolled down and Simon leaned over.

"Not very patient, are you?"

I yanked the back door open and let Abe and myself in.

"Move," I said. "This is only going to buy us long enough to get to the next town if we are lucky."

"Already on it, darling."

My eyebrows shot up. "I think not."

Simon laughed and got the car going again. I leaned back in my seat. "Wake me if you need me."

I closed my eyes, Simon flicked on the radio to a local station and I pretended to sleep.

CHAPTER TWENTY-TWO

We drove across country in a little under two days, switching off with each other enough that we never stopped for more than taking care of the necessities of life. Eating and shitting. Changing vehicles twice more.

The plan we developed as we drove was simple. We knew the name of the business my father was operating under. We knew it was going to be some illegal magic shit just based on the amount of money coming through. Blue Hills Studios was a brand-new movie studio that was already making three to five million a month with no movies to its name that we could find.

Simon assured me this was what he was good at, that he could find it in no time.

We would go in, strip the business of its goods, take the money we found, and leave a nice note for Romano so he knew exactly who to blame.

Me.

A part of my brain pointed out that it was suicide. That the Stick Man would find me.

A form of bringing the heat down on me that eventually I wouldn't be able to outrun.

I didn't care. Even when Simon pointed out the same thing. "You realize if you tell him it was you again, he'll send all he's got at you? Possibly all three guardians."

"Yes," I nodded, my heart rate spiking at the thought, "I'm counting on it. I have to kill the guardians at some point; might as well bring them to me."

"You got bigger balls than me," he mumbled. I almost smiled.

We were getting close to LA but still hadn't nailed down the details of the plan. Mostly because as far as we could tell, Blue Hills Studio didn't exist except in name.

Simon tapped his phone. "Website is here, but it goes nowhere. Doesn't even link to projects they are working on. No address either."

"In other words, they aren't trying that hard to prove they are legit."

He grunted. "Yeah, they got nothing like that."

"Any pictures of the place?" I glanced at him. If we could get a layout that would help.

"Nothing."

I frowned. "How the fuck is the IRS not all over them?"

"Bought off. It happens, though no one talks about it." He leaned back. "Romano has got to have at least three people under his thumb in the IRS. I've seen it before with Mancini. Abnormals who can make paperwork disappear."

That got him a longer look from me. "How long have you worked for Mancini?"

"Only here and there." He stared at the tiny screen as he shook his head. "I'm a freelancer, like you."

"I'm not a freelancer," I said.

"Maybe you weren't, but you are now. What else are you

going to do? Finish this job and go play with your ponies again?"

His words cut through some of my own thoughts. I wasn't going to try for a normal life again; that was beyond stupid. Which left me this—a life I'd run from.

"I don't know."

I think my honesty surprised us both because neither of us spoke for the next hour.

Finally, I broke the silence. "I need to stretch my legs." We were on the outskirts of LA and I knew traffic was about to pick up. More than that, though, something niggled at the back of my mind.

LA was Noah's home base, or as much of a home base as he had.

Noah had been in on whatever Justin had been dealing with, and he had info on Romano.

I stretched as I walked around the car, thinking. I kept my head down and a ball cap pulled low to shade my eyes from the bright sun as I searched through what I knew, looking for the answer that dodged me.

I pulled my cell phone out and dialed Noah's home number. It clicked through to his answering machine. "Noah, here, leave me your details and I'll get back to you asap."

Asap. Who the fuck said that anymore. I waited for the beep and then took a long breath I knew would pick up on the machine. "Noah. You lit my house on fire, you bastard. You have info on Romano I want and now you owe me." I paused and thought about what would bring him to me. "I don't have the coded papers, but I know who does." I clicked the end button.

Hell, I hadn't even left him a number to reach me, but I didn't think that would matter. Noah would find me if the papers meant anything.

Abe sniffed around the edges of the pull-out, but didn't go far, his eyes always coming back to me, to check on me.

I snapped my fingers at him, then let us both back into the current rental vehicle, a crappy older van that smelled vaguely of vomit. The only good thing was all the room in the back for Abe.

Simon climbed into the driver's seat, put his hands on the steering wheel and waited.

"I have a place we can start," I said.

He smiled. "See, I knew you were more than a pretty face."

I ignored him. The whole trip had been like that with him complimenting me and making flirtatious remarks. I knew men like Simon. Men who, whether they were abnormal or not, thought I would be flattered by a nice word or two, that I would let my guard down because they were charming. I didn't dissuade him of the idea, but let him continue thinking he was winning me over. I knew his game.

He had no idea how deep mine was being played.

Nor was I such a fool as to believe he had any actual interest in me. Men who worked in the circles of hell we lived in did not have women they took home. They had women they fucked once and left.

I nodded more to myself than to him. "Head to Lincoln Heights. There were a few apartments where the landlords don't ask a lot of questions and it's close to the 10."

Simon tapped his fingers on the steering wheel. "I know the area. Smart to be close to the highway if we have to run." He flashed me a smile, and I looked away.

I'd let him drive while I tried to straighten out what was running through my head. Would Romano realize I was coming here first? If he was smart, he'd try to see if he could figure out what files I'd taken from the office. Try to figure out where I would go next. And if he had someone working for him now, taking my place, they might already be onto us. Who was I kidding? He had three guardians that were hunters in their own right.

He'd stopped needing me the second they'd come online with him.

"Is it true that Romano made a deal with the devil?" Simon asked as he navigated traffic as well as one could here in LA.

"Yes."

"Nothing more than that, just yes? Come on, Phoenix, give me the dirt."

I looked out the window while I found the words. Because I'd been there when the deal was signed, the scene so impressed on me that I doubted I would ever forget it.

"He had a dealer in death magic use some ancient texts to call up the devil into his office."

"Like as in Lucifer?" Simon asked.

I shrugged. "He called himself Bazixal. A demon, a kind of devil. He offered my father steadily growing power and money for as long as he lived. The cost was simple. A soul that would be given at the end of my father's life."

"Shit. That seems a high cost."

I had to agree. Until that moment in my life, I wasn't sure I believed in souls, because if I had, I knew mine would be black. "He signed the paper in his blood. Bazixal gave Romano a mark on the inside of his wrist, and it was sealed."

Simon let out a long, low whistle that made Abe perk up in the back. "Your father's soul for money and power."

"My father did not offer his own soul. He offered *a soul*." I shook my head. It had not been Romano's name on the paper, that was all I knew.

"Happy?" I asked.

Simon shook his head. "Not really. The three guardians he was given?"

"A second deal around the time I stepped out. I wasn't there for it. The Stick Man, the Shadow, and the Strike. In that order of dangerousness."

"And they are immortal so they can't be killed." He shook his head.

I didn't tell him what Rose had said to me, that blood fire would kill the Stick Man. Because he was the only abnormal around me, and my reputation was such that he would likely think I kept him around to use his blood to save me. And that wouldn't necessarily be incorrect.

Minutes later, we were in the Lincoln Heights area. Simon pulled into a small parking lot attached to an Oriental grocery store, Pho Bong, and we both got out. Abe, too, as it was far too hot to leave him in the car even with the windows rolled down. Early May and already Hollywood was warm enough for T-shirts. Even though those who lived here were still bundled in coats and pants.

As always Abe stuck close to me. He didn't need the leash but the law was the law, and the last thing we needed was some beat cop asking questions about us.

The apartment we procured was small, one bedroom with a single bed. I lifted an eyebrow at Simon, but kept my thoughts to myself. From the banter between him and the owner—all in Mandarin—there had been a two-bedroom rental available too, but Simon had declined.

We tossed our small number of belongings into the room.

"Okay, let's nail down this plan then, shall we? Bits and pieces is all well and good, but I'd like to keep my skin attached if possible." Simon leaned against the door with his arms folded over his chest. His facial hair had grown in over the two-day drive and it made him a far more interesting looking person. Less of the unobtrusive blend into the world face he had first presented to me.

I arched an eyebrow. "We have a break-in to plan and a

studio to find. I think I have a guy who can get me the info and tools we need to accomplish both."

Simon pushed off the wall.

"You need me to come with you?"

I snorted at him and held up the list we'd made. "Got my grocery list."

He paused after he opened the door, and looked over his shoulder. There was something in his eyes, and I held up my hand, stopping him.

"No. Don't go there. We aren't those kinds of friends. We meet back here. If you don't show up, I'll assume you're either dead, or turned on me."

He winked at me. "We may not be that kind of friends yet, Nix. Give me time, I'll win you over."

Before I could tell him to go fuck himself, he shut the door behind him and was gone to take the car back to the rental place.

I put him from my mind in seconds.

The thing was, covering your tracks was never as simple as the movies made it look. Nor nearly as glamorous. Things like returning a vehicle to a rental place, rather than blowing it up, or some shit like that. A returned rental was never suspected. It was only the missing ones the police tracked down.

"Head on straight, Nix," I said to myself.

From my stash of things, I tugged out a wad of cash, a little over ten thousand dollars, and stuffed it into a cheap-looking purse. Small enough to not carry anything important. I glanced over the list.

Cameras, tablet, two USB storage drives, wireless hookups, night vision goggles, detonators, C4, a couple of GPS tracers, and a few things I hadn't used before, being that they were on the magical spectrum. Simon insisted on them.

Gag jam, spider's bolt, bit boom, smarm, and blinding.

The words were weird and they made me uncomfortable just looking at them.

Didn't matter, I knew where to get it all, hot off the market, as it were.

Barron wouldn't be expecting me. I just hoped he was still where I'd last seen him. Knowing him, as long as he wasn't dead, he wouldn't have moved. Lazy didn't even begin to cover the man.

I settled Abe in the room with water and an open window, told him to guard, and put a note on the outside of the door for Simon saying if he went in without me, Abe would eat his balls.

Smiling to myself, I was out of the building in minutes and off to my next stop.

Los Angeles was hardly my home turf, but I'd been sent to the West Coast more than a few times for jobs. During those trips, I'd met people who could be key in making things happen.

The best part about Barron was that—if he was still alive —he wouldn't ask questions like "What do you need this high-end, night-vision camera for? Why do you need this much C4 wiring? Are you trying to blow shit up? What kind of magic shit is this?" Those were the kind of questions we needed to avoid.

I flagged a cab and directed the driver to the higher-end side of town where Barron had set up his home and shop loaded with smart people, and smarter thieves. He'd bought a house on the dividing line between Brentwood and Encino.

The cabbie was happy to take me as it was an hour drive and easily a hundred-dollar fare.

"Visiting Hollywood for the first time?" He looked in the rearview mirror.

I didn't answer him, just stared out the window.

He tried once more and when I didn't answer, he gave up.

The hour passed slowly.

"That gate there." I pointed out my destination to the cabbie and he dutifully pulled over. There was no number on the gate, no name.

"Want me to wait?" The cabbie arched an eyebrow at me.

I handed him his money and got out.

He muttered under his breath, then left me there with a squeal of his tires. I stood in front of the gate, wondering if Barron still lived here. He had been an interesting one. A little older than me, he was quiet, thoughtful, and far too polite for being a thief. At least, that was what I'd always thought.

I hit the call button on the gate, buzzing through.

"NO VISITORS," a voice roared through the speakers, rattling it until the words were nearly indistinguishable from each other.

I pressed the button again. And again, and again. Best way to get a bee to come out of the hive was to keep poking at the nest.

"FUCKING LITTLE SHITS, GET AWAY FROM MY HOUSE!" It sounded like Barron. Though, I didn't remember him being such a spaz.

"Barron, is that any way to talk to a friend?" I spoke clearly, and just loud enough to be heard.

There was a static silence for a solid twenty seconds before he answered.

"Who is this?"

"You can't see me?" I turned to wave at the small camera tucked into the top of the twelve-foot gate. Small enough that if you weren't looking for it, you'd miss it.

"Holy shit. Phoenix?"

The gate buzzed open and swung inward. I started up the long drive, the heels of my boots a soft patter on the concrete.

The walk to the front door of the mansion was short, and yet . . . I felt like I'd stepped back in time. Like I was twenty years old again, and ready to run from my family.

Barron had been key in helping me escape, and at the time, I'd thought he was going with me. Stupid fool that I'd been.

He flung the door open before I could even knock.

Not smart. He'd lost some of his edge since I'd seen him last.

"I thought you were dead." He looked me over, his eyes wide.

I gave him the same once-over. Tall and thin, his dark hair had gone from the slightly messy unkempt surfer locks to a full-on long shag with some gray at the temples. It didn't look good on him.

He'd filled out some, living on good food and booze; his body had slid into the softness of middle age. Maybe not to anyone else's eyes, but I could see he was not keeping up with his regimen he'd claimed he had before. There were no more sit-ups before his morning coffee.

"Not dead yet," I said. "You still selling?"

His eyes flickered. "Of course not. Come on in. I'll put coffee on."

"Tea, actually," I said.

"Sure, you got it."

Look at us, chatting away like old friends, I thought. A game between us, which meant he was still suspicious of who was watching him and when. That he was still alive had been a gamble. The last I'd seen of him, Barron had been working for Romano, Mancini, and Killian Fannin, the pain in the ass Irish gangster trying to revive the old-school power of the Irish abnormal gangs. Fannin currently was costing Romano money by undercutting him in the various skeevy trade deals they ran. Which made me like him more, even though he claimed connections to the fae. But that was a load of horseshit as far as I was concerned. His cause was a lost one, despite what his current success at irritating Romano looked like. Still, I gave Killian credit for not only being stubborn, but for being a shot of shit in Romano's morning cereal.

For that alone, I would root for him.

Barron, juggling the three powerhouse men, had been a stupid thing, but profitable. He claimed he didn't help one of them over the other, that all had equal access to the same arsenals, etc.

I made sure of it when I'd asked him to help me get away from Romano, telling Barron the darkest side of my family to secure his help. I'd begged, I'd thrown myself at him . . . and it had worked.

Barron had wiped away any record of my existence and helped me create a new name, a new life, a new world that I'd run to as fast as I could.

I followed him through the main part of the house, taking in the high ceilings and gaudy artwork. Nothing had changed.

"Sorry for the mess. The housekeeper won't be here until later." He looked over his shoulder. "You look good. What are you going by now?"

I tipped my head. "Nix is just fine." I paused. "No wife yet?" I asked.

He snorted. "Nah. Women are trouble. You know that."

"They are," I murmured as I stepped into his kitchen. As massive as the rest of the house, it held a certain warmth the other rooms lacked. Barron made me tea and poured himself a cup of coffee, all while saying nothing.

And yet it told me a great deal. He was being watched everywhere, and he knew it. Which meant we needed a safe place to talk.

"You want to come downstairs with me? I still have the lingerie you like." He smiled over the rim of his coffee cup, a dimple appearing in one cheek. Yeah, he was still a little swoon-worthy. His eyes were kind, and that had been the draw then. I'd met very few kind men in my life, and Barron had been the first.

Justin had been the second, even if he'd turned out to be a con artist.

I took a sip of my tea, grimaced and added another teaspoon of sugar. "Sure, I haven't had a romp in a while."

Again, I followed him. A game for anyone watching. We weren't being exactly subtle, but in our world, women rarely were. It was fuck or be fucked.

From the kitchen, he led me downstairs, past a big open room with a TV and multiple gaming systems set up.

"Still with the games." I wasn't questioning him, just surprised. I'd run away and grown up, he'd stayed behind and remained being a kid.

An uncomfortable twitch started in my heart region. I'd asked Barron to come with me, and he said he would, until the morning after. That had been the last time I'd fallen for a man's line about loving me.

I blinked at the sudden prickle in my eyes. Not for Barron. But for Justin . . . I'd believed his lies too. I clenched my mug and forced the emotions down. No place for them in my life right now.

Maybe not ever again.

Barron went to a steel door with a punch code beside it. He fired in some numbers, then pressed his thumb to a black pad. The square beeped green twice, then the steel door opened. I kept close to Barron knowing—

The door slammed hard behind me, the edge of it brushing against the back of my shirt. The room was as it had always been. Walls covered in a variety of equipment, shelving units filled to bursting, cables, computers; everything in here was black, white, silver and glimmered of red. One wall was dedicated to magic and the aura around that shelving unit all but buzzed with electricity even though the panels on it were closed.

Well organized, but loaded literally to the ceiling. Barron was the kind of thief who could waltz into a bank and walk out without a single camera catching him on it, without a single clue, without the vault even looking like it had been tampered with. He was one of the best.

He'd joked once that Fort Knox would have been a cake walk, but what would you do with all those gold bars?

My eyes swept the room, looking for anyone else. We were alone.

Barron took a couple of steps, set his coffee down, and spun back to me. I braced myself until I saw his intent, and then I relaxed. He tucked a hand behind the back of my head and pulled my mouth to his. The kiss was only mildly unexpected but I let him do it, maybe I even wanted it a little, maybe I even kissed him back. It had been almost four months since I'd had any sort of physical contact with someone I cared about. No . . . I did not care about Barron. That was in the past. As was so much. He drew his lips from mine, but didn't pull further away. He pressed his forehead against mine, his hands cupping my face.

"Girl . . . I never thought I'd see you again."

I laughed and pushed him away, not hard enough to make him stumble, just enough to give me room. "You didn't want to come with me. That was years ago. And I'm hardly a girl anymore."

"I never stopped thinking about you. Wondering if you were alive." His eyes were wide and I knew him well enough to know he was telling the truth. A good thief he was, a good liar he was not.

A bad combination all around.

I shrugged. "I'm back now. And I have a grocery list." I

handed him the sheet of paper that Simon had filled out. Most of it had been his suggestions.

Barron looked it over. "Yeah, I've got it all. Looks like a big hit. You back working for your dad?"

I shook my head. The less he knew, the better for both of us. "Freelancing."

He barked a laugh. "Your father okay with that?"

I smiled and shrugged.

Barron's laugh died slowly. "Phoenix—Nix—what is going on? You swore you'd never come back."

"Stop stalling, Barron. I have the money." I pulled my backpack around.

"I'm sure you do. I have a few things I think you'd like to add to this too." He sat at his computer. "Some excellent new material. It's a type of spider silk created by the Yakuza. Done all in black, stronger than Kevlar." He tapped a few keys and then leaned back for me to look over his shoulder.

The material was black with the faintest of shine to it. "How do you stitch it then?"

"Magic." He winked at me. "You want it, don't you?"

"Hell, yeah." I breathed the words out. Stronger than Kevlar, and lightweight, and all in my favorite color. "A full suit?"

"You got it. Will take some time and it'll be costly." He pushed me back, leaned over the keyboard and his fingers flew across it.

"I've got cash. Not with me, but I've got it."

He grinned and ran a finger under my chin. "Measurements?"

I fired the numbers off. "5'9", 140 lbs, 36, 25, 35, inseam is 34."

"Damn." His eyes flicked to me and away again. I didn't move a muscle.

A few minutes later he nodded. "Done. Now to the rest of

it. I need to know who you are going after to make sure it's not my boss."

I frowned and took a step back. "You've decided to work for only one guy?"

The flicker in his eyes told me everything. I couldn't help the surprise from skittering across my face.

"Who did you sell out to, Barron?"

He grabbed an office chair and sat down heavily. "It was that or get killed. Things changed fast after you left. Your dad hired thugs to do his work and they were sloppy, getting caught and killed, or tossed in jail. Mr. Mancini didn't seem to care what was going on as long as he got his paychecks every month and . . ."

"Killian then?" I put my mug on a side counter.

Barron gave a short nod. "Yes. He's come up in the ranks fast, building an empire that is putting pressure on the old boys. Whatever magic he's dabbling in, it's working for him."

"He didn't seem more than a thorn in their sides before." I found a chair and pulled it up.

"True, but the thing is, he's hungry for it. He's our age, and he wants . . . well, it doesn't matter what he wants." Barron shook his head. "He's . . ."

He trailed off as he turned toward a row of security monitors. "Shit, speak of the Irish devil."

I stood and leaned over his shoulder, pressing my chest against his back a little. Reminding him that he'd wanted me once, and that he still did. He slung a hand backward, finding my upper thigh and giving it a squeeze.

"I have to meet with him," he said.

"I want to meet him, too. If he's in as far as you say, I might be able to use his help," I said.

Barron startled. "You think that's a good idea?"

I stared hard at the monitor as Killian Fannin let himself

into Barron's house as though he owned the place. Maybe he did.

"Yes, Romano hates him. I hate Romano."

Barron shook his head but I was already turning away to the door. "I will still need that list of things. Barron, get them together and I will greet Mr. Fannin."

"Phoenix—"

"Trust me." I looked over my shoulder. Slowly, he nodded.

"Okay, just . . . play nice. He's smarter than he lets on."

He hit a button and the steel door slid open. I stepped out and headed toward the kitchen. No wonder Barron had signed on with Killian. My ex-lover had apparently no business sense when it came to the dark side.

There would be no way a Romano would have let someone he was working with go and greet someone he thought of as an employer. Barron was showing just how low on the ladder he was by letting me greet Killian on my own.

I kept my mug in one hand and did a quick check over Dinah and Eleanor before I stepped into the kitchen. "Girls?"

"Ready," they spoke in tandem.

Footsteps echoed through the house.

"Barron, where you be, lad?"

Lad. Like Killian was that much older than Barron. I snorted.

"He be busy, lad," I called out. "Sent me to welcome you to his humble home."

The footsteps slowed and the audible click of weapons being drawn and cocked slid through the air. A hint of ozone and coffee floated on the air and a few sparkles danced around me.

Sparkles that looked suspiciously like tiny fairies.

I stared at them, letting the darkness in me swell. They squealed and shot away at rapid speed.

I sat at the kitchen table, leaned my chair back and set my

boots on the glass top. Mug still cupped in my hands. Who sent fairies to check things out for you? If I'd been so inclined I could have smashed them flat. Apparently the connection to the fae was not so full of horseshit as I'd thought.

Two men swept into the kitchen first, ahead of Killian. Dressed in jeans and leather jackets, their heads were covered with caps from the local ball team. More than that, I focused on their weapons. The guns were up and trained on me right away, steady. Both carried Smith and Wesson. Not terribly original, but they'd do the job, and I had no doubt the two men would pull the trigger if they thought I was a threat. I smiled at them over the rim of my mug. "Hello, lads."

They didn't smile or respond. I looked past them to Killian as he walked into the room.

This was my first up-close and personal interaction with the man, though I'd known of him for years. The aura around him crackled and danced. Abnormal through and through; the only question was, what kind?

Taller than me, he cut an imposing figure and stood easily over six feet. Where Barron had let his fitness regime go, Killian looked as though he'd not only kept at one, but increased it regularly. Muscles slid under his almost too-tight clothes, showing off every cut angle of his physique.

His dark brown hair was slicked back, and as he pulled off sunglasses, green eyes flicked over me. Dismissing me as just another woman. I was about to change that.

"Your pictures don't do you justice," I said and took a sip of my now-cold tea. This was all about appearances, though.

Killian pursed his lips. "Where is Barron?"

I slowly placed the mug on the table. "In his room downstairs. He was naughty and needed a time out."

Killian arched an eyebrow and his lips twitched as though he would like to smile at the innuendo. What I knew of him was that he had a wicked temper, but also a ridiculous sense of humor.

I shrugged. "You know how it is, you don't see someone for years and years, and then when you show up on their doorstep, you have to remind them of their place."

"And what does his place be with you?" The Irish accent was light enough that the words held a soft burr.

I raised an eyebrow. "No guesses? I heard you liked games, Killian."

Killian waved a hand and the two thugs with him lowered their weapons. "Depends on the game, lass."

"Ah, lass, that's the nicest thing I've been called lately." I leaned back a little further in my chair. "Let me make this simple for you. I believe we have a common enemy."

He stepped around the island in the center of the kitchen, and leaned back on it. Mimicking me. Trying to put me at ease with psychological games. I looked around the room as though I wasn't worried about him at all. Waiting for him to ask.

Finally, he broke. "What enemy would that be?"

I ran a hand through my hair and looked back to him. "Romano."

One of the thugs grunted as though I'd hit him, but otherwise there was nothing from the three men. That is if I discounted the sharpening of one pair of very green eyes.

From the kitchen entrance, Barron cleared his throat. "Killian, meet Nix."

I stood slowly, unfolding from the chair. Hell, I even held my hand out to him. An offering of peace. "You might know me better as Phoenix."

Barron groaned softly. But he didn't know how this was played. He didn't understand.

Three guns were up in a flash, and the aura round Killian

brightened, but I didn't move, didn't withdraw my hand an inch.

"You are a royal pain in Romano's ass, Killian. And that means I like you. If I'd wanted you dead, you wouldn't be standing now." I smiled at him.

Barron groaned again. "Please, Nix, don't pick a fight."

I sighed and shook my head. "Killian, Barron does not understand this world, even now after all these years. But you and I do."

Killian took several swift steps toward me, his gun trained on my face as he pushed me back until I was against the wall, his palm flat between my breasts, hot and angry, prickles of energy flying from him to me.

"Why shouldn't I kill you? Why shouldn't I use you as bait for your father? You'll be worth something to him."

I kept my eyes on his. "Because I'm going after him. Because I'm about to make your job to take your place in the hierarchy of the underworld much easier. Because he wants me dead as much as he wants you dead. Because he deserves to suffer."

He frowned. "Why would you kill him?"

I wasn't sure Killian would care that my son had lost his life. These kinds of men rarely did. But they understood power and possession.

"He took something very valuable from me."

"Enough to make you kill your own father? Your brothers will just take over the Romano holdings."

I didn't blink. "I'm taking *everything* from him, Killian. Every fucking last thing."

He stepped back, the heat from his hand still imprinted on me through my shirt. "And you want my help."

I burst out laughing. "Not really. Just stay out of my way. I'm sure I'll see you and yours around, and if you see me," I shrugged, "you know where I stand."

Killian lowered his gun and looked back to a pale-faced Barron. "You trust her?"

"If she gives you her word, she'll hold to it. She isn't like him." Barron clutched the edge of the counter. I had a sudden image of him flat out on the floor, pale, lying in a pool of his own blood. That it hadn't happened already was a damn miracle.

But it was coming for him one day.

Killian tucked his gun away and held out his hand. "You stay out of my way, and I'll stay out of your way."

I nodded. "Done."

His hand tightened over mine and his muscles tensed. I braced for the pull.

He yanked me hard toward him so we were literally nose to nose. A powerful intimidation tactic, if it worked. Not so much on me. The air between us was hot and made my skin itch. He was doing something with his magic, and I didn't like it but I held still.

Killian stared down at me, his jaw ticking. "Lass, you be treading dangerous waters. This is not the same ocean you swam in before."

I smiled up at him. "You're right. Then I was a fish on a hook, trapped. Now I'm one of the sharks and I have a set of teeth that will gut any man in my way."

CHAPTER TWENTY-THREE

Killian and I stood in Barron's kitchen, measuring each other for another five seconds. Five seconds that felt like an hour. The intensity between us crackled and before I could catch the words, they were out of my mouth.

"I bet you're fun in the sack."

His eyes went wide and he stepped back from me. "That an offer?"

"Not at all." I shook my head. "I'd never actually bed an abnormal. Just making an observation." One that also made it so he let me go. Too close, that had been too close for my comfort.

I'd both complimented and insulted Killian in two sentences. Dangerous ground indeed.

"You got my stuff ready?" I looked past him to Barron who was as pale as before.

He nodded. "At the front door. Along with your empty bag."

He'd taken *all* my cash. "Nothing left for my cab ride home? You are a greedy prick, aren't you?"

He flushed as I strode past him.

I waved at the men. "Nice meeting you, Killian."

"Charmed, lass." He gave me a nod.

Good enough.

I reached the front door and the bag of gear Barron had set out for me in a large backpack. I slung it up onto my back, testing the weight. Thirty pounds. Maybe a little more. Everything would be wrapped individually, but hiking back into Lincoln Heights was going to be a bitch with that much weight. The drive had been over an hour, which meant the walk would take me into the night.

The murmur of deep male voices rolled from the kitchen to me, as I let myself out the front door. I didn't care what business Barron did with Killian. It kept my old friend alive, which was good for me. I had a feeling I was going to need him again, so whatever kept him on this side of the dirt was in my best interest.

Killian's SUV was massive, almost more Hummer than SUV, and as I walked by, I couldn't help but peek in the front seat. No one waited for the Irish gangster. I pulled my bag off my back and dug around fast. Just because I wasn't going to fight with Killian, didn't mean knowing where he was wouldn't hurt.

I slid the bag off my shoulder and dug around in it until I found one of the magnetic GPS trackers. I flicked it on and tucked it underneath the passenger side door. The magnet in it was strong enough that it jumped from my hand to the metal.

I smiled, stood, and started down the driveway. Always good to keep an eye on your allies in case they decided to become enemies.

I was at the front gate before the sound of a large engine starting up turned me around. The big vehicle did a fast U-turn in the driveway and headed my way. I stepped off the path.

The SUV slowed and the back window rolled down. Killian crooked his finger.

"We need to talk, lass." He opened the door to the big black SUV.

"Nah, I'm good. Thanks."

He reached out and I stepped back, and pulled Eleanor before he could so much as blink. "I said, I'm good."

He stared at me. "I'd heard you were a fast draw."

"Fastest in the west." I didn't lower the gun. "We are not friends; we are not enemies. What I do will benefit you. That's all you need to know."

His gaze didn't waver from me. "I want to know what it takes to turn a Romano on their own."

"Why does it matter?"

"Because I don't trust that he took something from you. Which means I don't trust you. Which means you might be an enemy after all."

"Again, what does it matter? I'm not working for or with you."

He smiled. "The enemy of my enemy is my friend. So you are my friend, or you are my enemy. Which is it?"

"Neither." I flicked the tip of my gun at him. "Get going, Irish. I have work to do. People to kill. I'd prefer for now you weren't on that list." I paused for effect, thinking fast. "Unless you want to tell me about a certain movie studio."

He leaned back. "One that belongs to your father?"

"To Romano, yes." I nodded and let my gun fall. "You know where it is?"

"I might," he gave me a slow smile. "What will you give me for the information you're looking for?"

"An exchange of information. And I want a ride out of here,

seeing as Barron took all my money." I tucked Eleanor away and stepped into the truck, over him. I set the bag between us, but did not put on my seatbelt. Who knew when I might have to jump out the window, or over the middle seats to take the wheel?

Killian shook his head. "Where to?"

"Outskirts of Lincoln Heights will do fine." Close enough that my walk would only be twenty minutes to the apartment, far enough away that I wasn't taking them to my doorstep.

"You heard her, lads." He didn't look at his two men as they grunted in unison to his command.

"They got names? Or should I just call them Grunt and Ugh?" I asked.

He laughed, his eyes crinkling around the edges. "Grunt and Ugh will be just fine."

I cut back to business. "You tell me where the studio is, and I will tell you about a merger coming up."

His eyebrows lowered. "What do I care about a merger?"

"It isn't legit, which means Romano is trying to outpace someone. You, most likely, since the merger is with Mancini." I shrugged.

Killian nodded, and surprised me by giving me my information first. "The studio is called Blue Hills but there is no sign on the gates. And from the street it looks more like a factory than anything else. It's not far from one of my safe houses."

I already knew that much about that studio, he was telling me nothing new so far. Of course the exterior was more factory; it was myst magic being made, not movies. "What's being developed there?"

He frowned. "Diva."

My turn to frown. "What is that exactly?"

"Diva's effects give the user strength and speed, like an abnormal. It's an oil that comes in a single dropper. Very easy to take, and for human's it gives them a high along with the perks."

I watched his face. He didn't seem impressed by a new magic hitting the market. Was it because it wasn't his idea, or because he didn't dabble in the dealing of magic? I had a hard time believing that last, but you never knew. Some people had a moral code no matter what, even if they didn't mind killing people.

"What is the merger for?" Killian leaned back in his seat, turning just his face to me.

"Gabe is going to work on the Yakuza to bring them into line with Romano and Mancini. One big powerhouse magical conglomerate." Sure, I was sort of guessing, but he didn't know that.

"Fuck."

"My thoughts. I believe Romano is going to try and oust Mancini at some point." My thoughts tumbled out of my mouth. "He's had delusions of grandeur for a long time. He fancies himself his own mob boss, and the power of the Yakuza behind him could help him do that. They are going to blindside him."

Killian shook his head. "Why not tell Mancini your suspicions?"

"Because he's currently in on the deal, and I have no proof that Romano will turn on him. I'll look like a vindictive spoiled child trying to get her father—" I struggled to call him that, "—in trouble with his boss. If I can find proof, I can do that. Without it, Mancini will try to kill me and my father wins. That is unacceptable."

"What is your plan exactly then? Get proof from the studio?" Killian was already shaking his head. "That place is lined with security up the arsehole and out its mouth."

"There is more than one way to make things happen, Mr.

Fannin." I glanced at where we were. Close enough to the edge of Lincoln Heights. "This will do, Grunt."

Grunt grunted and pulled the SUV over. I wrapped my fingers around the door handle, but Killian stopped me. "Here." He handed me a card. Not unlike the one Simon had given me.

Only this one had his full name on it, and an email, of all things. I raised an eyebrow. "No Facebook profile?"

He gave me a half-grin. "Maybe next year."

Dinah snickered, and Killian's eyes shot to my side. "Who is that?"

"Dinah," I said. "You don't want to meet her."

"Not as bad as meeting Eleanor," Dinah snickered again and I rolled my eyes.

His eyes sobered. "I'd heard about your guns. So, they do talk?"

I nodded.

His eyes darkened. "Black magic is dangerous, lass. Even when you think it's your friend."

I shrugged. "It's funny to me that you think I'm not dangerous without them."

His smile was back and he switched gears. "To be clear, I'm not offering help, lass. But . . . the safe house of mine would be a good place to set up if you need to be getting into that studio."

"Then why the card?"

"The address of the safe house is on the back." He grinned at me. "And just in case you want to see if your prediction is true, the number is my private line." He winked and I struggled not to flush under the sudden surge of heat between us. Nope, that was not happening. Whether or not he was good in the sack . . . that had just been to throw him off balance. And I hadn't been lying either—he was an abnormal. I wasn't touching that for nothing.

Unfortunately for me, it looked like he thought my comments meant I was interested.

Which I was not.

The vehicle doors unlocked with a click loud enough to make me jump which pissed me off. I grabbed my bag and slid out of the SUV, slammed the door behind me and headed straight for the closest side street that took me away from my apartment.

When I looked back, the SUV was still there. Fucking meddling green-eyed Irishman.

"Was he cute? You're acting like he was cute," Dinah said. "I liked his accent."

"What does it matter if he's cute? He's an enemy," Eleanor snapped, surprising both me and Dinah.

"What's jammed up your muzzle?" Dinah grumbled.

Eleanor didn't answer.

I ducked down a cross alley and ran to the end, from there putting myself into the hollow of a doorway while I waited. In my mind, I went over the events of the day so far. From Barron and getting the goods, to meeting Killian, to planting the tracer on the SUV, and our little chat. All and all, a rather productive day. I could only hope that Simon had found as much success.

Weaving my way through Lincoln Heights, I finally made it back to the apartment, sure that I hadn't been followed. The note on the door was still there. I gave a soft knock with my knuckles.

Abe woofed.

I opened the door and he greeted me enthusiastically as ever, sniffing me all over and licking at my hands.

"Good boy, Abe." I rubbed his ears, then took him out for a quick relief of his needs. He watered the few weeds in the alley behind the apartment and then we headed back inside. The day was waning, and Simon was not back yet. Dropping off the car shouldn't have taken that long. An hour or two depending on traffic and how he found his way back here.

Unless something had happened.

Or unless he *had* turned on me.

"Simon, you shit," I whispered as my heart ratcheted up a notch. Simon knew enough to turn me in to my father for a fair chunk of money. They could have the Stick Man here in no time flat.

I went to his bag and rifled through it. Clothing, a few chocolate bar wrappers. I frowned. I didn't remember him eating chocolate bars at any point. I spread them out on the table, flipping them over to see the insides of them.

A few numbers that when I moved them around, whatever speed I thought my heart capable of, I was proven wrong. The studio address. How had he gotten it? Unless he still had an in with Romano somewhere. I closed my eyes. More than once he'd been on his phone, doing what I thought were web searches. What if they'd been texts with an informant?

Fuck.

Had he gone in ahead of me then? And why?

The answer was obvious. He didn't think I would let him have all the money. Greedy-ass bastard that he was.

But I knew where the studio was now, too.

Did I need Simon? A lot of the gear I had in my bag was useful for surveillance, and I had no clue how to use the magical stuff. But I didn't need any of that now. This *go get the groceries* had been just to get me out of the way so Simon could go in on his own.

I knew where I was going.

I took a slow breath and let my heart rate settle. Simon was gone. Wherever he was, he wasn't coming back. I knew it with the acute senses that came from years working in the underbelly of the world. He'd gone in alone, and maybe he'd gotten his money and left. Or maybe he was still stuck there.

Or maybe he was dead.

"Abe."

He was at my side in a split second, his ears perked and tail still.

This time I was taking him in with me. He was my real partner.

"What happened to Simon?" Dinah asked.

"He's either been taken by Romano's gang or he turned on us." I spoke as I grabbed the backpack with the gear and the bag of weapons and clothes.

"Son of a bitch," Eleanor growled. "He's mine then."

"Yeah," I said, "he is."

Time to rain some chaos down on my father.

I couldn't help the grin that spread over my face.

"This one's for you, little Bear."

CHAPTER TWENTY-FOUR

Blue Hills Movie Studios was a sham, and a good one. Vehicles went in and out at regular intervals, there were guards at the main gate and in the distance up the tree-covered driveway. I could see the edge of a big blocky "studio." From where I sat in my—yet again—stolen vehicle, I used the binoculars to watch what was going on without being seen myself. Of course, I couldn't sit long where I was. I needed to move after just fifteen minutes, a map stretched out in front of me.

"I wanna get down," Dinah sang softly, "I wanna get down and dirty, baby. I want to see you beg for mercy."

My eyebrows shot up. "What is that song?"

"I made it up," she said. "Do you like it?"

"Actually, it's kind of catchy. You should sing it with Eleanor."

Both guns wiggled in their holsters, and seconds later they were belting out the words, harmonizing as they went.

I wanna get down.
I wanna get down and dirty, baby.
I want to see you beg for mercy.

Yeah. That could be a top one hundred hit.

I shook my head thinking once more of Simon. He'd wanted to go in using one of the delivery vehicles. I'd argued that we needed to recon first. This was not meant to be a quick job, but one done with good insight and deliberation. That was always how I'd done things.

Not for the first time, I cursed him. The thing was, whether he'd been caught, or he'd slipped in and out without being caught, the studio would be on full alert. Which made my job that much more difficult.

"Fucking idiot."

I pulled over into the entrance of the studio. I got out, map and phone in hand, the tightest short shorts I could find clinging to my ass cheeks. Anything I could use to distract the guard was worth it. The map caught the breeze.

The guard stepped out. Not a fat, old man guard, but a young, fit, eagle-eyed fellow. Eyes that shimmered with some sort of magic. Shit.

Romano had real guards on board then, not the local rent-a-cops.

"Hi," I smiled, "I'm super turned around. Can you help me out here?"

"No visitors. The studio is closed."

"Oh!" I went to my tiptoes. "Is that a movie studio? Oh, my God! That would be *so amazing*. Do they do tours? Have you met Brad Pitt? He's single now, you know."

He rolled his eyes. I stumbled forward as if I'd tripped on something, all but launching my weight at him.

The guard caught me, stumbled back with the force of my "fall" and we were inside the guard house. A set of schematic maps of the building were laid out. I caught them in my fist and I giggled up at him. He wouldn't fall for such a fake performance, even he wasn't that dumb, was he? But I kept going, because I had nothing else unless I was going to shoot him right there and rush in right this second.

"God, I am such a klutz! Wow, do you work out?" With my free hand, I molested the bicep closest to me while I carefully tucked the papers down the back of my shorts, flipping the hem of my long-sleeved shirt over them.

He grinned at me, his eyes on my tits. He was buying this? What a fool, and a lucky break for me.

"Yeah, a little."

"Wow. Do you think you could get me in? I've never seen—"

He was already steering me back to my car. "No, sorry."

I sighed. "I understand. Hey, do you think I could come back later and keep you company? I promise to be good." I got into the driver's seat and forced myself to bat my eyes up at him.

He leaned in. "Maybe. I get off at midnight. Want to pick me up, we can go for a drink after?"

"Perfect. I think that would be so cool. Can you tell me about all the actors you've met?"

"Sure thing." He shut my door. I leaned out.

"My name is Danielle."

"Jim." He settled back into his seat. "Go on now, you're too much of a distraction."

I waved at him and backed the car out. I drove down to the next intersection and turned left, then left again.

I pulled right up to the front of the place that was apparently Killian's safe house and around the side. There wasn't much cover here, but the side of the house would have to do. I let Abe out, then grabbed my two bags of gear.

I hated to say that it was nice of Killian to give me the use of this place. And while I didn't trust him, I also didn't think he would hand me over to Romano. Killian was a curious man, and I had intrigued him despite insulting him.

Good enough for me. I used the key code written on the back of the card, and slipped into the house. Not huge, an average house with two levels.

If you discounted the red flashing light that flicked on when I stepped through and the camera that swiveled my way, you'd think it was a family home waiting for the kids to get back from school. I blew a kiss to the camera and headed deeper into the house. I didn't flick any lights on, and Abe roamed ahead of me sniffing the air.

He stopped on the threshold of the hallway and what I thought was the living room with a low growl.

I pulled Eleanor and Dinah from their holsters and crept forward. They were humming their favorite song. "Beg for mercy," Dinah whispered.

Abe dropped to his belly and slunk along the floor without needing to be told.

I stepped into the room and quickly lowered the gun.

Killian sat on the couch across from me.

"What the hell are you doing here?" Exasperated, I lowered the guns.

"I came to see you in action. You see," he rolled his shoulders, "you were the threat your father used against the rest of us. The Phoenix will come for you, if I send her. Behave yourself, she's a killer of abnormals." He paused. "You don't look like I thought you would, and that bothers me a great deal." He leaned forward and put his elbows on his knees. "You can draw a gun at speed, and your guns talk, but that is no great skill."

"We sing, too," Dinah said.

I rolled my eyes. "This is your house, so do what you want. Watch me kill them, get off on it. I don't care."

"Cold. Very cold. What did your father take from you?" Killian hadn't moved from the couch.

I didn't answer him. I set my bags on the coffee table and

pawed through until I found the clothes I was looking for—ripped jeans, a tube top and a light pink coat.

I laid them out, and then started gathering what I was going to need for this hit. Weapons for the most part and ammo. A set of knives. Explosives and their timers—primarily C4. Flash bangs. Ropes. Gas masks.

"What are the ropes for?" Killian leaned over. "You think you're going to have time to torture someone?"

I shrugged. "Possibly."

He leaned over my bag. "Ah, a pack of gag jam, spider's bolt, bit boom, smarm, and blinding. Classic tools of a thief who dabbles in magic." He pulled the five packs out. "You know how to use these?"

I shook my head. "Nope."

"Then may I make a suggestion?"

I waved a hand at him. "Go ahead."

"Don't take anything but the gag jam with you. It's easiest to handle, and the only one you'd want to use as a normal, the rest have a kickback that could hurt you." He unscrewed the small plastic container and something swirled in it. "Its base is sugar. Mixed with wax and a touch of magic, you put some of this on a person's mouth and they aren't talking for days. Nose and mouth . . ."

I held my hand out and took the jar from him. "Thanks." The word almost stuck in my throat. I pushed the rest of the magical stuff to the side.

Killian didn't ask who was supposed to be handling this since I obviously didn't have a clue.

He sat back. In the shadows of the room, he was hard to read. Then again, I couldn't be sure what he gave me before in terms of readability was even true. How much of a master was he over his facial expressions? Hard to say.

Abe hadn't moved from the floor.

"Your dog is well trained?"

"Very. I don't suggest touching him."

Killian stood and Abe stood with him, placing himself between us. The Irish gangster let out a low laugh. "He don't be trusting me."

"Because I don't trust you." I kept at my bag, laying things out. Checking my ammo. Checking everything I would need as if Killian weren't there.

"Ah, that isn't very nice. I thought we were being friendly."

I slammed the weapon in my hand onto the glass table, cracking it, my stress levels peaking. "Why are you here, Killian? Want a kiss goodbye? I am not the one you want to fuck with on any level." The words snapped out of me in a torrent. "Romano is too good for death. I'm going to pull apart what he loves most, piece by piece. This is one piece of that. There will be others. You want him gone, you can keep helping me."

He stood straighter. "His sin against you must have been great."

"Like no other." I didn't take my eyes from him, the tension rising to a heady top. "I have to get ready. So, unless you are coming into the studio with me, I suggest you fuck off and stay out of my way."

He took a step, then another. "Too bad. I'd have liked to see how you perform in the sack. A woman who can make Barron stand up to me? You must be something special."

My eyebrows shot up, both at his words and his change of conversation. "Barron stood up to you?"

Killian grinned. "Told me to keep my hands off you."

I rolled my eyes. "Tell me he didn't threaten you at least?"

"Nah, his balls don't be that big." Killian was still grinning, obviously enjoying this tête-à-tête.

"Barron . . ." I shook my head and stared into my bag.

Mostly so I didn't have to look at Killian. "Barron is in love with a ghost."

"Aye, that's my thought, too. You aren't the way he remembers, but he wants to love you still. You aren't what I remember being told you were either, though."

"You think I'm weaker now?" I couldn't help the question, or the snapping heat it was delivered with.

He shook his head. "No. No, I think whatever happened to you, it's made you more dangerous."

I stood, waiting for more words, my back to him. Not afraid of the gangster when so many others would be. There was a moment when he stood, and took a step toward me, and the air between us crackled once more. Would he draw on me, or worse, try and use whatever magic he had to put a spell on me? I didn't think so . . . I was his best hope for taking down a man who had plagued his life for years.

"Good luck . . . Phoenix."

My shoulders tightened but I said nothing. Quiet filled the room, quiet except for Abe's displeasure of this man who had sat in the dark and irritated the shit out of me.

There was no sound of boots on the floor, or the push and pull of a door opening and slowly closing. Killian, for all his size, was a quiet bastard.

Only when Abe stopped his low rumbling growl was I sure the Irish gangster had left.

I let out a slow breath. He put me on edge, and I knew I intrigued him, which was dangerous in and of itself. Even as it was, taking the small help from Killian put me in his debt. An unspoken cost that would come knocking on my door at some point.

But I wasn't lying when I said I would need all the help I could get. I was still familiarizing myself with the world I'd run from. With Killian, at least I knew what I was getting into. I knew where I stood.

Letting out a sigh, I went through the equipment I needed. Without Simon, I had to make changes on the fly. I'd go in at midnight to "pick up" the guard. From there, the flash bang and I'd knock the guard out, take his key cards, and head in.

I bounced the jar of gag jam in my hand. This might come in handy indeed.

Next I ran a hand over the small explosives. As per Barron's written instructions, they would go sky high, a new brand of big bang that was still being tested. That made me nervous. Still being tested meant there were hitches and hiccups. I tucked four of the new C4 bombs inside a compartmentalized backpack. I made sure they were packed tightly, with lots of layers between them and the rest of my gear.

For the rest of my weapons, I kept it simple. Two handguns besides Dinah and Eleanor, matching knives, several smoke grenades, a mask for myself and a great contraption Barron had that would work for Abe if we got caught in the fire that was likely going to ensue. I didn't bother with the bigger guns; the bombs would do most the work.

I ran a fingertip over the schematics I'd snagged from the guard house. A simple outline of the building and the floors. Two levels above ground, three below. Unusual, and similar enough to the Lounge that I wouldn't be surprised if it was the same designer. There were little red dots here and there that I thought might be guard points. If they were, I counted fifteen, not including Jim at the front gate.

There would be a mix of abnormals and normals. How many, though? I had no way to know, but if I'd been able to do recon this wouldn't be an issue. Idiot Simon.

I went over possible entrance and exit points while I waited for the time to pass. I picked two of each, a primary and a backup.

I forced myself to eat, and then the clock finally said eleven thirty. I dressed first in my skin-tight black suit and weapons, and then over it I put on my ripped jeans, pink top, and slip of a shawl. I didn't bother with the flak jacket Barron had put in without asking me. His assumption was that anyone would be able to see me.

I did put Abe's flak jacket on, tightening it over his chest and neck. "Let's keep us both alive, okay?"

He woofed and bounced, picking up on my excitement.

I rolled my shoulders and closed my eyes.

There was no fear in me.

I had nothing left to fear of death.

My heartbeat slowed as I brought up the image of Justin and Bear, together, in my mind. Smiling at me. Loving me. Loving me despite what I was. A shudder slid down my spine, turning the emotions into a pure sense of purpose.

I put all my gear into a single pack, zipped it up, and tucked it inside the back door of the house. While I hoped I wouldn't have to make a run for it, the reality was there was going to be smoke, fire, bullets, chaos, magic of all kinds, and death everywhere by the time I was done if I had my way.

Having done as much as I could to prepare both the assault on the studio and my escape, I snapped my fingers at Abe. "Let's go, buddy. We've got work to do."

CHAPTER TWENTY-FIVE

I pulled the car up to the guard house at the side of the gate and sidled out, my hands behind my back holding a flash bang. A tiny thing, one wouldn't expect much from it. Flash bangs, though, put on a hell of a show. I already had my ear plugs and Abe's in.

I smiled up at the guard . . . what was his name? Jim, damn it, I almost panned on his name. "I know I'm a bit early, Jim, but . . . I'm *excited*."

I didn't have to fake the way my heart beat far too fast, the way my breath caught. The rush of a job was better than sex in some ways, and on more occasions than I'd care to admit, far more enjoyable.

Jim took one step out of the guard house, his eyes traveling up and down my body several times in quick succession. "We are going to have some fun tonight."

"Fun like fireworks, Jim." I grinned up at him, he grinned back, and I flicked the flash bang forward, releasing the handle as I did.

The flash bang hit the inside of the guard house and

exploded with a roar that would make any momma proud. The concussion slammed into my chest and I stumbled back, going to one knee. I kept my eyes glued to Jim as he spun around, pulled his gun and headed into the smoke. Had he not seen me toss it?

Damn.

I'd give him that, he was braver than most hourly wage guards. Then again, I suspected he hadn't found this job at the local rent-a-cop. And he was an abnormal, which meant he believed he was special, and less likely to die in shit like this.

I followed him, stepping into the smoke that filled the tiny space until I had my bare hand against his back.

"Get out, woman!" He coughed around the words.

I held my breath, found Jim, and pistol-whipped him with Dinah across the back of the head.

"Weeeeee!" Dinah screeched.

He grunted, went to the floor like a lump of potatoes. A three-hundred-pound sack of lumpy potatoes.

"Abe!" I yelled for him and he rushed in, belly to the floor. "*Nimm.*" Take it.

He hesitated and I pointed again, repeating the command. The flash bang had him rattled. Finally, he grabbed Jim's leg and together we pulled him out of the smoke.

Several more guards ran toward us from inside the fenced perimeter. A reaction I'd banked on.

I frisked Jim at high speed, taking a card and set of keys from his waist and slipping them inside my shirt before I stood up. "Hey, he's hurt! Help me, please!"

I coughed and motioned for Abe to stick to my leg. We stepped away from Jim as the other guards came through the large gate. Three guards, all three of them abnormal.

Dressed in ratty clothes, jeans, torn leather and vinyl jackets, two of them held larger than needed guns for a simple guard job. AK-47s were not what I'd call typical guard weaponry. I took a few more steps to the side, and they barely looked at me.

The moment slowed as I pulled Eleanor out first, my left hand diving to my lower back and coming out with her, closely followed by my right hand bringing Dinah back to the game. I aimed at thug number one's chest, and squeezed the trigger as I let out a breath, aimed and squeezed at thug number two as I breathed in. Thug number three dived at me, tackling me around the waist.

We hit the pavement so hard the wind was knocked out of me. I clung to Dinah and Eleanor, but the abnormal had my arms pinned to the side. As I stared at him, his mouth expanded, teeth filling it like some sort of crocodile. He snapped his mouth at me. I had no air to call to Abe to help me.

My lungs burned and I kicked my legs up, slamming them into his back while I twisted my upper body. The teeth snapped again, reared back and raced forward right at my face.

With all I had, I jerked to the side. I saved my face, but not my shoulder. The same side Mary-Ellen had hammered.

His teeth sunk deeply into me, tearing through flesh. I needed my arm intact for this.

"Abe!" I had my breath back despite the pain flying through me. "*Fass!*"

Abe hesitated, whining, and I screamed for him. "*Fass!*"

Right when the bones began to grind, Abe shot forward, latching onto the abnormal's arm and freeing my hand that held Eleanor. I had her up and the trigger squeezed before the abnormal so much as growled at Abe.

The abnormal flopped backward and I sat up. My

shoulder was bleeding and the skin on the back of my head had split against the cement.

"Shit." I forced myself to my feet, stepped over the bodies, and scooped up a walkie-talkie attached to the hip of thug number one.

"Abe," I called him to me and rubbed his head. "Good boy."

I clipped the walkie-talkie to the front pocket of my jeans and walked through the partially open gate. I jogged up the driveway sheltered with trees in the dark of the night, knowing cameras would be watching even now. Not truly caring, even though I knew it was going to make this a hell of a lot harder than if Simon had stuck around to work with me and helped to flick the cameras off as he'd said he could.

I scanned the thin bush as I jogged, but saw nothing. Was it possible that Simon had managed to take some of the surveillance out? I shook my head. He had nothing with him as far as I knew—no equipment to make it happen.

But he was an abnormal and had tricks up his sleeve that I was sure he kept from me. Hell, I'd not told him everything either.

My jaw ticked as I kept my body moving at a quick pace, Abe trotting beside me.

I could see the edges of the building clearer with each step, the lights around it lighting up the parking lot like it was the middle of the day. A few vehicles were parked outside, and there was activity. I slowed and stepped to the side, sliding into the shadows just as my walkie-talkie squawked.

"Billy boy, what's going on up front."

I deepened my voice as much as I could. "False alarm."

"Get your ass up here. We're expecting that bitch any time now."

My eyebrows shot up as I depressed the button to talk and gave a noncommittal grunt.

I put the walkie-talkie back on my pocket. That fucker, Simon . . . he had turned me in then? That was all it could be. Son of a bitch . . . I shook my head. They were expecting me, but not right that second.

Hard and fast, that was going to be the only way to go in now. There would be no finesse.

"Abe," I crouched to him. "*Fuss.*"

He licked my nose and I gave him a tight, fast hug, feeling death at my back, watching. Mine, or theirs, I never was sure until the job was over. My body was already aching, especially my shoulder, but I couldn't stop now.

I stood up. Four men were out front. Two at a vehicle having a smoke, one at the main door, one looked like he was grabbing his crotch. Had to pee, did he?

Moving fast, I slid through the thin bush toward the far edge that the full-bladder man was headed for. He would make a good shield against the others. I did not need any more injuries.

I made it to the section of bush only seconds before he did. He unzipped, flipped his dick out and started to pee.

"Boo," I whispered and he jumped and tried to get his dick in and a gun out at the same time, managing to do neither.

I slid around behind him and wrapped my arm around his neck as I pressed Dinah to his temple. "Shhh. No talking now."

I turned him around and pushed him ahead of me. "Move it. And try to act normal. I might let you live."

He was shaking as he walked with his dick bouncing against the front of his jeans. One of the other guys saw him and started to laugh, not seeing me behind his friend.

I stepped out to the side and shot the laugher in the head, the silencer doing its job at keeping the noise to nothing more than a pop.

Still, the others were trained to know the sound of a silenced gun.

They knew that noise as well as I did.

Their guns were not silenced as they shot at me, and hit their friend. He bobbed and jumped where he was with each bullet that sliced through him. I waited until he began to slump before I opened fire on the other two idiots.

I picked the first one off with a single shot.

The other ducked behind the truck they'd been leaning on. I bolted forward, dropping to my knees as I reached the front end of the vehicle. I grimaced as my knees took the brunt of the fall, but I held my breath. Abe whined softly beside me, trembling, ready to dart forward or run away, I wasn't sure. This was pushing him to the edge of his training.

I held two fingers at Abe, as if flashing him the peace sign. Not yet. I didn't want him to move yet.

His breathing slowed and we waited.

The sound of feet on the pavement. I lowered to my belly, seeing the guy's legs. I squeezed off a round, nailing him just above the ankle. The sound of the bone cracking was louder than the gunshot itself. The guy screamed as he fell to the ground, one hand going for the wound.

"*Fass!*" I gave Abe the command and though he hesitated again, he did race around the truck. He'd go for the gun hand first.

The guy screamed a second time as Abe latched onto his left hand and began to shake. I stood and stepped around the truck. "Hold."

Abe went still, his teeth still buried deeply in the forearm flesh. The man looked up at me, his face twisted up with pain. "Bitch."

"As if sweet talking will save you now," I said.

His body jerked just once as Dinah's bullet slammed

between his eyes. I ran my hands over his body, checking for anything useful.

Nothing.

"*Fuss.*"

Abe let go of the arm and trotted to my side. I went to the front door, slid my backpack off and opened it. Pulled the first of the tiny C4 bombs at the top of the pack. I twisted the bottom half of the round explosive and attached it on the lintel of the door. There would be no easy escape for anyone. I set the timer for fifteen minutes. If it took me longer than that, I deserved to go down with the building. Barron had given me a remote he said could set them off one by one if I needed. I checked the number on the bomb. 35T.

I put the pack on, and winced as the straps dug into my bleeding shoulder. Carefully, I held Eleanor in my left hand, the door knob in my right. There was no chatter of talk on the radio. I wasn't sure if that was because they knew I was here, or they thought nothing was wrong. I was banking on the latter.

The doorknob opened easily and I stepped inside in a crouch, gun raised.

A quick sweep left and right of the small room. An office. A waiting room. A false front.

I let out a breath, and Abe and I stepped into the room. I went to the computer first. It was on, a message blinking in red on the black screen.

Welcome home, Phoenix.

I smiled. Romano knew I was here. The question now was simply which of my family was here to greet me? Romano himself or one of my brothers? I prayed for the first time in a long time that it was Romano. Even though I'd said I wanted him to suffer, I wanted to see what he was doing up close and personal if I could.

I stripped off the bag and the jeans and pink top to the

skin-tight black clothing underneath. From my bag, I pulled the lace mask that covered my eyes and a pair of gloves that rode up to my biceps. The only skin showing on me now was a small patch between the gloves and the short sleeves of the black shirt. I slid a pair of night vision goggles around my neck, ready if necessary.

I left the civilian clothes behind and slid the backpack on once more. One bomb set, three more to go.

"Here we go," I said quietly.

I could see the schematic of the building inside my mind. The interior greeting room led into a false studio with panels, lighting, cameras . . . everything to look like an actual Hollywood setup if someone did force their way in.

The electrical panel in the wall of the office beckoned to me. I went to it, flicking everything off. Such a simple thing to do, but darkness still scared so many. There was a single yelp from the other side of the door and Abe gave a low growl. I reached down and put a hand on the top of his head.

"*Fuss*," I whispered and went to the door that would lead into the rest of the massive building. Thirty thousand square feet was no small space . . . and that was only the main sprawling floor. I slid the night vision goggles up and turned them on, sending my vision into a world of green and black.

I kicked the door open, jamming the heel of my boot next to the knob, sending it flying. It thudded into a body on the other side, a gun went off, the flash of the muzzle lighting up the dark space here and there.

"*Fass*." I sent him around first, for a moment my heart clenching. But he darted around the door and there was a scream as his teeth found flesh.

I was around the door a split second after him. The man was on the floor and I put a bullet through his head without hesitation.

From there, we crept through the main floor, my back to

the wall as much as possible. There was no one waiting for us around the panels, no one else hiding.

I couldn't help the snort. Cocky bastards.

The lights came on suddenly and I dropped and rolled under a table to my left, pulling the goggles off. Abe stuck with me.

The hiss and bite of static filled the air before a voice boomed over speakers that filled the place up.

"Baby sister, you didn't really think you'd be able to take Dad on, did you?"

Gabe had been sent to deal with me then. My hand clenched around the handle of Eleanor. The other I placed on Abe's back, keeping him still.

"Phoenix. I'll make you a deal. Walk away now, and I'll tell Dad you left on your own. I'll tell him you aren't coming after him. I'll tell him you're dead if you want."

I kept silent. The worst thing for the men in my family to be treated to was silence. They hated being ignored.

"You answer me, Phoenix!"

I smiled. Right on cue, his temper showed up to play.

From the backpack, I pulled the tiny remote and flipped it open. Only one bomb was set, and though I hadn't wanted to blow it so soon, I needed the cover of darkness. "Don't fail me now, Barron," I whispered as I hit the button that should only set off the one bomb. If Barron was wrong, or I'd taken note of the wrong number, then Abe and I were in for a very short trip to hell.

The front entrance of the building erupted in a boom that shook the foundations. The floor beneath me rippled and the lights went out. I waited for the dust to settle before I slid from under the table, pulling the night vision goggles on. From the schematics, I knew the stairwell was to the right at the very back of the oversized warehouse. That was where the rats would come from to escape the burning house. That's where most of the red dots had been on the plans.

That was where I was going down to find them.

I moved through the semi-darkness, using only the shadows of tables and paneling to guide me. The door came into view and I drew a slow breath. Into the depths we went.

CHAPTER TWENTY-SIX

The warehouse groaned around us, the last remnants of the first bomb going off settling into the bones of the place. There would be no way out the front door. I knew there was another door, though, another way out that was hidden. The schematics showed it as being in an office on the second floor that led to a ventilation pipe out to what looked like a sewer lid in the back of the lot. A ladder was shown as the way up to a narrow passage that led outside. That would make a good backup escape for me, and with a little help I was sure I could get Abe's furry butt up it too.

Eleanor in hand, I went through the first door, shocked that it was unlocked. Seriously, was my family that dumb? Or was it a trap?

The stairwell was made up of steel steps that went straight down, no landing between floors. I moved fast to cover ground. Getting caught on stairs was a bad idea.

Abe's nails clicked on the steel, but otherwise we were silent. But not quiet enough.

I was body-slammed from the left when I stepped onto the second floor, the scent of Obsession heavy on the body that hit me. Obsession belonged to one of my father's thugs. Barco. Barco who liked to make his women submit, who liked to play with his kills before ending them. Barco who was an abnormal who liked the taste of human flesh.

His meaty hands worked to get around my neck. I was not going to be his next meal. I rolled hard to the side, forcing him under me. Knives, he liked knives. The memories rolled up and I worked hard to get his hands under control. The first blade of his caught me on the upper arm, slicing through the thin mesh and flesh underneath. At least it was my uninjured arm.

"*Fass!*" I called and Abe was on Barco's left arm in a flash, biting deeply. Barco snarled back, and Abe *let go*.

"Shithead." I got my hand on Dinah's grip and pulled her free, but not fast enough. Barco smashed the side of my head, snapping it sideways, making my vision blur. I twisted my wrist, pointing Dinah at him as best I could.

"Squeeze the trigger!" Dinah yelled. "I can't shoot without you!"

I was trying. Fuck it all, I was trying. I flexed my hand with all I had, and the trigger squeezed. Dinah went off, and Barco was hit, but not mortally. He roared and looked at his upper arm where the bullet had taken him. I should have told Dinah to switch out. Barco shook his head. "Killing you is going to be my pleasure."

Tough bastard, but that didn't mean I was going to let him win. His right arm shot up, sliding along my forearm; a blade cut through my glove and the first layers of skin and flesh.

I gritted my teeth against the instant pain while I twisted hard, throwing him off me. Eleanor was in my good hand, and I squeezed off two rounds while Barco tried to dodge. Both bullets took him through the neck.

He scrabbled at his bleeding flesh, blood gurgling out of

the wound and his mouth as he fought for air. I didn't waste another bullet putting him out of his misery.

Footsteps echoed down the hall.

Abe growled low. Abnormals then. I was bleeding from both arms, my head pounded and I knew I was fighting odds that were no good.

I didn't care. I wasn't stopping.

Barco had busted my goggles, and I tossed them off to the side. I kept Eleanor out and put Dinah back into her holster. Mostly because my right arm was throbbing and my fingers were numb.

From the schematics, I knew this level was broken into offices, small rooms all over the place. But it was the main mechanical room and cutting floors I was looking for.

The cutting floor was where the magic was made, and where the best bang for my buck was going to happen when it came to setting the C4.

The offices, though . . . that was where the money would be, where I would give my father his first taste of my rage. Take his money, make him bleed out in a way that mattered to him. Then to the manufacturing floor, and I would be able to take the money machine out at the head.

But for the first step, I would need to find my brother.

I had nothing of his to set Abe on. No piece of material, no bit of blood. I half-turned back to where I'd left Barco's body.

Gabe would have been with Barco, of that I had no doubt. Barco was one of his favorite bullies.

I hurried back to where I'd left the body, pausing at the edge of the hall that would lead me back to Barco.

Two voices whispered low enough that I couldn't make out the words. But that was all good; I didn't need to know what they were saying to know they were in my way.

I pulled Dinah back out of her holster, and held both of my ladies up, drew a breath and stepped out into full view.

"Hey." I snapped the word, and the two men lifted their guns in what looked like slow motion to me.

Dinah bucked against my hand first, making my shoulder scream, and then Eleanor went off right behind her. Bullets ripped through the air and drove into the man on the right, then the one on the left. They reeled back in unison, hit the opposite walls to each other and slid down.

I let out a slow breath and shook my head. "Abe." He took a step, his face lifted to mine as he waited for his command.

I pointed at the still-bleeding corpse of Barco. "*Such.*"

Abe pressed his muzzle against Barco's clothing for a moment and then he swept the room, looking for the trail.

Hesitating here and there, he started off down the hall. This would be the most dangerous part. Letting Abe lead me through the semi-darkness with nothing but the odd emergency light flickering for light.

Doors on either side of me flashed by and my heart picked up speed as we weaved through the dimly lit office halls. The backup generator had the occasional light going. Enough that you could find your way out, I supposed, if you knew where you were going.

I ran into another of my brother's thugs. Eleanor made short work of him and he dropped before he likely even realized what was happening. I was breathing hard, my body humming with pain. I made myself touch the wounds.

Both were hot, on fire and sending waves of nausea through me. There was nothing to be done about it now. I had to keep going.

No, that wasn't right. "Linx," I stopped and slid my pack off. The magic tool was in the bottom, quiet like a mouse. I pulled him out. "You got anything you can do for infected wounds?"

Linx shivered in my hand. "Nope, sorry."

I shoved him back in the bag. So much for that idea.

Once more we were moving.

At a T-intersection Abe paused, and then spun to the right. He moved at a good clip, but not so fast that he would lose me. The lights around us flickered, dancing as the generator fought to keep them on.

Abe slowed, tipped his nose up and then was off again, only to slide to a stop in front of a set of double doors engraved with my brother's name.

Gabriel Romano.

I might have found it eventually, but not at the speed Abe had brought me. Not with enough time to get this done and get the hell out of here before the rest of the place blew.

I rubbed Abe's head quickly, then pressed my ear to the door, listening. Voices, muffled, came through. There was a light to the left of me. I reached up and broke it with Dinah's grip.

I didn't think the tinkling of glass would be loud enough to be heard through the doors. I waited to the side, just in case. No one came to inspect the slight noise.

I stepped up to the door, and gave it a soft knock with the back of one hand. Abe and I moved to the side once more, waiting. My vision narrowed to the doors.

A man stuck his head out and he was barely a dark shadow against the lighter gray shades, illuminated from the room. I sent a bullet through the side of his head, splattering brains and blood on the far side of the door. Before he could fall, I stepped in front of him and hooked an arm under his, with a sharp hiss. Hefting his dead weight while I pointed Eleanor in front of me was a stretch of the last of my reserves.

How was I going to get through the rest of this?

My brother stood beside his desk, a gun pointed at me.

His face was lined with fear, with anxiety, and the shitty lighting didn't really help.

"Phoenix, Phoenix, you really came back?"

"You know why." I kept the dead man up, propped against my body. Abe stayed behind me, his nose tucked into the back of my knees.

"I don't, actually." Gabe didn't lower the gun. "I don't really want to kill you."

"The feeling is not mutual," I said.

He shrugged. "Such is life with abnormals."

I snorted. "You aren't abnormal, you dumb fuck."

He smiled, the light catching the edges of his mouth, making it sinister. "You've been gone a long time, Phoenix. You have no idea what's changed. Dad made it his goal to become part of the abnormal world, you know that."

I stepped sideways, keeping my back to the wall. "He's not as good as Mancini at keeping his people alive. He's too damn lazy."

Gabe frowned. "You were always uptight about security. Nothing ever happened."

"Because no one was ever gunning for us, you moron. And I killed those few who tried." I snapped the words. Part of me hated that he'd pulled me into a conversation, that I hadn't just shot him in the gut as I'd planned. I needed to shoot him. I needed to get this job done as fast as I could.

A gut wound would take time to bleed out, and I was sure I was going to need him to break into the computers. To find the money. To transfer it out.

"Your boyfriends are waiting for you on the bottom level. One of them told us you were coming. Thought we might pay him good for it." Gabe smiled again.

I frowned and for a split second, I thought he meant Killian. But of course, he didn't. Gabe meant Simon. But boyfriends? Who else was down there?

I forced a laugh. "Please, Simon was a tool and not a very good one."

"Not any good in the sack? That's disappointing. He was bragging about how amazing you were. I remember that about you." Gabe smirked. Trying to put me off balance.

I lowered my gun a little, and he did the same. "He's not the only shit around here." I squeezed the trigger, the gun bucked and a bloom of violent red opened on Gabe's belly. He flew backwards, his ass hitting the desk behind him.

He lifted his gun but I was too fast. I shot him in the hand and he dropped the weapon. "You have a choice, Gabe." I let go of the limp body and walked toward my brother.

"What's that, you cunt?" He sneered up at me, but his eyes were full of fear. As well they should be. Of all the people I knew, my family had the most reason to be afraid of me. They created me, and they knew what I was capable of.

I grabbed a handful of his belly skin around the wound and pulled him upright. He wobbled as he cried out, but when he pushed on my hand I only tightened my fingers, digging into the wound. The blood made my grip on him not as good as I would have liked, but it was working for now. He stopped fighting me. Hell, he didn't even try to return the favor and slap at my wounds.

Dumb, just too dumb.

"Your choice is simple," it was my turn to smile, "you have the bank codes to the money flowing through this place. We need to move it now." Still holding him, I directed him around the side of the table. I set up a mobile hotspot with my phone, and forced him to turn the laptop on.

Beside him, I laid out a single account code. A temporary one that would bounce the money three times before landing back in the original account in two days. By then, I would be able to pull out.

I didn't give a rat's ass about the money. But it would piss my father off to no end to lose millions more to me.

Gabriel slowly—so damn slowly—logged in and began moving the money. "You're just as greedy as ever." He spat the words at me and they splattered the screen with a bit of blood and saliva.

"Save your breath. You're dying, Gabe, and if you want to live, you're going to need all your strength to get out of here." I watched what he was doing closely. Abe guarded the door, his ears pricked. My brother had implied he was an abnormal, but I didn't see any indication of that.

There came the sound of wood crackling, of branches being formed at rapid speed as they grew unnaturally. My problems had just multiplied like all those damn splinters.

The Stick Man was here.

CHAPTER TWENTY-SEVEN

A few more clicks, and the transfer of money was in progress.

The scrabbling of wood on the wall had me turning around. The Stick Man stepped out of a side room, ducking to fit through the doorway. His hands stretched outward, wide with a welcoming embrace I didn't want.

I let go of Gabe, wiped my hand on the back of his shirt and stepped away, training my eyes and guns on the overgrown toothpick, but speaking to my brother. "I'm blowing this place up. This is the only warning you'll get. It's the last thing I will ever do for you."

Not watching him was a mistake.

The click of the gun a split second before it went off was the only warning I had. I threw myself to the side, but it wasn't enough to avoid the bullet completely. It caught the edge of my neck, slicing through the first layers of skin and muscle, and leaving a burning trail in its wake.

I spun as I dove to the right, and brought up Dinah, because Eleanor was in some ways too good for my brother. He didn't deserve to see the light. He deserved judgment.

Gabriel's dark eyes were all I saw as I pulled the trigger. Watched as the bullet slammed between them, and the eyes went wide and then blank, his body slumped and fell forward on the desk.

I had no time to consider what happened, to register the pain in my own body.

The Stick Man shot forward.

"Dinah, switch!"

I squeezed the trigger and the bullets slammed into the Stick Man, exploding on contact once more. I shot him four times. Torso, both legs, and his head. The branches shimmered all around my feet and several worked toward me. I stumbled back, shaking. I put a hand to my neck. Painful, shocking, but not deep. I pushed to my feet and hurried to the door.

"Dinah, how many more you got?"

"None for at least an hour," she said. "You know I need time to recharge on those."

I did, I'd just been hoping my memory was wrong.

Moving as quickly as I could, I headed to the mechanical room on this floor.

I chose not to think about what had just happened. I forced Gabe's dead eyes from my mind. He would become a nightmare to haunt me, of that much I was sure. And the Stick Man was still here, he'd respawn or whatever it was he did to pull himself together and I'd be fighting him without any big ammo.

The mechanical room was at the end of the hall, the door jammed shut. I tried the key card I'd taken off Jim. The door clicked and opened.

I placed the second of my C4 bombs in the room, next to a great deal of explosive things that did not belong there. Things like a propane tank. I ran a hand on the tank, noting three more.

I shook my head and cranked the propane tanks open. Extra explosions were not a bad thing when trying to take down a monstrous factory, a guardian, and a whole lot of magical drugs.

I should have been careful with what I wished for.

Abe and I were off again, working our way back the way we came to the office that led into the ventilation shaft. It was time to go.

I paused. Simon was still in here, and he'd apparently turned on me, along with someone else Gabe thought was with me.

My heart chilled. Not Zee? Could they have grabbed Zee? I scrabbled at my cell phone and dialed Zee's number.

It rang and rang, over and over. My breath came in hitches. No, this was not happening. I tried his cell phone.

Nothing.

I slammed the phone shut.

I flexed a hand, knowing I could leave Simon behind and feel nothing. But if Zee was down there, I was going after him without another thought.

I pulled my backpack off and lifted out a pack of C4. Attaching it to the wall, I set the timer. If all went as planned, it would cover our retreat, and if the Stick Man was behind me, maybe the C4 would be enough to keep him down for good.

"Come on, Abe. Let's go get them."

We jogged through the office, the blood on my neck cooling, sticking, and pulling on my skin. Both shoulders on fire and my head throbbing. This was not the best time for me to pursue a rescue mission. But here I was.

The next set of stairs going down had an open door. There were two floors below me. The only question was, which one was Simon and Zee on?

There was no one between us and the second basement floor. Not a single person.

The area held nothing but open tables and lab equipment. I searched until I found a collection of propane tanks and set the third of the C4 bombs against them, setting it for eight minutes. Sweat trickled down my body, the air not cooling the lower we got, but instead heating up.

I paused at the far table and the vial droppers there. Killian's words echoed through my mind. Diva gave the user speed and strength like an abnormal.

I grabbed a vial, and tipped it into my mouth before I could second-guess myself.

The effect was instantaneous. My heart began to race at a speed that should have scared me. But the pumping adrenaline washed away the pain in my body and the last vestiges of fear.

I took off running, feeling the power in my muscles and the strength in every part of my body.

At the top of the third set of stairs, I hesitated, listening. The lowest level was also the smallest at only a few thousand square feet. Built like a bunker, it had only one way in, and one way out. Which meant whoever I left down there was going to die a terrible death, trapped far below.

I deepened my voice as much as I could. "Gabe is coming down."

"'Bout fucking time. This asshole is a mouthpiece. I want to shoot him." There was the sound of flesh on flesh, a hard slap and then a clatter. I could see it in my head. Simon was tied to a chair, his guard had knocked him down. Good place for him when the guns started blazing. Zee would keep his mouth shut. There was no way he'd say one single word.

"She isn't coming," Simon said, his voice tight. "I keep telling you she isn't coming, you shitheads. She's too damn smart for you."

A grunt, the sound of boots slamming into his body.

I jogged down the stairs, heart picking up speed with each step. I had both guns out, a flash bang hooked into my right hand and I was as ready as I was going to be. From where I stood, I could see that they had some light at least, so I wouldn't go in completely blind. That being said, I wanted them to be at a disadvantage.

I hit the bottom stair and tossed the flash bang in.

The hand bomb went off bursting into the room and stealing their vision for a precious few seconds.

I fired off two rounds into the two guards. They slumped to their knees, their AK-47s clattering to the ground.

"There's a third!" Simon yelled. I dropped with a speed that shocked even me, turned sideways and a bullet ripped through the backpack. My breath hitched as I waited for the last C4 bomb to explode.

Waited to die.

There was the clunk of a bullet going through plastic and I closed my eyes.

Above us, the two bombs I'd set went off, but not the one in my bag.

The remote had been hit.

From where I was, I shot the last guard in the chest. He fell backward. I scrambled to Simon as I searched the room for Zee. I pulled a long knife and held it up.

"What happened and where is Zee?"

"They jumped me at the rental place, dragged me here. No Zee. This guy over there says he's FBI." His eyes were steady, but I couldn't be sure he was lying.

FBI . . . I spun on my knees. There was Noah, tied to a chair, his eyes on me. "Hey, Bea."

"Don't you 'hey' me, you asshole. I should leave you here. You burned down my house and helped get my husband and son killed." I turned my attention back to Simon, doubly pissed. I'd only come because I thought Zee had been caught. I'd taken a magical drug to make it happen, and now here I was rescuing two men I would have gladly left behind.

I suspected one had turned on me.

The other burned down my house and shot my dog.

Neither had any chances left as far as I was concerned.

There were bruises all over Simon's face and he'd obviously been at their mercy for the last day, maybe he hadn't turned on me. Damn it, I did not want to feel bad for him. I slashed through his bindings, rope and zip tie, then stalked over to Noah and did the same. I didn't hand either of them a gun.

I didn't trust them not to shoot me in the back.

"Let's go." I snapped my fingers and Abe was at my side first.

"Did you get the money?" Simon asked and that made it easier to keep the anger flowing at him. Always the money with that one.

"No." I led the way up the stairs, and the two men followed slowly. Simon had not worked for the money, and other than helping me drive across country had done very little to help me. Which meant he got nothing.

Simon grunted. "That's what will piss your father off, so—"

At the top of the stairs, I looked back at him. "This building is coming down around us. I don't know if *we* can get out even now."

I helped him up the last few steps, ignoring the limping Noah, and together the four of us made it to the next level, the one that had the propane tanks. Had, definitely past tense when it came to the tanks. The massive cutting room was engulfed in flames. I couldn't resist a look toward the vials.

"Fuck, I'm a fool." I reached over and grabbed two more, stuffing them down the front of my shirt.

Abe whimpered and wormed at my side, fear lacing his vocals.

"We've got to run through." I put the leash on Abe and looked at Simon. He gave me a tight nod and then we were off, running. Noah had to work to keep up, but I didn't care. The reality was, right now, I liked him even less than I liked Simon.

That was the plan.

The Stick Man changed it.

He stepped through the flames, his limbs on fire but seemingly unbothered by it.

We all stepped back.

The buzz from Diva took that moment to tank and my body sagged worse than before. Noah caught me.

I reached for the vials in my shirt and drank them both down at the same time.

The world snapped into focus, my senses in overdrive. I spun away from Noah and it was if the Stick Man was stuck in mud as he moved to follow me, his arms flailing.

I jumped at him, feet first, driving him back into the flames. At the same time, I pulled Dinah and Eleanor, firing hard and fast into the guardian.

"Go, go!" I screamed at the two men in order to be heard over the crackling of the flames.

Outrunning the Stick Man was a stall, but I knew he wouldn't be killed by the flames. There was no choice here.

I kept moving, kept running, herding the other three, as I guarded our rear.

Twice we were forced to go through a wall of flame. Abe yelped but kept moving. Simon balked.

I let him go.

"No, wait!" He screamed for me, but Noah grabbed and dragged him.

I kept moving. The bomb I'd set in the mechanical room had lots of time for the flames to reach it.

There was no hope for this place if the C4 in the escape room had been set off. If so, we were royally fucked.

At the set of stairs up to the second level, I paused and looked down.

The Stick Man was at the bottom of the steps and coming fast.

"Get my dog out," I yelled at Noah. "Ropes and gear in office 419. Panel behind the wall is an escape hatch."

Noah reached for me and I shook him off. "Get the hell out of here, Noah."

He turned away, taking Simon and Abe. Abe was on the leash and Simon all but dragged him away. He kept turning his head to look at me.

I could save all three of them.

Damn, I was getting soft in my old age.

CHAPTER TWENTY-EIGHT

The Stick Man raced up the steps toward me, pulling himself along the railing. I turned in the opposite direction of where I'd sent the men.

Rose's words were the only clue I had to go on. Blood fire. The only blood that was good in a fire was abnormals'.

Barco was an abnormal who had no need of his blood if I could get to him. I bolted down the hallways, finding my way back to Barco with an ease that surprised me. It was only when I stopped that I realized I'd been following the smell of his blood. Honey and cinnamon. I shuddered and spun as the Stick Man stumbled through the narrow passage. There were no words from him, no dire warning. Just the inexorable path to take me down before him, and that was where he stayed. He swung a clawed hand at me.

The Diva in my system began to sag once more. Well, this was not good.

I dropped to the floor, grabbed a knife from my boot and jammed it into Barco's chest. I opened him up in a single cut —stronger than I'd ever been before.

Blood and guts spilled out and I scooped at them, flinging

them at the Stick Man. He was splattered with the viscera. The Stick Man shook his head once, shot toward me, and swiped me across the leg.

I screamed as the splinters—twice the size as the first time he'd nailed me—drove high under my skin.

I fell to one knee and scrambled forward, slipping in Barco's blood and guts.

The Stick Man reached for me again and I flung myself away from him so hard I slammed into the side wall. The wall was so weakened by the fire that I fell through and into a tiny office with one desk, and one chair.

The Stick Man leapt through the hole I'd made and all I could do was get the desk between us. I picked up the chair and used it like a lion tamer, holding the creature at bay. "Burn, you asshole, just burn!"

He slammed his arms into the chair's legs, sending it flying out of my hands.

"You better move!" Dinah yelled.

"I agree with her," Eleanor added in.

I leapt for the door, and grabbed the handle. The knob was hot under my fingers, but I turned it and was out in a split second. I slammed the door behind me as the Stick Man slammed into it. He'd be out the hole in no time but I'd bought myself the seconds I needed.

Barely, but I had done it.

Moving as fast as I could, I raced back the way I'd come. But there was a problem that I'd been ignoring until that moment. The fire was licking along the sides of the wall and I was covered in accelerant.

No choice now. I stripped my clothes off with the last of the speed from the Diva magic. Down to nothing but bra, underwear and holsters, I ran for the fire. The heat licked along my bare skin, feeling like each touch stole my energy from me.

Behind me the Stick Man roared. I was clear of the flames, the last of my abnormal strength and energy faded and I struggled to breathe.

The Stick Man flailed behind me, his body eaten by the flames cutting through him.

Good enough for me.

I could not move faster than walk, though I knew I needed to run.

Other than the flames, the wounds over my body, and the threat of C4 going off at any moment, I faced no other challenges as I headed to the office with the escape hatch.

I opened the door and the C4 was still there, not set off despite the heat that was rapidly growing.

What surprised me, though, was that Noah, Abe and Simon were there, waiting for me.

"What the hell? I told you to go!" Fury trickled through me.

Noah stared at me. "You were gone like three minutes."

My jaw dropped.

That Diva was a damn miracle.

Both Simon and Noah were sweat-soaked and limping badly. "You can be a callous woman, you know that?" Noah said.

"And you're fucking lucky I don't shoot you now and leave you behind. It's a damned miracle I'm taking you out alive." I motioned for him to shut the door, and I went to the paneling in the wall that was a whiteboard. A few seconds later I had the false door pried open, showing the real door behind it.

Steel, and locked.

"No lock pick, I suppose?" Simon asked.

I took my backpack from Noah and dug around in the bottom. "Linx, lock pick."

The silver tool shifted and shimmied until he was a perfect pair of lock picks.

"Thank you."

"Any time, sweet cheeks," he said. If an inanimate tool could wink, he would have. "We'll get those splinters out next."

"I'll do it, you're spent." Simon held his hand out and I let him take Linx. He was right, I was fighting to stay on my feet.

He bent to the door and I slumped against the table.

Noah couldn't look at me. I wanted to tell him to grow up, but I had no energy left. I was done in.

"Got it," Simon said and opened the door with a flourish.

I took Linx and put him into my bag.

I stepped through the door first, Abe followed, then the other two.

The climb up the ladder was a bit of a bitch, and I resorted to slinging a rope around Abe's back end to help him up. But he never hesitated, never looked back. Unlike Simon, who kept up a running litany of how hard it was, how tired he was, how much money he was out. At least Noah kept his mouth shut.

Noah was smart enough to see that as badly as Simon might have been hurt, I was in far worse shape.

Simon's whining brought him close to being shot in the head, just for the blessed peace and quiet I wanted.

At the top of the ladder there was a room—if you want to call it that. A four-foot ceiling narrowed to three-foot which had me on my back and the backpack on my belly. We crawled for at least a hundred yards before we came to a dead end. Above my head was the flat plate of the false sewer cap. I pushed on it and the thing was open. I flipped it up and Abe shot out first.

I was out next with Dinah pointed and ready with only

some difficulty. We were at the far back of the lot, the building right in front of me burning like a son of a bitch.

The two men followed me all the way to the front gate where the guards were still laid out and Jim was just beginning to sit up. He had a hand to his head. "What the hell happened?" His eyes were semi-glazed when he looked at me. Widening as he took in my state of undress and the guns.

I didn't look anything like the woman he'd been prepared to go on a date with. I pulled an envelope from my bag and handed it to him.

"For Romano."

He took it with trembling fingers and I walked away.

CHAPTER TWENTY-NINE

Killian's house served as a stopping point for us. Simon hit the couch and I left him there as I cleaned up the wounds on my body as best I could. I locked the bathroom door behind me and pulled Linx out.

"Tweezers, Linx."

He shimmered and shifted and then I held him at an angle so he could work the slivers that had crawled from my thighs up through my belly and to my ribcage.

With those removed, I set to washing the bite on my shoulder. In the cupboard, I found an arsenal of medical supplies including some heavy duty antibiotics of which I downed three with the lukewarm tap water, then stuffed the remainder of the bottle into my bag. That would have to do for any infection brewing.

Next I washed the bite, using a medical grade cleansing solution. The tooth marks were ragged and were going to scar badly.

I hated to ask for help.

"Can either of you do stitches?"

"I can," Noah called back, and I let him into the bathroom.

He said nothing as he stitched me up, and I wasn't feeling chatty. He stitched up the knife wounds on the other side of me as well.

I let out a breath and waited for him to leave. He stepped out. "You're welcome."

I almost killed him right there. But I still wanted answers so I kept Dinah and Eleanor on the flat of the counter even though they both grumbled on my behalf.

My extra clothes were hard to get on over all the wounds, but it was the best I could do for now. I needed to find a place to sleep and heal and decide what I was going to do next. Where I was going to hit Romano.

I thought about Noah in the other room with Simon. He was my best shot at knowing where to go next. But I wasn't sure I trusted him at all, even though I thought he had the bible that would decode the papers from Justin's desk. He'd burned my house down. He'd killed Abigail. Yet, Justin had worked with him for years.

Could I do the same?

I couldn't stop my shoulders from tensing or the resulting pound of a headache starting behind my eyes. The same headache I'd gotten after every job. After every major kill.

Cleaned up and dressed, I walked into the living room. Simon was passed out on the couch. Noah stood quietly against the bar countertop.

"You going to tell me what's going on, or am I going to have to convince you to tell me?" I tucked my fingers into my belt loops, and cocked a leg as if I didn't want to lie down and sleep for days. I could outwait him.

Noah's blue eyes danced over me and away. Looking for a

way to lie his way out of this. "You figured out that Justin wasn't a ski instructor."

I nodded. "No shit. Keep talking."

He let out a big breath. "He'd heard a rumor that Romano's oldest daughter had died, but he didn't believe it because of the rumors around your death that the body went missing. He went looking for you, Bea. He thought..."

I finished the thought for him. "He thought he could score big with Romano if he brought the oldest wayward daughter home." Which was a joke because I was the reason Bianca's body was never found. The note she'd left for me with Dinah and Eleanor had asked that I hide her body away. A last request I couldn't refuse even though I was only eighteen. That had been when I'd begun to wonder about my life. To wonder if it was everything it should have been.

Noah nodded. "But he met you, and couldn't do it. Couldn't turn you in. He always said it was the look in your eyes, this mix of hunted and hunter that drew him to you."

I remembered the first time Justin and I met. How when I'd told him my name was Bea, his face had lit up like I'd just handed him a stack of cash.

I didn't give Noah any sort of indication how I felt, but let him keep on talking.

"He never went back to your father for the money. You need to know that."

The ramifications rolled through my mind, the first and foremost that Justin had loved me enough to try and hide me from my father. To fool a man who could pull the trigger on him at any time. Just like Romano had.

Noah watched me closely for a moment, then went on. "I work for a division of the FBI trained to infiltrate Mancini's crew, to find out what they are doing with myst magic, to work undercover with them."

"Lancaster is your real last name?" I said, recalling the badge in his room in Jackson Hole.

He nodded. "Yes."

"And the score Justin was after this time?" I frowned. What did he think he was going to do?

"He was blackmailing your father. He told him that he would go to the police with information of all your father's holdings, money, underground dealings, the illegal magic usage. Names of everyone he was working with, which government officials he was connected to. Everything. That is why the hit was called out on him. I caught wind of it but too late to warn him."

"Romano has lawyers; he would have fought Justin's papers and won." I waved my hand in dismissal.

"Yeah, well, Justin wanted to hurt him, and he thought he could do it. I did too, I thought we could take Romano out." Noah's words were weighted with meaning. Justin wanted to hurt my father for what he'd done to me. A lump formed in my throat and I struggled through it.

"I burned your house down because I couldn't have anyone else getting that paperwork. I . . . I know you wouldn't have found it. Justin told me it was well hidden and that you'd never noticed. I didn't have time to do much more than take a cursory look before I—"

I glared at him, the gaze intense enough to shut him up.

"You were the one in my house, you took the bible?"

His eyes didn't lower. "I was."

I narrowed my eyes, thinking about how the steps of the man in the house had been wide and staggered. The gortex in Abigail's teeth suddenly made sense. "Abigail got a piece of you, and made you limp, didn't she?"

He nodded. "She did."

"Thank you for your honesty, Noah. Now where is the family bible?"

His eyes widened. "Why would you want that?"

"Because I have the coded papers." No point in lying now.

He sucked in a sharp breath that seemed to pain him. "Justin wouldn't have wanted you to go after—"

"This isn't about Justin. He didn't know all of my story. He didn't know who I really am. He thought I was my sister, Bianca. I let him believe I was her. I let him believe I was not the other sister. You know the one I mean."

Noah visibly paled. "You're not . . . Bianca Romano?"

"No. I'm not. I'll let you figure out who that leaves me to be. Surely even you can manage that much." I kept my eyes locked on him. "Where. Is. The. Bible?"

He swallowed hard. Abe growled.

"You can't do this on your own," he said.

I knew what he was saying. He wanted in. "The bible."

"I don't have it." Noah shook his head. "I took it from you, and someone stole it from me."

"Who stole it?" I stared hard at him.

He shook his head. "I don't know."

The lie was so obvious he might as well have painted it on his forehead in neon lights. "Right, you expect me to believe that shit?"

He turned away, then back to me, his face twisted with anger. "I think it was one of Romano's men. An abnormal that was so well cloaked I couldn't get features on him." Noah growled the words. "

The Shadow then, the second of Romano's guardians. With that I knew that the chances of getting the bible back were zero to none.

Simon let out a groan and sat up. "Are we leaving, yet?"

I grabbed Simon's arm, yanked him to his feet. "Your bedside manner leaves something to be desired, my love."

"You want to stay with the dirty cop?" I let go of Simon and he wobbled where he stood.

"Nah, I think I'll pass on that. Rather go with the dirty assassin."

I grabbed hold of him again and dragged him to the back door. I scooped up my waiting bag, my body groaned, and in seconds we were in the car.

I left Noah there, not caring what happened to him. I had bigger fish to fry. For months, I'd stared at the coded papers from Justin's desk. Wondering what they were. Wondering if they were worth breaking.

"You know a code breaker who can deal in magic codes?" I steered us onto the main interstate that would take us out of LA and back to Brentwood. Barron was my best bet. Not a code breaker himself, but he had connections. Maybe even Killian could help if Barron couldn't.

A name was all I needed . . . my foot eased off the pedal as we pulled up to Barron's home, shock filtering through me.

The entire place was on fire, exploding here and there, glass shattering as the flames escalated. On the front porch was a single body, slumped against one of the ugly statues. I had no doubt who it was.

I backed the car up and hit the gas, ramming through the gates.

Simon yelped, and Abe let out a whine, but otherwise they were quiet.

I hit the brakes, sliding sideways as we got close to the front steps. I leapt from the car and was around the side in a flash, on my knees, next to Barron. A note was stapled to his chest. I put a hand to him, his eyes closed as if sleeping.

He groaned, surprising me. "Barron," I said. "Hang on, I'll get Killian—"

"No. Romano did this. Because I helped you."

"How did he know?"

His eyes fluttered open. "Watching me. All along. The Shadow."

My guts clenched. Romano had sent his guardian after Barron. "This is my fault. Because I came here."

He gave me a tight smile. "No. My fault. I was still helping him. On the side."

I sucked in a sharp breath. Damn him and his greed.

I blew out a breath. "Code breaker, Barron. I need a code breaker."

"Talia Lovstark." He breathed her name. "Seattle."

Seattle. I leaned down and kissed him on the lips. He kissed me back. "Love you, Phoenix. Never stopped."

I lied to him, because he was dying. "I love you, Barron."

He smiled and the last breath of air slid from him. I stood, took the paper from his chest and read it.

I will kill everyone you know, bitch.

I snorted.

"That makes two of us, fucker." I crumpled the paper and threw it down beside Barron.

Luca Romano paced his office in downtown New York, the Shadow in the corner not moving, not even breathing under his dark hooded cloak.

Luca looked at the papers on his desk again. The bank records had to be wrong. They showed the entire two months of money from the deal in LA was gone. He'd had his two hackers on it for the last three days and while they'd traced the money in a circuitous route, they hadn't been able to stop it from moving. Or figure out where it had ended up.

Romano slammed the flat of his hands onto the desk in front of him. The entire operation had been a clusterfuck the second that bitch of a daughter had stepped foot into it. Gabe was dead. The money was gone. The Stick Man was missing.

And Mr. Mancini was again going to expect answers from

him. Answers along the line of where the hell was the money and where was all the Diva that had been promised to him? Romano ran a hand over his head and the intercom on his desk buzzed. He hit it harder than necessary.

"What is it?" He didn't know his secretary's name. Only that she was an ugly fat cow. He wouldn't have kept her around if she hadn't been so good with the filing system, and the occasional blow job didn't hurt either.

"You have a Jim Gordon here to speak with you, from LA."

"Send him in," Romano growled.

A big man dressed in a nice suit that was far too tight over his oversized muscles stepped into the room. An envelope was clutched in his hands.

"That it?" Romano barked the question. Jim nodded.

"Yes, sir."

"Open it, and read it to me." On the off chance Phoenix decided to leave a nasty surprise in the envelope, he would not be opening it himself.

Jim didn't seem to realize the danger he was in. He peeled the envelope open and flipped open a single sheet of paper. His face paled and his eyes flicked to his boss and to the paper again before he cleared his throat and spoke slowly.

"This is war. You took what was mine, and I will take everything you love. Your money. Your power. Your family. Remember that you made me who and what I am. Karma is a bitch, Romano, and she's come full circle to ram her vengeance up your ass so hard, you'll choke on it."

Romano didn't react. The words were all Phoenix. Tough. Hard.

But he knew her, he knew where her weaknesses were. With a quick dismissal, he sent Jim away and brought his secretary in. He stared down at the small 4X5 picture in front of him. The boy with the dark hair, the dark eyes, the dimple so like his own. In his new school uniform just a week prior.

"Take this picture of the boy."

His secretary blinked several times. "Sir?"

"Take it," he handed it over to her, "and make sure it's sent to Zee Preston in Jackson Hole, Wyoming."

AFTERWORD

Coming September 2017
Blood of a Phoenix
(The Nix Series Book 2)

Want to keep up to date? Sign up for my newsletter. New releases are the only thing I will email you about

Click here- Newsletter

Want to see my other books? There's a shit ton of them, you can check them on my website

www.shannonmayer.com

Last but not least, please consider leaving a review for "Fury of a Phoenix" the more the better!

Made in the USA
Middletown, DE
24 May 2021